THE WEBS YOU WEAVE

Shade Owens

Edited by Maggie Morris
www.indieeditor.ca

ISBN: 978-1-990775-45-1

CHAPTER 1

Meghan - One Year Earlier

"Meg, can you hear me? Oh my God. Meg, honey?"

Rapid footsteps echo around me. They sound hurried, yet calculated, like they've traveled this same path countless times before.

The pungent scent of rusted lemon slips into my nose. In what world do lemons smell like rust? I inhale deeply, and a nauseating ache spreads from my neck to my shoulders and all the way down my back.

When I try to turn my head sideways, I can't. Something solid has been firmly wrapped around my neck.

"Meg, Oh God. Meg."

My husband's words sound like they're coming in through a giant funnel. Why does he sound so distraught? So worried?

Hazel—is she okay? The thought of my daughter sends a motherly dose of panic through me, and I try to sit up. But I can't. Someone, or something, is holding me down.

What the hell is going on?

And why can't I see anything?

I try to blink, but my eyes are sealed shut. Did someone tape my eyes shut? My heart starts hammering so loudly in my chest that my husband's frantic cries in the distance now sound as if they're coming from someplace deep underground.

What if I'm going underground?

Into my grave.

I've heard about out-of-body experiences many times

before. If I *am* dead, I can still hear him. I suppose my death would explain why he's freaking out so badly.

But . . . there's pain. Blinding pain coming from inside my head. If I were dead, I wouldn't be in pain, right?

My attention is drawn to the sound of the footsteps around me. They seem to be moving faster and toward something. Some important destination. And I'm being pulled along with the crowd—I can feel it.

And judging by the uncomfortable pressure against my back, I think I'm lying on a flat surface.

A gurney?

Okay—I'm definitely moving.

And fast.

Cole's voice keeps swelling over everyone else's. "That's my wife. That's my wife. Please . . . Help her!"

Well, that confirms it—I'm not dead. If I were, he wouldn't be begging people to help me. But what's he freaking out about?

And why can't I see anything?

Using all of my energy, I force my eyes open. Crust, possibly blood, flakes away painfully. All around me are several figures in white coats and several more in pastel-colored scrubs. Above them is a bright-white light that hurts my eyes.

I may not be dead, but now I'm starting to wonder if I'm about to be.

Because isn't that what people say when someone is close to death? To *follow the light*? Well, that light seems unnatural. Unearthly. It's so bright I swear it's burning my retinas.

I seal my eyes shut again, but now all I see are bright circles behind my eyelids. I don't want to follow the damn light.

Hazel needs me.

That rusty scent assaults my nose again. What is that? Blood? And if so—is it mine or someone else's? What the hell is going on?

"Meg, baby!"

An authoritative voice tells my husband to back off the way they do in medical shows. I've never seen it happen in person before. But now I get it. He's almost annoying, and I imagine it's making it difficult for the doctors to do their work.

"What's going on?" I ask.

Actually, I don't think I asked it at all. No words came out of my mouth.

Hello? Someone say something. Please.

I'm thinking these words, but I can't form them.

Now, I'm freaking out on the inside. Suddenly, I wish my husband's irritating voice were still echoing through the halls around me.

I try to sit upright. Maybe if I move, someone will pay attention to me. But I'm strapped down, which only makes my anxiety worse. Little prickles poke at my toes and my right arm. But not my left arm.

In fact, I can't feel my left arm at all.

I try to wiggle my fingers.

Nothing.

I hear a faint mention of a *surgery room.*

The lights overhead flicker as I'm rolled around a corner and rushed into a room with even brighter lights and shiny silver tools sprawled across flimsy-looking metallic tables.

But the second I'm brought into the room, the lights around me begin to dim.

Wait—no. Those aren't the lights. They're my eyelids. They keep fluttering, and I'm not certain how much longer I can keep them open.

"We've got you, Meg."

Those are the last words I hear before all sound fades from around me and I'm immersed in a vast pool of blackness.

CHAPTER 2

Meghan

Little raindrops assault my windshield as I pull into the east parking lot of Bayton Valley High School. They're calling for a severe thunderstorm, which is something I used to love.

Now, they give me migraines.

I watch my daughter in the distance as she runs toward my freshly washed car. I can't tell if she's holding her arm up to shield her hair from the rain or if she's trying to shield her face due to embarrassment.

I get it.

Hazel's fourteen years old, and getting picked up by your mom isn't *cool*. But it's more than that.

Hazel is embarrassed to be around me more than other kids her age. I feel like Frankenstein's monster when I'm with her.

She waves goodbye to some of her friends from soccer—thankfully, no boys of interest. I'm not ready for that.

The moment she rounds the hood of my red Jeep Cherokee, the raindrops double in size. A muffled mewl escapes her mouth on the other side of the window, and she swings the door wide open.

Water droplets splash against my leather seats and atop the vinyl of my dashboard. Not that I care. Hazel often makes me out to be one of those uptight moms who shriek over a forgotten coaster, but when it comes down to it, the little things in life don't bother me. I couldn't care less about water rings on my tables or droplets on my Jeep's leather.

That's Cole's territory.

Hazel is just too young to understand the *bigger things* I have to deal with daily.

Now that the rain has completely engulfed my car, I feel silly to have thought that showing up with a clean car would somehow lessen Hazel's embarrassment. I should have checked the weather forecast before spending money on a car wash.

I'm certainly not strapped for cash, but I don't like senseless waste.

Rain or shine, my Jeep's level of sparkliness has zero bearing on my daughter's embarrassment of me. I have a nice Jeep. She becomes perceptibly uncomfortable when I'm anywhere near someone she knows.

Hence me feeling like Frankenstein's monster.

Because I know the truth—her discomfort is due to my physical appearance.

But I can't change my appearance. I didn't ask for this. And it's not like I can fix it. The doctors already did everything they could.

Next week will be one year since my accident, and I still have a hard time looking at myself in the mirror.

My mother has told me that it really isn't all that bad. But all she's seen is a picture, and to be honest, I don't think she wants to hear about any of my problems, even if those include permanent disfigurement. She'd rather talk about herself.

When Hazel buckles herself in and flattens her wet hair over her head, I flash her a smile but instantly regret it. Did she just wince? I get that my smile looks funny, but you'd think she'd be used to my new face by now. She sees it more than I do.

"How was soccer practice?" I'm now hyperaware of my speech impediment. Although subtle, it's detectable.

I should shut up, not talk, and drive us home.

Her lips sharpen into a pinched smile. "It was good."

At least she's making an effort. I don't think she wants

things to be strained between us. But they have been lately. Painfully so.

I'm not ignorant of the fact that Hazel is fourteen years old and her body is flooded with hormones, but some days, I'm certain she hates me.

"That's good," I say.

Did I shout? It felt like I was shouting. I clear my throat and shift my Jeep into Reverse.

"Mom!" Hazel yelps.

At the same time, my collision sensor screams at me.

The sound of her voice, combined with the high-pitched alarm, sends what feels like high-voltage electrical shocks up my right arm and into my steering wheel. I slam on my brakes, eyes wide at my rear camera screen.

Two girls Hazel's age cross behind my Jeep, scorning me with their hateful eyes.

"You almost ran over Tash and Fatima!" Hazel says. She's now swiveled in her seat, gazing over the rear headrests and through the back window at the ambling teenagers.

I swear, they're walking even slower now. It's like they're trying to taunt me.

I'm tempted to lower my window and scold them for acting like a bunch of entitled snobs. If I were in their shoes, I would have quickly moved out of the way. Not walked with a slow gait, eying the back of someone's car with attitude all over my face.

Teenagers, these days.

Honestly.

"They came out of nowhere," I say.

Little bitches.

I push this thought away. My husband, Cole, has patiently—and repeatedly—pointed out that my accident has led to unwanted psychiatric symptoms, such as irritability and anger.

He's not wrong.

I have been angry. Very angry. But I don't think it's

because of the trauma to my head. My whole life has changed. Hazel barely talks to me, and even Cole has become extremely distant, which is saying a lot given that I lost him a long time ago.

To make matters worse, my left arm doesn't function at all. Thankfully, I'm right-handed, so I can still do most things, such as drive. But my disability still bothers me every single day.

How can I not be angry?

I miss the old me.

I miss my family.

"Are we going, or what?" Hazel snips.

I glance into my rear camera screen to ensure it's safe to move. As an extra precaution, I go old-school and look over my shoulder.

We're clear.

Hazel sighs and rests her head against the window, then reaches into her bag for a pink ball cap and slips it over her head. She lowers it as much as possible until it's masking half her face. Her long, wavy brown hair drapes over her shoulders, blocking part of her soccer team's logo on the front of her shirt.

I don't bother trying to make conversation anymore.

She'd probably rather die than talk to me.

CHAPTER 3

Meghan

"Ziggy, would you relax?" I hiss.

Ziggy nibbles on my pant leg before zooming out of the kitchen, into the living room, and then hurrying back. He moves so fast that he skids across the kitchen tiles, slamming into my ankles.

Thankfully, he only weighs fifteen pounds, which is about as much as my cat used to weigh.

Personally, I'm not a fan of Jack Russells. Although they're adorable, they're high energy—really high—and yap a lot. But I love Ziggy, in my own way. When he's calm, anyway.

What I wanted was a pit bull, especially now that I don't work and I'm home alone most of the time, but Cole went off about how they have lockjaw and how they're illegal in some states for a reason.

But there's no statewide ban against pit bulls in New York.

Regardless, Cole is set in his ways, and no matter how much I tried to explain that the whole lockjaw thing was a myth and that pit bulls are actually extremely sweet and loyal when raised by loving dog parents, he wouldn't budge.

I blink down at Ziggy, who is now panting ferociously.

He's always hyper when we get home.

I set my frozen chicken aside and plant my functioning arm on my hip. "What is it, buddy? You want to play?"

His yap is so high-pitched that I wince and turn my face away. Ziggy may not be as big and strong as a pit bull, but I suppose his big mouth would alert me if anyone were to break into our home.

I cross our kitchen of custom white cabinetry that cost more than Cole's Lexus. The project took about three weeks a few months ago. I couldn't be happier. Especially with the white marble countertops and drop-in copper sinks.

Cole may not be a great husband, but at least he remembered the dream kitchen I've always wanted.

I step into the dining room and slide the back patio door open. The moment a little crack appears, rain droplets patter on the tip of Ziggy's nose. He doesn't mind. Instead, he shoves his snout into the opening and starts hopping up and down as if capable of further widening the gap.

"It's pouring out there," I say. "You really want to go?"

Now he's clawing at the glass.

Fine.

I pry the door open wider, and out he goes, zipping and zooming around in our backyard despite the thunder and torrential downpour.

He'll probably be back in about thirty seconds, once he realizes how wet it is out there.

Thankfully, the yard is fenced, so Ziggy will tire himself out on his own. All I have to do is pop my head out every ten minutes or so to make sure he didn't dig a hole under the fence or somehow unlatch the pool gate. It wouldn't be the first time I found him swimming in our inground pool. Right now, the pool looks like it's being stabbed by thousands of invisible knives.

It's really nasty out there.

I return to the kitchen and start prepping supper. With only one functioning arm, it's not an easy feat. But Hazel deserves to eat, and now that I'm on disability, I'd feel pretty useless if I didn't contribute around the house.

As I'm carefully inserting my cream of mushroom chicken into the oven, my phone dings on the marble counter.

It's either Cole, Hazel—who is too lazy to come downstairs from her room—or Chels, my best friend.

I suppose it could be my mother, although we don't exactly talk anymore.

So when I see Cole's name gliding across my screen, I'm not surprised. I pull my arm out of the oven and answer the phone, then press the Speaker button.

"Hey, honey," he says.

"Hey," I say back.

He clears his throat awkwardly. What does he expect? For me to be sweet? My husband and I haven't been close for years.

He's put me through hell.

"Listen," he says, and even though I can't see him, I can picture him rubbing the back of his pale neck. "I'm so sorry. I have meetings booked late this evening that I didn't know about. Vincent asked me to stay late for those."

Vincent is the CEO of AstroWyre, a tech company that recently launched some highly advanced antivirus software. He's a short man with and olive complexion who tends to wear way too much hair gel and way too much cologne. I never liked the guy. He's arrogant and acts as if he's God's gift to women.

"Okay," I say, biting my tongue.

Cole clears his throat again. My husband is a good actor. He acts like he cares. He doesn't.

Ever since AstroWyre's Chief Operating Officer, David Chernyak, went missing, Cole has been filling the gap. Vincent even offered him a temporary interim position, which came along with a fifty-thousand-dollar pay raise.

And if David doesn't return, then Cole will assume the role permanently, which means he'll also be next in line to earn the title of CEO once Vincent chooses to retire. Vincent still has several working years ahead of him, but he's taken a liking to Cole. The company will have to hire more people to fill the vacant positions once that happens, but Cole doesn't seem stressed about it at all.

"Eat supper without me?" he says.

Yeah, that's what I planned to do. I may even overeat so there won't be any leftovers for him. As the thought crosses my mind, I realize how petty I'm being, but Cole has been home late nearly every night these last few weeks. I barely see him anymore.

And it wouldn't be a huge deal if I loved my husband—if I trusted him, and we had a healthy relationship.

But I don't trust him. Not in the least.

That, and we have a daughter who deserves to spend time with her father.

"Yep," I say.

An awkward silence hangs between us until finally, Cole says, "I have a meeting. Sorry."

Before he can say I *love you*, which are words I know he doesn't mean, I hang up.

CHAPTER 4

Cole

Sighing, I slip my cell phone into my pocket.

Why does Meg always have to give me such a hard time about working late? She knows that my interim position is very demanding. But along with that comes more money.

You'd think she'd be a bit happier about that. A bit more grateful.

Instead, she's snippy, and cold, and treats me like I'm a piece of shit.

I'm getting really tired of it.

Footsteps echo near my office's entrance, so I glance up to spot Frank and a few other sales managers huddled together.

They're all looking at the same thing.

Valeria Cruz.

Her name sounds like it belongs to a movie star. Actually, she looks like she should be a movie star. Either that or a model for some high-end fashion magazine.

She certainly has the body.

I grab my coffee off my desk—a blue ceramic mug that reads *Best Boss*, which was a gift from one of my former assistants—and casually make my way over to the small crowd.

"Hot, right?" Frank says. "I'd do anything to get a bite of that ass."

A few other men nod, salivating like dogs. When Frank spots me, he nudges me hard in the bicep as if we're still on the same level, as if I'm not *his* boss, even though I surpassed him in rank three years ago.

"Don't you wanna sink your teeth into that?" he asks me.

I blink at him. "I'm a married man, Frank."

He laughs, and a piece of donut flies out of his mouth. Frank is the last person who should go around talking like he's some hotshot player. He doesn't give a shit about this health, thinks his greasy comb-over is fooling everyone, and has a horrible mouth-breathing habit. And it's loud. Every time he breathes, you want to reach inside his throat and remove whatever obstacle is causing that raspy rattling sound.

My best guess is a deviated septum combined with oversized tonsils. Either way, it's maddening to listen to.

He licks his chops, and his brown eyes glaze over as he watches the new secretary set up her workstation.

"Show a little class, will you, Frank?" I say.

His eyes narrow on me. "Oh, I get it. You want dibs on this one, too."

I don't appreciate his tone.

Ignoring him, I turn around and head back into my office. Frank doesn't have an office—he works in the cubicles where I used to work years ago.

But as the director of the Sales Department for AstroWyre, I get certain privileges. And now that David decided to go MIA, I'm technically the interim chief operating officer, which means I'll be getting *his* office, and that's twice the size of mine.

It's pretty damn sweet.

What's even sweeter is the pay raise.

Thanks, David.

I almost raise my coffee to salute him, even though he's not here. When I realize how creepy that would make me look, I keep my coffee at waist level and leisurely make my way over to my desk.

"Excuse me?"

I swivel on my heels to spot Valeria leaning against my doorway, her breasts pressed up against the doorframe.

Frank and the other sleazeballs have all dispersed with bowed heads and scissoring legs. It takes a lot of self-restraint to ignore her chest.

But I manage.

I'm not blind. The woman is . . . Well, she's hard not to look at. For her first day at work, she has decided to wear a bright-red V-cut top and a snug black skirt. The buttons at the center are barely holding on. It accentuates her curves, and this woman is very curvy despite her petite frame and small waist.

Even more than Meg, who has always been rather curvy. Over the last few years, though, she's really let herself go. In all fairness, Meg has also been through a lot and is still recovering from her injuries.

When I don't answer right away, she plays with the tips of her long, tousled chestnut hair and blinks several times at me.

"How can I help?" I ask.

She smiles, and it's impossible to look away.

But I need to control myself. I don't want to be gross like Frank. Besides, I'm married. Although, it doesn't feel like I am. It hasn't in a very long time.

Some days, Meghan is like a distant relative. She's a comfort, but even that's a stretch. Her mood has been all over the place, and I never know what I'm going to come home to.

I'm starting to think she hates me.

Sure, I'm not perfect, and I've made mistakes, but who hasn't?

"Do you know where I can find a longer HDMI wire?" she asks. "For my monitor. The one I have seems to be defective."

Beautiful *and* tech-savvy.

She beams at me again, and I mirror her expression.

"Actually, I have a few spares in here," I tell her.

She lets go of the doorframe and walks in, her heels ticking against the floor. With hands clasped together, she approaches me slowly. I can't tell if she's shy or uncomfortable.

"Welcome to AstroWyre, by the way," I tell her. "Nice to have you on the team."

"Nice to be here," she says. "I'm so thankful Vincent hired me. The place is huge, though. I almost got lost this morning."

I chuckle softly. She has a point. This glass building can be rather intimidating. It's only five stories high, but it's wide and made entirely of glass and sharp edges. Access to our offices requires navigating through two different security checkpoints.

"It's definitely a big place," I say. "But you get used to it." I pause, then add, "And Vincent is a good judge of character, so I imagine he chose right."

I set my coffee down with a clink, then lead her away from my large wooden desk and toward a storage closet tucked away in the corner of the room. She follows me quietly.

When she abruptly stops behind me, a subtle breeze sweeps past her, and her intoxicating scent floats up into my nose. She smells so good. I shouldn't be so focused on her perfume, but it's not like I can block my sense of smell.

I open the closet door and rummage through a few boxes. "I have a bunch here, somewhere."

"Take your time," she says sweetly.

I pull out a long cable that still has a tag on it and hand it to her. "Here you go."

She grabs it and thanks me. We stand awkwardly for a moment, and then she says, "Well, I'm gonna finish setting everything up. I should be ready to start work in about an hour."

Her gaze flickers down to my left hand. Is she looking for a wedding ring?

"You know we have an IT team for that, right?" I say. "They were supposed to set up your station this morning."

She shrugs. "It's okay, I enjoy hooking stuff up."

I run a hand against the back of my neck. "Well, I'm going to give them a call anyway. You'll need their help to get access to the system."

She nods knowingly, then raises the HDMI cable as if to say, *I better finish hooking everything up before they get here, then.*

I flash her a tight smile. When she turns around, I'm captivated by her swaying hips underneath that tight skirt of hers.

They're taunting me.

No.

I'm not going to be that person.

Not again.

CHAPTER 5

Diary Entry

I've never been more attracted to any man in my life.

Cole . . . My God. He's everything I ever dreamed about. He smells like . . . perfection.

Honestly, Cole has got to be the sexiest man I've ever laid eyes on.

He's tall, probably at least six feet. He's not muscular in a pretentious way, either. He probably works out, but he isn't jacked. I prefer men on the slender side, and that's exactly how he's built.

His dark hair looks like it belongs to a Ken doll. It's longer on top, and he keeps it coiffed meticulously and out of his sculpted face. And those icy-blue eyes . . . My God. They're so penetrating. Beneath his thick eyebrows, they resemble crystal marbles.

When he smiled at me today, his lips pulled up higher on one side. It didn't appear forced. He seems to actually have a crooked smile, which is both so hot and so cute.

He also has a perfect nose. Some people don't pay attention to the little details of a person's face, but I do. His nose is neither pointy nor round—it's right in the middle, which is my favorite.

This morning, his face was cleanly shaved, but by the afternoon, a bit of stubble was already growing in.

I'd give anything to have that stubble tickling my thighs . . .

I'm getting worked up just thinking about it.

How can one person do this to me? I don't even know the man. Yet, I feel like he knows me. I wish our hands had touched during our short and brief interaction this morning.

He was smiling at me like he saw me. Like I wasn't just some new secretary here to serve everyone in the office. He saw me for me.

I really didn't know what to expect from my first day of work, but this wasn't it. This was so much better than I could ever have imagined.

I swear, if physics weren't a thing, I would have melted into a puddle when Cole smiled at me the way he did. But if that happened, I'm sure Vincent wouldn't be happy. He hired me to do a job here. An important job, according to Vincent. He said I'll be managing administrative tasks around the office and helping management when they need anything.

That includes Cole. That man could ask me to wash his feet, and I'd do it.

I want him to tell me what to do.

I want him.

So damn bad.

Anyway, I can't keep thinking about it. Otherwise, I'll have to take another cold shower. I'm going to bed early because tomorrow can't come fast enough.

I can't wait to see Cole again.

Chapter 6

Meghan

When Cole comes home at eight thirty, the storm has subsided. Still, a dark and wet gloominess clings to the air all around me.

Despite the unpleasant weather, I've propped myself onto the living room's creamy leather sofa to read a book about zombies. It's not my usual go-to, but this one has me fully immersed.

So when Cole steps in through the front doors, I don't bother looking up at him from my book. I'd rather read about some rotten corpse losing its head.

Ziggy, however, immediately abandons me and jumps off the sofa and right over the coffee table before landing midrun.

Cole sets his shiny suitcase on the foyer bench, right beneath an ugly black-and-white painting he paid way too much for. To me, it looks like a monster's face with hollowed eyes and a mouth stretched beyond normality.

Cole says it's a tree.

He bends to greet Ziggy, whose butt is now waggling harder than it has all day. He pats him on the head while mumbling a bunch of incoherent words.

Part of me wishes I could be better for Cole. He's been working hard to pick up the slack around here. It's not exactly fair that I punish him for his overtime shifts, especially when he's the only one working between the two of us.

Feeling a tinge of guilt, I rest my book on my lap and forcefully crinkle my eyes at him. Hopefully, he can't tell that I don't mean it. "Hey, honey. How was work?"

He seems pleasantly surprised that I'm even speaking to him. He pulls his shoulders back a bit and flattens a few lines out of his expensive business suit. "It went well. How was your day, sweetheart?"

Ugh.

The conversation is so strained, you'd think we were actors in a sitcom: husband comes home and politely asks his wife how her day at home was. That's when she starts talking about how the vacuum malfunctioned and a bird hit the window.

This isn't us.

We used to be passionate, and fun. We used to spend our Friday nights bar hopping and coming home with our hands all over each other in the back of a cab, only to then have passionate sex in the living room.

But that was eons ago.

We'll be married fourteen years this summer. I can't keep hoping for things to go back to the way they used to be.

If he hadn't betrayed you, you wouldn't feel this way.

Then again, if he hadn't betrayed me, my life wouldn't be what it is now. I have so much to be thankful for.

Cole watches me intently, waiting for my answer.

Oh, right. We're being polite.

"My day went well," I say.

He nods absentmindedly and removes his tie. "Listen, I'm sorry again that I was so late today. Vincent has been—"

"I don't need to hear the full story," I cut him off. "I get it. This is how it is now, with your new title."

"It's not always going to be this way," he says.

I repress a scoff. "You've been home late every night for the last two weeks. You think that's healthy for Hazel?"

His forehead scrunches. "Two weeks? Meg, I was home every evening last week."

I dig my nails into the back of my book. Is he serious right now? He was late. Every night. I remember it clearly.

I wouldn't be so upset if he weren't calling me a liar.

He looks at me with pity, and I want to tell him to stop. He's been giving me that look a lot lately. It makes me feel like a young child who doesn't know the difference between an apple and a pear.

He approaches me one deliberate step at a time, then gingerly sits at the edge of the sofa. "Honey, do you think we should go see Dr. Tang?"

We? He doesn't mean we—he means me. I should go see the doctor because I'm not okay.

I let my book fall beside me and get up off the sofa, away from him. "I'm not injured anymore, Cole. I don't know why you keep treating me like a child. I think I'd remember if you were home late or on time."

He's calm—too calm. Rather than say anything, he locks his fingers and nods slowly. "I understand. I'm not trying to treat you like a child, Meg. But I'm telling you—I was home last week for every supper. Do you want me to ask Hazel? I can call her down."

"Don't bring her into this," I say.

The last thing I need is to give Hazel another reason to pull away from me. If Cole is right, and my memory is out of whack, I don't need Hazel knowing about it. She's already been through so much.

"You've been forgetting a lot of stuff lately," he says. "And I'm not judging you, or anything, Meg. I want to help. But lately, all you do is lash out at me."

"Lash out at you?" I say, holding back a full-blown yell. "You're the one staying at the office late, probably fucking your secretary—"

He raises a flat palm. "Okay, whoa, stop. I'm not doing this again. Every night, you accuse me of cheating if I have to work late. Do you know how insulting that is? I'm loyal to you, Meg. You were in a coma for several weeks, and I stood by your side. I took care of you for several more months after that, even through all the angry outbursts."

He's breathing hard through flared nostrils now. But I know my husband—he isn't angry. Not with me, anyway.

He's frustrated with this whole situation. And I don't blame him. I know I haven't been easy to deal with since my accident.

After a long pause, Cole lets out a sigh. "I think your paranoid delusions are back."

Did he seriously just say that to me?

I clench my teeth so hard it hurts my jaw.

Paranoid delusions were a symptom that came out of *his* mouth during my assessment. He said I kept accusing him of cheating. But let's face it—my husband is a cheater. How does that make me paranoid or delusional?

I suppose there was that one time I saw a dark silhouette of a woman standing at the dining room window peering through. Ziggy didn't bark, and Cole went out with a flashlight to confirm that no one had stepped on our property.

Another time, I heard footsteps in the house and called Cole.

No one was there.

So, yeah, I've had a few issues. But those were months ago. Thinking my husband is cheating on me does not mean I'm having paranoid delusions. He has a history.

And the fact that he's using this right now means he's deflecting. So now, I'm even more upset at him, and I'm even more certain that he's screwing someone at work.

"There it is again." He throws his palms in the air as if he's given up conversing with me.

"What?" I say coldly.

"That look. You're doing it now. It's like you hate me."

Right now, I do hate him.

He basically called me crazy.

When I don't respond, he bows his head, then rakes both hands through his dark hair, brushing it all back on the top of his head.

If I didn't know my husband was a cheating piece of garbage, I'd still think he was the sexiest man alive.

But I know who he really is.

And to me, that makes him repulsive.

CHAPTER 7

Hazel

I shove my earbuds into my ears and listen to my favorite band—Escape the Fate. Their music calms me. It's so powerful, so meaningful.

Right now, I can't take another minute of listening to Mom and Dad fight downstairs. They think I can't hear them since they aren't yelling. But Mom sounds like she's on the verge of snapping.

I don't understand why.

Dad hasn't done anything wrong. He tries to be here for her in so many ways, but she's always angry.

If I weren't so hungry, I'd stay in my room for the rest of the night. Mom made cream of mushroom chicken for supper, but that was hours ago.

With my earbuds still in place, I get off my bed and make my way downstairs. If I ignore my parents, they might ignore me, too.

"Hazel."

My name slips in with the lyrics blasting into my ears. Great. I was really hoping I'd sneak by without getting noticed. Rolling my eyes, I pull out one of my earbuds. The screaming music blasts out of the little speakers.

Mom and Dad are both watching me. Dad looks like he always does—happy to see me—while Mom, on the other hand, is trying way too hard. Her smile is fake. I swear, sometimes, I think she doesn't really like me. That secretly, the soul inside my mom's body isn't really my mom anymore, and this woman resents me for whatever reason.

Last week, I googled signs to watch out for in sociopaths. Ever since her accident, she's been different. Can people *become* sociopaths? Is that even possible? Because her emotions don't seem to be real. Not anymore.

Some days, when she smiles at me, I picture her standing in front of a mirror, practicing that smile over and over until she gets it just right. Then getting frustrated when the paralyzed part of her lip won't cooperate.

I'm afraid if I keep looking at her, I'll see her lip twitch, or something, and it'll confirm to me that my mother no longer exists in there.

I don't want that confirmed.

I don't think I could handle it.

"H-hey," Mom says awkwardly. "What're you doing up this late?"

"It's only nine," I point out.

Her smile fades instantly. *See? It wasn't real.* "It's past your bedtime."

"It's okay," Dad says. "Honey, what do you need? Bedtime snack?"

I nod.

"I'll make you something," he says.

"Seriously?" Mom says. "Cole, she's fourteen. She can grab herself a snack."

Why does Mom have to be so mean?

I glance over at Dad, who fluffs her off with a playful pout and says, "It's just a snack, Meg."

"No, it's not just a snack," Mom says. "It's everything. Her laundry. Helping her with her chores when she's tired. She needs to learn life skills, Cole, not have someone hold her hand through her entire adolescence."

I clench my jaw. She's making such a big deal out of nothing. Like Dad said, it's just a stupid snack. I swear, I think she's jealous of me. Probably because Dad's nicer to me than he is to her. But if she wasn't so mean with him all the time, he'd probably be nicer, too.

Dad looks at her pointedly and says, "Let's talk about this later, okay?"

I can't see his face from where I'm standing, but I imagine he has both of his big eyebrows raised on his forehead. He does this when he's really serious about something but doesn't want to talk about it in the moment.

Like the day I got in trouble at school for calling Mrs. Lamishki a cunt. Another teacher overheard me and sent me to the office. When Dad came to get me, I started explaining to him that Mrs. Lamishki went out of her way to torment me, and that's the look he gave me in front of Mrs. Laurier—our vice principal.

And it wasn't until we got home that he gave me a huge speech about respecting authority even if I didn't feel they deserved respect, and even if the teacher *was a cunt*. I laughed when he said this, and the corner of his lips pulled up on one side, but Mom didn't think it was very funny. She rolled her eyes at him and walked away.

Dad leads me into the kitchen and pries the fridge door open. "What do you want, honeybee?"

I love it when he calls me that.

It makes me feel loved and cared for. Mom used to call me bunny, but she stopped doing that after her accident.

I'd be lying if I said I didn't miss it.

We used to be close.

I miss her so much. But some days, I also hate her. Because accident or not, it's like she's doing this to herself. She should be better by now.

So why does she act the way she does?

CHAPTER 8

Meghan

I hate it when Cole treats Hazel like a five-year-old princess. He'd do anything for her. And while that's sweet, in a sense, he tends to go overboard, like last night. Any time she's hungry, he offers to make something for her. When she laments about being tired, he says he'll do her laundry or help her with her chores.

She takes advantage of it.

I love my daughter, more than she'll ever know, but I don't want her growing up to be an entitled snob. I want her to be independent and to be able to take care of herself.

Hazel's eyes light up when Cole comes sweeping into the kitchen in a freshly pressed suit, his hair slicked back with gel.

He's put a little more effort into his appearance today. He's clean-shaven, although he shaves every morning. But that's not it. It's his hair. It's like he spent an hour getting it perfect. And his cologne—I can smell it from here. He isn't supposed to wear cologne at work, but every now and then, he does.

There's more.

His red power tie.

He only wears that when he has a really important meeting with big clients that could bring in millions of dollars.

"Big meeting today?" I ask.

"Sorry?" he says.

How could he forget about some huge meeting?

"Do you have any big meetings today?" I repeat.

"No, why?" Then he catches me looking at his tie. "Oh, well, sort of."

Right.

He's full of it. He probably has a new secretary working there. Or he's about to interview potential candidates. Either way, I'd be willing to bet there's a beautiful woman involved.

"Why don't you sit down?" Cole says to Hazel. "I'll make you a tomato sandwich."

I clench my good fist. Here I am, trying to make us both some coffee with one arm, yet Cole doesn't offer to help me. Instead, he offers his princess breakfast when she's perfectly capable of feeding herself.

I was too angry last night to have a conversation with Cole. Instead, as he made Hazel a snack, I went to bed. But we really do need to discuss how quick he is to help her. He might mean well, but he's being an overfunctioning parent. His actions aren't helping Hazel. They're hindering her. I've tried telling him this. I've even shown him over a dozen articles from renowned psychologists about how overfunctioning robs kids of the ability to develop healthy life skills.

That doesn't make me crazy, yet they both act like I am when I get angry over these things.

It makes me a mother who wants the best for her child. The best doesn't always mean making your kid smile, either. But when he acts like this, he makes me out to be a bitch. Like I don't want him taking care of her.

That's not it at all.

Hazel happily accepts Cole's offer.

I should bite my tongue. Hazel already views me as the bad guy. I'm about to turn away when I realize that I'd rather be the bad guy and raise a good child than hinder my teen's development to protect my own ego.

"Hazel, you're fourteen years old," I say. "In a few years from now, you'll be out of the house and on your own. I think you should start making your own breakfasts in the morning."

"But Dad wants to," she says.

She's sitting lazily at the dining room table with her white wireless earbud case resting next to her elbow. Today, she's chosen to wear jeans with fewer holes than yesterday, which is an improvement. While I don't like her mostly black style—something kids refer to as *emo*—she does, and that's all that matters.

She's trying to find herself, and these things take time.

"It's not a big deal, Meg," Cole says.

"Yeah, it is," I say. "How many times do we need to have this conversation? Clearly, it isn't getting through to you. Hazel needs to learn life skills, and she can't very well do that if you're constantly catering to her every need."

It takes everything in me not to slam my coffee mug on the counter. But if I do that, I'll be the *irrational* one. The *crazy* one. The person who *gets angry over nothing*.

"Meg, honey, it's just breakfast," Cole says. "Hazel is learning plenty of life skills—"

"Hazel, get up and make yourself breakfast." My tone is clipped now. "Cole, get out of my face."

I pour myself a coffee and don't bother to extract Cole's mug—a bright yellow #1 Dad mug I bought for him on behalf of Hazel a few years back.

Like Hazel, he can serve himself. They both have function of their arms. Both arms. And it's about time they started using them.

"Come on, Ziggy," I say.

Ziggy gets up from his little blue plush bed and comes darting across the kitchen and into the dining room. He hops a few times around my ankles as I walk to the patio door.

Stay calm. Don't slam the door.

To my own surprise, I manage to step outside without causing a scene, even though all I wanted to do back there was throw my coffee mug at the wall and then ask them both to pick up the shards.

All right—I do have pent-up anger. Dr. Tang did say

that brain injuries can often lead to anger and irritability. But it's not just that. Cole is testing my patience. He's constantly making me the bad guy in front of Hazel when all I want is the best for her.

I sit on our outdoor patio sofa and breathe in the fresh morning air. But I wince when a rancid smell hits my nose, ruining my serenity. Then I catch Ziggy's back fully rounded as he takes a poop on the lawn.

"Ziggy!" I yell at him. "Not there!"

He has a designated potty area, and he knows better.

The moment he hears me, he runs to his potty area with half a turd dragging behind him.

At least *someone* around here listens to me without arguing.

CHAPTER 9

Hazel

I plop myself down into the bus's leather seat, next to Alex.

"What's up with you?" he asks.

I'm too angry to compliment his new pink hair. But it is nice, especially at that length—right past his ears.

"My mom," I say. "She's being a bitch."

He sighs through his nose, then rests his cheek against the seat in front of us to look at me. When he breathes, the dark-gray leather gets even darker, but only for a split second.

He watches me quietly—knowingly—with those pretty green eyes of his. I hate it when he does that. It's like he's amused.

"What?" I snap.

"You don't mean that," he says.

He's referring to me using the word *bitch* to describe my mom.

I shouldn't have done that.

I feel bad about it. But she makes me so angry.

"She's just mean, okay?" I say.

"What did she do?" he asks.

Alex is always playing devil's advocate. And every time I point it out, he says he can't help himself because he's a Libra. That he has to consider all sides. And as annoying as it is, it does help balance me out when I get upset.

"She told me to make my own breakfast." As soon as the words come out of my mouth, I feel like an entitled little brat. Some kids get abused and beaten, and here I am, complaining that I have to feed myself.

Alex raises a brow at me. I can see the judgment all over his face. He thinks I'm way out of line.

But before he can comment on how childish I'm being, I raise a flat palm in front of his bright eyes to cut him off. "Look, it's not what she said, it's the way she said it. My dad was about to make me breakfast, and she got all pissed off like he was doing something wrong."

Alex stays quiet, so I keep talking. "Every time my dad offers to do something nice for me, she butts in and tells him to stop."

"Does she say why?" he asks.

"Something about life skills," I say.

I'm feeling more stupid by the second. I should have kept my mouth shut and not told Alex what was bothering me.

Alex shrugs a bony shoulder, and his light-blue cotton shirt drags upward. "She isn't wrong, Haze. I mean, you're fourteen. I started making my own breakfasts at, like, eight. You're lucky your dad even offers to make any food for you."

Is he for real right now? Isn't my best friend supposed to have my back? He's been on my mom's side a lot, lately.

"Sounds like your parents have different parenting styles," he says.

I roll my eyes at him. "I didn't realize you'd gotten a degree in psychology."

He chortles loudly, and a few heads turn our way. "Haze, this isn't advanced psychology. Every parent is different. Look at Anna. She lets me do anything. Like, anything. She doesn't care. I could come home at three a.m., and she wouldn't say anything."

Anna is his foster mom. He never calls her mom.

I snort. "I wish I had that sort of freedom."

"Do you, though? Anna doesn't care where I am or what I do because she's too busy drinking. She doesn't care about me."

I go quiet.

Alex has it way worse than me. Both of his parents died of overdoses when he was young, and he ended up in the foster system.

"Ew. Don't look at me like that," Alex says.

"Like what?" I say.

"Like you feel sorry for me, or something." He smacks my shoulder, then rakes his medium-length hair backward, and it fluffs on top of his head. "Besides, things are looking up for me. I met Anna's sister last week. Charlotte. She's nothing like Anna. She's already made me supper, like, three times and taken me to the movies."

My jaw drops. "Seriously?"

Alex nods proudly. "Yeah, I hope she sticks around."

For his sake, I hope she does, too.

Some kid squeals at the front of the bus, and Alex perks up momentarily to make sure everything is okay. Some stolen toy. The kid will get over it.

"Sounds to me like you have two parents who love you," Alex says. "And they both show it in different ways."

"Yeah, well, if you were around, you wouldn't think my mom loves me."

He reaches for my shoulder. "I know things have been hard since her accident."

He thinks he knows, but I don't tell him everything. Almost everything, but not everything. Because how can I tell my best friend that I think my mom *did* die from her injuries and that someone else took over her body?

Because if Alex knew what my mom did, he'd probably call the authorities or something and have her taken away from me.

CHAPTER 10

Cole

Valeria sits quietly at her sleek white desk, riffling through papers. What are those? How-to guides? There's zero privacy around here unless you have an office with a door, so I can even see her purse, her lunch, and her cell phone sitting upright at the edge of her desk.

"Everything all right?" I ask.

When she sees me, she tucks a strand of her hair behind an ear with a hoop earring. She doesn't smile. Instead, she looks surprised that someone is even talking to her.

"Oh, yeah, I'm okay," she says. "Just trying to set up the printer."

"IT didn't do that for you?" I ask.

She shakes her head. "They set up my server access, but that's it. It's okay, really. I've done this countless times before."

"You sure?"

This time, she smiles at me, her plush red lips pulling up above a row of perfectly white teeth. "I'm sure."

I give her a polite nod and head into my office. Frank, who is yet again lingering near my office door, winks at me and lets his jaw hang loose.

Some days, I wish I could knock the guy in the face. Teach him to stop being such a dog. Missing a few teeth might set him straight. He could also be forced to join the marketing team for a few months. It's a small yet powerful team of only two—Rob and Joaquin. They're both devoted husbands and fathers. All they do is talk about their wives and children, and I've never once seen them gaze at any of the young, beautiful women in the office.

That might be exactly the kind of influence Frank needs.

When I don't acknowledge him, he waddles toward me. The guy isn't even that overweight. It's a bad habit of his. He always walks like he's trying to balance something on his head. "Hey, Cole. My man."

His comb-over looks even greasier than it did yesterday. You'd think he lathered it in petroleum jelly. The guy could really put more effort into looking the part of a sales manager.

"What is it, Frank?" I ask.

He fidgets with his stubby fingers. "Was just wondering if my request was approved."

Oh, right—his request. He wants an additional two hundred thousand dollars to expand his team. But his team sells hardware, not software, and it isn't exactly an expanding market right now. Not with all the cheap competition out there.

"Sorry, that's denied," I say.

"What?" he blurts. When Valeria looks our way, he smooths a hand over his red hair and flashes her a sleazy smile as if to say, *Nothing to see here, sweetheart.*

"Vincent agrees," I tell him before he can try to go over my head.

And with that, he storms off like a child being told they can't play an extra hour of video games.

The moment he's gone, Valeria gets up and approaches me sheepishly. "Must be hard being the boss."

"Not really," I say. "I can deal with men like Frank."

She watches me carefully. "Does the team have any female sales managers?"

I'm embarrassed to admit that we don't. My thoughts must be all over my face.

"That's a shame," she says. "I'm really good in sales."

A playful smirk curves my lips. "Did you join the company to move up, Valeria?"

"Would that be so bad?" she asks.

I shake my head playfully. "No, not at all. I'm just surprised, that's all. We've had countless secretaries join. A few had ambition, but not many. Some preferred to stay comfortable."

"I don't like comfort," Valeria says. "I'm sick of it. I want better, for Emiliano and me."

A boyfriend? Husband?

When I don't say anything, she smiles sweetly. "My son."

I part my lips, but nothing comes out.

I don't ask her whether she has a boyfriend or a husband because I don't want to come across like I'm flirting with her. I'm sure that's the last thing she needs. That's something Frank would do.

"Single moms aren't exactly rolling in money," she adds.

"Well," I say. "There are positions around here. If you're looking to move up."

Her brown eyes widen almost imperceptibly. "Oh?"

"I have a meeting this morning, and it will probably last into the afternoon. But if you're free at three, I'd love to talk to you about it."

Her eyes drop to my red tie, and she wiggles a finger at it. "Is that why you're wearing that tie?"

I let out a faint scoff, even though I don't mean to. But it's nice to be questioned civilly and not interrogated as if I've committed some heinous crime.

"Sorry, I didn't mean—" she starts.

I raise a flat palm. "No, you did nothing wrong. Honestly. My wife—" But then, I stop myself. This woman doesn't know me, and I don't know her. It wouldn't be appropriate to talk to her about Meg and how she berates me. So instead, I force a smile. "Never mind. Yes, the tie is for today's meeting."

"It's nice," she says.

Our eyes lock for a moment, and then I run my hand down my tie to flatten it as much as possible. "Thank you."

"Would you like me to schedule the meeting in your

calendar?" she asks.

"You already have access to my calendar?" I say.

She raises a brow. "Of course I do. That's my job."

Still, I didn't expect her to have everything organized so quickly. And this is exactly why I want to meet with her this afternoon. I already planned for it yesterday after I saw how she set up her own computer and monitors, but today only further validates that I'm making the right move.

She's the one I want.

And I need to snatch her up before anyone else does.

CHAPTER 11

Diary Entry

Today, Cole proved to me that he's exactly what I thought he was. An amazing man. I don't know what compelled me to open up to him about my struggles with money, but I did. And I could see it all over his face. He cares about me.

There's something in those icy-blue eyes of his that makes me feel so safe. Like he's going to take care of me.

Like he'd move mountains to make sure I'm happy. Even though he barely knows me.

There is one problem, though. He mentioned he has a wife.

I can't lie. That tidbit of information upset me.

But it sounds like he and his wife aren't close. Something's going on between them. I can sense it. I'm willing to bet they'll get divorced in no time.

There's something between us.

I think he feels it, too, but he's being such a gentleman about it. He's not like those other weirdos in the office who won't stop staring at me with their jaws practically touching the floor. It's disgusting. Some men are dogs. But Cole . . . he's not like that.

He's a good guy.

And that only makes me want him more.

So if his wife is too stupid to realize what she has, then she's too stupid to know what she's about to lose.

CHAPTER 12

Meghan

"What's her name?" I ask the moment Cole steps through the door at seven o'clock in the evening.

I've been thinking about this all day. Nonstop. I haven't eaten or bothered to make supper for Hazel. I've literally sat on the sofa, imagining Cole's hands on some young woman's hips while he takes her on his office desk.

It's all thanks to that stupid red tie of his.

He wore it for *her*.

I know it.

I considered not saying anything at all. I mean, I've gone this long without leaving Cole.

But I need to know.

It's eating away at me.

"Excuse me?" Cole says.

He's already on the defense. He used to come home and grab me in his arms. But that hasn't happened in years, and it's never going to happen again.

Not after everything.

"Your new secretary," I say.

He raises a brow at me. He's confused and probably thinking, *How did you know we hired a new secretary?*

But it doesn't take a rocket scientist to do the math. His previous secretary, Mia, left two weeks ago. And God forbid any of the suited businessmen at AstroWyre do any menial work around the office. So they must have brought in a new girl.

"Are you accusing me of something?" he says.

He stands a little taller. I despise it when he does that.

It's like he's trying to remind me of how big he is. Not that he's ever laid a hand on me. He wouldn't dare. I may not have followed through on some of my previous threats to him before, but if my husband ever touches me or my daughter, I'll end up in prison.

Well, if I get caught, I suppose.

"I just want to know her name," I say.

"I'm not cheating on you," he says through gritted teeth.

I let out a half-hearted scoff.

Right.

Because I haven't heard that one before.

"If you think I'm such a cheating piece of shit," he says, "why don't you divorce me already?"

I hate it when he says that. He knows damn well why I haven't gone that route.

"Have you called Dr. Tang?" he asks.

My nostrils flare. Does he really want to play that card again right now?

"Why are you getting so defensive, Cole?" I force my eyes to remain open despite them wanting to narrow on him. "Do you, or do you not, have a new secretary?"

"I do," he says.

He freezes like he's afraid that I'm going to ask if she's hot. Because if I do that, his face won't be able to lie to me. But I don't care to ask. I know the woman is hot. Otherwise, the company wouldn't have hired her. It's what they do—what they've always done.

"I'm asking for a name, Cole. I'm not accusing you of anything."

"Why bring it up at all, then?" he says.

Asking me that was a mistake. I cross my arms, a disingenuous smile tightening my already very tight lips. "Oh, I don't know, Cole. You've been acting more chipper than usual this week—"

"Our new secretary's name is Valeria," he says quickly.

I tap my chin, feigning deep thought. "Valeria. Sounds Hispanic. She must be gorgeous."

His eyes narrow on me. "Why are you doing this, Meg? Nothing is going on between us."

"Maybe not yet," I say. "But that's how you lure them in, isn't it? It's how you lured me in. You play the perfect gentleman." I pout my lips and dramatically tilt my head until my cheek is resting against my palm. "The man who can be trusted and who wouldn't dare do anything to make a woman feel uncomfortable."

He throws his arms up in frustration. "Meg, it's not my fault there's such a high turnaround at work. We have to hire a new secretary every few months."

I slap the wall next to me, the impact of it painfully warming my palm. The sound echoes throughout the entire house. "Well, maybe if you stopped screwing them all!"

He retreats from the conversation. I can see it. He's looking at me like I'm a lunatic.

"Have you stopped taking your meds?" he says. "Because you've accused me of cheating on you with every one of my secretaries this year."

"Because you have!" It takes everything in me not to slap the wall again. I realize I must look like a monster. I haven't showered in a few days, and my blond hair is a total mess with the roots having grown in at least an inch.

His nostrils flare.

I wish I had video footage of him or something. But I don't. In fact, I don't have any concrete evidence to shove in his face. But I can't tell him that. If I do, he'll be sure to tell Dr. Tang to double my bipolar medication.

I don't trust that doctor. Honestly, I've never had bipolar in my life. Yet she's convinced that my little brain injury caused me to develop the disorder.

"Meg?" Cole says as sweetly as possible.

I don't realize I'm breathing hard through my nostrils until I catch his shrewd gaze. "You're disappearing on me, Meg."

Although I very much dislike it when he tells me that, it does cause a switch to go off in my brain. He's warning me—I'm about to black out.

And when that happens, things get ugly, even though afterward, I rarely remember what happened during the episode.

I stare at Cole for a moment, trying to sort my thoughts. But I can't. All I feel when I look at my husband is contempt and rage.

I turn away from Cole and run my fingers through my greasy hair, then walk away.

"Where are you going?"

"Don't talk to me right now," I warn him.

He knows better, and he keeps his mouth shut.

I need to be alone. I need to calm myself out of this before it's too late and I do something I might regret. The last time this happened, I tore a steak knife from our kitchen block and threatened to cut Cole's throat. He still has a tiny mark from it.

I don't remember it. Not really. It's a giant fuzz. So all I have are pieces.

But those pieces are enough to terrify me. How could I have lost control like that? I'm not even a violent person.

But the worst part about that day was that Hazel saw me. She says she didn't, but I remember her being there. Faintly—but she was there.

She must have been standing right around the corner.

No wonder she hates me.

I spent two weeks in the psychiatric unit after that incident and was placed on different medications to help balance out my brain chemicals. I haven't had an episode since, but tonight, I came a little too close.

Have I missed my medications lately?

I need to be more careful about this.

The thought of losing total control of my own mind and body is beyond terrifying. And if that happens again, I might do something worse than last time.

Something that can't be undone.

Chapter 13

Meghan

I wake up to a soft pitter-pattering sound against my bedroom window. Next to me, Cole is sound asleep, snoring with his lips slightly parted.

I didn't want to sleep next to him after the fight we had, but I started to wonder if I was in the wrong. Did I go overboard?

I didn't mean to get so angry, but I spiraled.

I lie in bed, staring wide eyed at the ceiling above me. A strip of white light peeks through our bedroom curtains, illuminating the tips of my toes underneath our king-sized comforter.

Now, all I can think about is this Valeria woman. Has he already slept with her? If not, he must be planning to do it soon. My husband can never seem to keep his dick in his pants.

Sighing internally, I push the comforter off my legs and roll out of bed.

I'll never fall back asleep now.

I make my way downstairs and into the kitchen to pour myself a glass of chilled white wine, even though Dr. Tang told me not to mix alcohol with my new medication.

But it's one glass.

It's not the end of the world.

As I move into the living room, I flick on the light switch and dim the light until the room feels like a cozy cottage. Thankfully, all of the blinds are closed. I hate having the lights on in the house at night. It always feels like someone is standing outside peering in.

And ever since I saw that woman at my window—nothing more than a *delusion*, as per Cole's repetitive assurances—I'm constantly looking over my shoulder.

I didn't have this feeling before. It all started after my accident. What if Dr. Tang is right? It isn't normal to be this paranoid about everything.

I constantly feel like someone is watching me. When I explained this to Dr. Tang, she said it's a symptom of my bipolar and that the medications should help.

While I don't appreciate being told I have mental health issues, I can't fight science. I *did* have a traumatic brain injury, and I haven't been the same since.

It just sucks. Royally. I want my old life back.

I take a sip of my wine as I slowly lower myself into our living room sofa. I snatch my slick new tablet from my least favorite piece of furniture in the house—an octagon-shaped side table that wobbles constantly. I reserve this surface for my tablet only, which is covered in a heavy-duty case.

I press the Power button, and the screen's brightness hurts my eyes, but only momentarily. This tablet has changed my life. It's my favorite go-to when I want to browse the internet mindlessly and forget about all my problems.

Smiling to myself, I sink deeper into the sofa, the grip around my wineglass unrelenting.

Before I manage to start watching funny animal videos, however, I spot a notification on my AnyT-Chat app. It's a relatively new app that stands for Anytime Chat, and so far, I'm very much enjoying it.

The only people I have on there are Chelsea and my mother. I've never been one for friends. That's not true. I always thought of my staff as my friends, but after my accident, everyone gradually stopped talking to me. I guess that just proves what I've always believed—people remain in your life if it's convenient for them.

Not Chelsea, though.

We've been through thick and thin together. I consider her the sister I always wished I could have grown up with.

If she'd been by my side growing up, I likely wouldn't have so many trust issues.

I tap the little speech bubble icon and open up AnyT-Chat. The app flashes open without delay, and I spot Chelsea's name next to a little exclamation point.

1 New Message

I'm not one to ever ignore messages, even if I'm not in a talkative mood. I can't bear having little notification icons on my screen. It's beyond grating. It drives me almost as mad as when Cole places our blue ceramic coffee mugs with the tall yellow ones. I organized them by shelf for a reason.

Everything needs to be clean and organized.

Chels always said that my "obsessive-compulsive disorder" was the reason I made such a good dentist—I'm very attentive to detail.

I tap open the notification.

Hey! Guess what?! Hired a new girl, and she's awesome.

To anyone else, this might not mean much. But I talk to Chels at least once a week, so I know all about her dilemma.

Ever since her pregnancy, she's been trying to keep her bakery open. Having given birth at thirty-three years old, she's a bit late into the motherhood game—but that also allowed her plenty of time in her twenties to build her business from the ground up.

But Chels is a lot like me.

She likes things organized and flowing seamlessly. Her business is no different, which is why she never bothered to hire another baker.

I'd rather it be done right, she's always said.

But after she gave birth, she just couldn't do it. So she's been struggling to find the right match to run her bakery.

Jack, her husband, is useless when it comes to baking. The guy can hold a drill and put together just about anything, but if it's dough-related, you might as well ask him to fly a plane. He'd probably do that better than he does anything that requires flour and an oven.

To be fair, he's the king of the grill and makes pretty mean hamburgers and steaks.

I tap the text box and type in my reply: *That's amazing! Where'd you find her?*

Instantly, her name lights up in blue at the top of my screen. She's online. What is she doing online at two o'clock in the morning?

A little chat bubble throbs on the screen as she types.

Friend of a friend. She's a student. Studying baking and pastry arts. She's better than I was at her age! OMG. So relieved. I think the bakery will hold up so long as she keeps working there. Also, it's 2 a.m. Why are you up?!

I send her a laughing emoji, even though I'm not laughing.

So freaking happy for you, Chels. Honestly. It's about time you find the right person. And I couldn't sleep. What about you?

She ignores my question and jumps into interrogation mode. Ever since my accident, Chels has been hyperalert around me. Honestly, she's been a godsend. More supportive than Cole, even though he tries his best.

What's going on, Meg? Is it him? Something happen again?

Chels knows me all too well. She knows about Cole and exactly the kind of man he is. When my husband first betrayed me, she was the first one to show up at my door with a crowbar. Not that she'd have needed it if it came down to a physical altercation between Cole and her.

The girl has a black belt in mixed martial arts. Before tearing her ACL, she competed in national tournaments and almost came out on top.

Honestly, I was afraid for Cole that day. But I told Chels to go home. It was complicated. Very complicated. And although she couldn't understand it at the time, she does now.

Cole's first betrayal was heartbreaking, but it also

changed my life.

I stare at her message for a little too long as I slowly tilt my glass back. Cool, tangy wine coats my tongue.

Helloooo??

I set my wine aside, and I write back.

Yeah. New secretary

She sends me a red-faced angry emoji, followed by a dozen more with steam blowing out of their noses.

What can I do, Meg?

Nothing, but thank you. I'll take care of it.

Her response comes back way too fast.

Will you, though?

YES. Promise

She doesn't respond right away, but there's a read receipt under my message. What is she doing? Thinking? Does she not believe that I'll handle this?

Then, her message appears.

When is megalodon coming back?

I smile wistfully at her little blue text bubble.

Megalodon. She hasn't called me that in years.

When Chels and I first met in my last year of high school, it was right after I'd gotten into a fight with Jessica Hans and her little posse.

There were no fists involved.

My mouth has always been my superpower.

Apparently, Chels watched me rip Jessica to shreds with my words, and from then on, she wanted to be my friend. She said no one in the school dared talk to Jessica like that, but I'd had enough. She'd picked on me throughout all of high school and needed to be knocked down a peg. Or ten. I think she actually landed somewhere in the negative.

Rumor has it she tried to commit suicide after all the awful things I said to her. I felt bad about that—really bad. It hadn't been my intention. Fortunately, she didn't kill herself. Instead, she stopped bullying everyone at school out of fear of pissing me off again.

"I always looked at you as a dolphin, or even a basking

shark, because, you know, they're so passive," Chels had told me after the fight (she has a fascination with sea animals). "But honestly, Meghan, you're a freaking megalodon. Wanna be friends?"

I ignore Chels's message about my megalodon self coming back.

A vivid image flashes in my mind—me holding a steak knife to Cole's throat; his watery, terrified eyes; his pleas for mercy.

I've never been one for violence, but with my new psychological symptoms, what if that changes? What if I really am capable of doing something horrific to Cole?

I don't want to hurt him.

I'm terrified that if I allow megalodon to come out, she might end up being a new breed altogether—something way more dangerous than I ever imagined.

I ignore Chels's last message about megalodon making her return, and instead, respond with a row of red heart emojis.

Chapter 14

Meghan - 15 Years Earlier

Chels isn't watching me the way my best friend should on my wedding day. There's a glimmer of anger in her small, dark eyes.

Uncertainty.

No, not uncertainty. I wish it were uncertainty. Quite the opposite—she's *certain* I shouldn't be getting married to Cole.

But it's my wedding day.

Where's the excitement? The joy?

"You don't have to do this," she says sharply.

She crosses her arms over her emerald-green dress—the one I picked out for her to wear as my maid of honor. I gave her the title, even though she doesn't have any bridesmaids to boss around.

I stare at her through the silver-rimmed vanity mirror, then turn around and rest my makeup brush on the glass table. "Yeah, I kind of do."

"But you don't." She approaches me quickly, her muscular arms dangling on either side of her petite frame. "Marriage is a lifelong commitment, Meg."

"So is a child." I rest a hand over my small round belly.

It's small enough that no one should notice it, but large enough that if my mother eyes me carefully, she'll spot the pregnancy belly underneath my wedding dress.

"There are other ways," she says.

I shake my head. "No, there aren't, and you know that. Cole may not be perfect, but he'll be a good father. And my daughter needs to have a father."

She doesn't argue.

How can she?

All I've wanted since I was sixteen is to be a mother. And now, it's finally about to happen. I'm not going to raise my child without a father. I spent years longing for my dad, who left us when I was nine. I never saw him again.

I can't do that to my future daughter.

I won't.

My marriage doesn't have to be perfect. But my daughter's well-being and happiness—that's a different story.

"Kids grow up with only one parent all the time, and they're perfectly happy," Chels says. She's about to say something else, but I give her what she calls my *megalodon look.*

If she continues this conversation, I'm going to get upset and put her in her place. This is my life—my decision.

"Fine." She raises two flat palms on either side of her face. "If this is what you want, then I respect your decision."

"It is," I say.

She sits on a glossy stitched-leather chair across from me. "Did you write the vows you said you were going to?"

A playful smile pulls at my lips. "Of course."

CHAPTER 15

Cole - 15 years earlier

My wife-to-be enters the hall, looking like a goddess.

Especially as she walks underneath countless hanging lights and draping green vines. I promised her a dream wedding, and I delivered.

It came with a forty-thousand-dollar price tag, but my wife deserves it. And my parents were willing to spend up to fifty, so it worked out well.

Her hair is pulled back and tucked underneath her bridal veil. She's so damn beautiful.

Then, I catch a glimpse of her best friend sitting at the front of the banquet hall.

Chelsea.

She's watching me with those dark beady eyes of hers and her manly arms crossed over her chest. That girl must lift weights every day. Meg mentioned she started taking mixed martial arts and dreams of competing. With how much anger that girl has bottled up, she'll probably kick a lot of asses.

She looks more feminine than usual today in her silky green dress. Meg loves green, and being that Chelsea is her only bridesmaid—or maid of honor, or whatever it's called—she asked her to wear green.

I wish I could tell her to stop watching me. Shouldn't she be paying attention to Meg? Instead, she's looking at me like I'm some horrible monster.

It was one mistake, for crying out loud. I've apologized to Meg countless times.

And besides, everything turned out fine. Better than

fine. We're getting married, and now, we're going to have a child.

I wish Chelsea would mind her own business. I still can't believe she threatened to break my legs with a crowbar a few months ago. What a psycho. Not exactly the kind of person I want my future daughter growing up around.

But Meg loves Chelsea. I'd never tell her not to see her or talk to her. I'm not that guy. Besides, Meg is a powerhouse. It's not like she'd listen to me anyway.

Meg walks down the aisle with her mom, looking slightly uncomfortable. They aren't exactly close. I've heard some pretty bad stories about Meg's upbringing. I can tell she's sad that she isn't locking arms with the father she doesn't remember. But Meg hides her feelings well when she's around people. I'm sure I'm the only one who can sense this tinge of sadness.

Okay—maybe Chelsea, too, since they're practically sisters.

The second Meg is standing in front of me, I reach for her hand. She doesn't hesitate the way she did months ago before I proposed to her. We're over that. We've healed from my mistake.

The officiant, a middle-aged woman with a short silver afro and vibrant amber eyes, goes on to welcome everyone with a smile that lights up the room.

But honestly, all I can focus on are Meg's big blue eyes and the subtle pink eyeshadow she smudged over her eyelids. Her lips are rose colored, and it takes a tremendous amount of self-control to not lean in and kiss her.

I'm pretty sure the officiant has to give us permission, first.

I smile at her, and although she smiles back, it seems a bit strained. Part of me still wonders if she really wants to go through with this.

But we've talked about it.

We both want the same thing—a family and a life

together.

The officiant talks for a while about love, promises, and something about an invisible glue that will hold us together for all of eternity.

Meg suddenly widens her eyes at me.

The entire banquet hall has gone silent. At the front, both my mom and dad are watching me with anticipation.

I bet they'd be happy if I asked to cancel the whole thing. My mom isn't a fan of Meg. I can tell she thinks that Meg isn't good enough for me, even though she'd never outright say it.

The officiant clears her throat. "Your vows, Cole."

"Oh," I blurt out, embarrassed. I reach into my pocket and start reading my chicken-scratch writing. "Meg." I pause to look up at her. "I know I haven't always been perfect, and sometimes, I can downright annoy you." She arches a brow like she's not quite understanding where I'm going with this. "But I promise you that as your husband, I will do everything in my power to keep you happy. To love you. Cherish you. To always be by your side, no matter what happens. I love you more than life."

I glance up at her again, and she smiles sweetly at me. There's a sparkle of love in her eyes that I haven't seen in a long time. I don't doubt she loves me.

Being the wordsmith that she is, Meg doesn't pull a note out from her dress. Instead, she grabs my hands.

"Cole, before we met, I didn't think I'd ever find someone to love the way I love you. I promise to always be here for you, through the good and the bad. I promise to be a listening ear. A best friend. And most of all, I promise to be yours and only yours. And in return, I expect the same loyalty."

I swallow hard. Why is she bringing up loyalty in her wedding vows? Isn't that a given? Isn't that what marriage is all about? Committing yourself wholly to another person?

She shoots Chelsea a quick look and my jaw tenses. Why is she looking at her like that?

Then, her icy eyes meet mine again. "And if you betray my trust, I'll break both your legs and bury you six feet underground."

I blink several times, my heart thudding loudly in my chest. Did she just say that? Or did I imagine it?

An awkward silence fills the banquet hall, until finally, Chelsea bursts out laughing, and so does Meg. Everyone else follows, and I turn to see grinning faces throughout the audience. Even the officiant is smiling at Meg's morbid sense of humor.

But as I stare into Meg's sharp eyes, I can't help but wonder: Is she really joking?

CHAPTER 16

Cole

Vincent already gave me shit for offering Valeria her new title so early into her new job.

But she's the one I need.

If he wants me to continue bringing in clients the way I do, then I need my things to be organized efficiently. And I also need someone pleasant to look at.

I hate to admit it, but most of the clients I deal with are middle-aged men who are easily swayed by beauty. Having Valeria in the room may not seal a deal, but it will definitely help.

"So, I don't help the other managers anymore?" Valeria asks me sheepishly.

I'm guessing someone already asked her to do something, and she didn't know how to respond.

I gaze up at her from my desk, then gesture her to come inside. She closes the door behind her by pressing it with her body, hands tucked behind her back.

Today, she's decided to wear high-waisted dress pants and a red blouse that looks custom-tailored for her. It fits her snugly in all the right spots.

"Vincent still has to hire a new secretary," I say. "Unfortunately, you'll have to juggle both jobs for now, but not for long. Once HR is done with the paperwork, you'll officially be *my* assistant. I have a lot on my plate, and I need all the help I can get."

She forces a smile. "What can I do? Coffee?"

"Oh." My idea of receiving help wasn't in the form of a hot coffee. My calendar is a mess, and I need to send follow-up emails on several leads. But a coffee would be great.

"I'd love that," I say.

"Two creams, one sugar," she says.

I arch a brow. "How did you know that?"

The corners of her bright-red lips sharpen. "Saw you in the staff room."

She watched me make a coffee? I'm not sure whether this is flattery or whether she's *that* attentive to detail.

"I hope you don't think this job is . . . beneath you," I say. "I will always treat you with respect. All I ask for in return is competency and that you be here as often as possible."

"I know," she says. "I can tell you're a good boss. That's why I accepted the offer."

We lock eyes for a moment, and it looks like she's fighting back a smile. Is she shy?

"How about we celebrate your new position?" I say.

Finally, those bright-red lips split into a grin. She has very white, glossy teeth that are no doubt the result of whitening strips. "Oh?"

"My treat," I say. "Lunch at noon. You like steak?"

Her eyes seem to double in size. "Um, yes, of course—"

"Meet me back in my office at eleven thirty, and I'll drive us to Blue Fusion Bistro."

Her jaw goes slack.

I'm certain she didn't expect to eat at a place like Blue Fusion Bistro during her first week on the job. Plates start out at fifty dollars each. But they have the best steak in all of Bayton Valley. People from all over the state come here to enjoy the food.

It's also my go-to when trying to hook in a new client.

"A-are you sure?" she asks. She's fidgeting with the multiple gold rings around her fingers.

"I'm sure." My mouth curves into a smile. "See you at eleven thirty."

***

There's something adorable about the look on Valeria's face. She reminds me of a kid being offered some new limited-edition candy. And a whole bucket of it.

She looks around the luxurious restaurant, her gaze clinging to the vintage paintings hanging on the charcoal wooden walls, the tables topped with linen tablecloths, the chandeliers overhead, and the buttery leather chairs all around us.

"This place is . . . wow," she says.

The server—a young man with wavy raven black hair—leads us to a small, intimate table tucked underneath a dimmed light.

I extend an open palm, inviting Valeria to be seated first. The moment she sits down, I pull my chair out and follow suit. Then, I open up my white napkin and rest it on my lap.

"Would you like wine?" I ask.

"Oh, no, that's all right—"

I glance up at the clean-shaven waiter, who is waiting patiently for any request we might have. "We'll have a bottle of your house wine, please."

He smiles politely and nods at us as if he's serving a table of royals.

"Red or white?" he asks.

"Red," I say.

The waiter bows politely, then walks away with calculated pride.

Meanwhile, Valeria looks petrified.

"This isn't a date," I tell her.

Her cheeks darken several shades of pink. "Oh, no, I wasn't thinking that—"

"You weren't?" I ask.

She bites her plush lower lip.

"This job doesn't come with a price tag," I say.

She's staring at me. I know exactly what she's thinking. That I offered her the job in exchange for sex.

"I'm a married man," I say.

A faint scoff escapes her mouth. Before I can ask her

what she's thinking, the waiter returns and delicately pours a bit of red wine into my glass. I swirl it around, coating my glass with a faint red film. The moment it touches my tongue, I analyze the liquid thoughtfully. There's a dark berry undertone, which is immediately followed by a peppery taste—almost spicy.

It's perfect.

I give the waiter a brisk nod and he proceeds to fill my wineglass. Valeria doesn't bother doing a taste test. She flicks a finger outward at the waiter as if to say, *Go ahead.*

The waiter fills her glass, places the bottle down, then stands with his hands tucked behind his back.

"Are you ready to order now, or would you like more time?"

"More time, please," I say.

He nods again as if he's Batman's butler, then walks away.

"Are you okay?" I ask.

She stares at me for a moment, like she's trying to gauge whether or not honesty is the best policy with me.

Finally, she says, "In my experience, men in power don't hand out freebies. They always want something. Usually—"

But she doesn't finish.

I sip my wine and shake my head at her. "I'm not going to ask you for sex, Valeria. All I want is an assistant who knows how to manage my calendar and my clients. That's all I want in return."

She eyes me carefully. I can tell she wants to believe me but that she's been through her fair share of bad experiences with men.

That's all right.

She'll come to see that I'm not like the rest of them.

Chapter 17

Cole

"I'm serious," I say. "Twenty-nine hot dogs. And that's with the buns."

Valeria's laughter fills the entire parking lot. "I can't see it, sorry."

"Is it because of my slender figure?" I ask, twirling awkwardly like a ballerina. But I almost stumble, so I stop midtwirl. "I trained for months to get my stomach to stretch."

She's still laughing.

I suppose the idea of me winning a hot dog competition does sound ridiculous. Especially as the interim chief operating officer of AstroWyre. But that's just a job title. It doesn't change who I am or some of the dumb stuff I did when I was younger.

I laugh with her as we stroll down the paved walkway leading away from Blue Fusion Bistro, then rub my face, which is rough. I hate how fast my beard grows. It's not even two o'clock yet, and I could already shave again. But unless I have a late evening event, I don't bother.

Meg used to love that about me. Actually, she prefers me with a beard, but with my job, I prefer to be clean-shaven. I once read an article that very few men within the Fortune 500 have beards.

There's something about a clean shave that just screams success. And that's where I want to be. At the top.

"What's that?" Valeria asks.

All trace of a smile has left her voice. I turn to look at

her. Not only is she not smiling anymore—her forehead is deeply puckered. It causes the smallest of bumps to form between her shapely eyebrows.

I follow her gaze to my shiny black Lexus LC.

On its hood are little brown-red specks. Or crumbs. Or . . . What the hell is that? Dirt? It's all over my windshield, too.

Valeria approaches my car, her heels ticking against the parking lot's freshly paved asphalt.

"It looks like leaves or something," she says.

I lean in closer, then reach for one of the brown bits. It crumbles between my thumb and index finger. Some are more red than others, but they're all approximately an inch in width and curled at the edges.

They're . . . rose petals.

What the hell are rose petals doing on my car?

"Cole?"

I look up to find Valeria standing across from me on the passenger's side. How long have I been standing here with crumpled rose petals in my palm?

"You okay?"

I tilt my hand, allowing the wind to sweep the little dry bits to the ground.

"What does this mean?" she asks. "Is this . . . Did your wife do this? She might have thought we were on a date."

It isn't like Meg to leave behind some cryptic message like this. She's direct and always has been. Just like yesterday—she didn't hold back when she accused me of cheating on her.

Still.

Despite all the accusations she's thrown my way, she's never actually done anything to me. She gets upset, then lets it go and makes it a point to emphasize how important it is that our family *stays together*.

When she first accused me of infidelity after we married, I was afraid to go to sleep next to her that night. It was one thing to have made a mistake while we were dating—but married?

I was terrified she might slit my throat in my sleep. But she didn't. She let it go, which was confusing, because she's always been very outspoken about her views on cheating husbands. She'd often say that if she had her way, she'd castrate any man who cheats on his wife.

Needless to say, I slept with two pairs of briefs that night.

But when I woke up, everything was fine. She was cold with me for several weeks, but eventually, she acted like nothing happened.

It's what I've learned to deal with—sudden accusations, fits of anger, and then, silence.

So if Meg did do this, she's changed her approach.

Her days of *letting it go* are over.

Chapter 18

Meghan

Cole steps into the house at precisely five o'clock while I'm boiling pasta for supper. The starchy smell has already filled the kitchen, and the warmth of the steam is comforting.

Ziggy is at my feet, waiting for me to drop something—anything.

And I will.

But now that Cole's home, I'll have to do it secretly. He hates it when I feed Ziggy. Says I'm turning him into a poorly behaved dog with all his begging.

But honestly, it's cute. I don't care if he begs. Besides, I'm the one who spends every day with him. So if the begging doesn't bother me, Cole has no business even having an opinion.

I grab a piece of cooked pasta with a spoon, rinse it with cool water, and flick it at Ziggy. His little jaws snap shut.

"Perfect catch," I whisper.

"Honey?" Cole calls out.

There's a faint quiver in his voice. He sounds scared, like he doesn't know whether he'll be greeted by a showered and friendly Meg or a bedraggled and emotionally unstable Meg.

But today, I decided to shower and freshen up. I spent the whole day cleaning, trying to remind myself of everything Cole has done for me and this family. He's been a good father, and he takes care of me despite all of my new mental health issues as well as my new physical disability.

Another husband might have left his wife.

I should be grateful.

"In here," I call out.

He enters the kitchen with a bouquet of flowers. Not the cheap kind. But something he picked up at a flower shop. Something that cost at least a hundred dollars.

They're beautiful. A mixture of reds, yellows, and purples. The wrapping paper around the stems looks more valuable than our tablecloth—and that thing wasn't cheap. Cole had it imported from Italy when I told him how madly in love I was with the design.

Without Cole, I'd be living in some shoddy apartment, living month to month on disability insurance paychecks. Thankfully, I was smart enough to purchase disability insurance when I started my dental practice. But without Cole, I wouldn't have had the funds to obtain my university dentistry diploma in the first place.

I may not be able to practice anymore thanks to my nonfunctioning arm, but I'm rather well off.

I do miss work . . . a lot. There's something about digging rot out of teeth and filling the hole with a clean white filling that always satisfied me. Some days, I drive by the building that started it all.

Rent alone was expensive, and no way would I have been able to get my business off the ground without Cole's help.

The place is still operating with the same hygienist staff and everything. But I had to partner with another dentist—Miriam Pelowski—who keeps things running for me and keeps raking money into my small corporation.

I have a *good* husband.

"Do you like?" Cole asks, drawing me back to reality.

I blink at the flowers, then move toward them and inhale deeply. They smell heavenly. "They're beautiful."

He watches me carefully like he's expecting a different reaction. Anger, possibly. But today, I'm feeling good. Much better than yesterday.

"What did you do today?" he asks.

He never asks me what I did.

"Stayed home. What else would I have done?" I say.

He shrugs. "It's a beautiful day. Thought you might have gone out somewhere."

The functioning side of my mouth droops down. What is he talking about? I've been a recluse for a year. I don't go anywhere unless it's to do groceries, pick up Hazel from soccer, or drive her to or from Alex's place.

"Like I said, I was here," I say.

He's looking at me like he doesn't quite believe me. Why? Cole only gets like this when he has something to hide, and he wants to test me—see if I know anything.

He thinks I don't see the subtle changes in his facial features, but I do. His nose does this very strange, almost imperceptible twitch when he's nervous. It's like several mini nostril flares that happen in succession.

I don't know what causes it. He might be trying to calm his nervous breathing. Regardless, he's been doing it for years.

And the flowers. It's all a red flag.

But then, he beams at me. "I'll put these in water for you."

"Hey, listen," I say. "I'm sorry about yesterday. I got in my own head, and—"

He brushes me off with a swift wave of his baby-smooth hand. "No need to apologize. I should have explained to you that I had an important meeting all morning, and that's why I chose to wear my tie."

I stare at him.

He sounds genuine. I want to believe him—I really do. But there's this nagging part of me that is warning me not to trust my husband.

I push this loud voice aside. "That's okay. I overreacted."

A cute smile lights up his face. He looks so sexy when his beard starts to grow in like that. It comes in dark and makes his light eyes pop so much.

I step toward him and curl a finger inside his belt, then

tug on it. "How about we make nice?"

The happiness on his face falters, and he pulls away from me. "I'm sorry, Meg. Honestly, I had a really long day, and—"

"Don't worry about it," I cut him off.

I turn around to stir my pasta in the pot. But I ignored it for so long that now it's overcooked and sticking to the bottom. I want to throw my spatula at the kitchen window and shatter it.

"Meg?"

He approaches me from behind and reaches for my shoulder, but I jerk away.

"I'm sorry," he repeats.

"You're always sorry." I slam my spatula down on the marble counter and turn to glare at him. "Is it my mouth? Am I so disfigured now that you have no interest in touching me?"

He pulls his face back as if I just backhanded him. "What? No. How could you even say that?"

He's either an amazing actor, or he's a total idiot.

"Seriously? Cole, we haven't slept together in over a year. You never want to touch me anymore."

His eyes widen, then narrow as he ponders this. "Has it . . . Has it really been a year?"

How has this not affected him? If we'd been sleeping together this whole time, I probably wouldn't feel like he's out getting it someplace else.

"Shit, Meg, I didn't realize—"

Bullshit.

He's a man. And every man has needs.

Actually, every person has needs, including me. And he hasn't been meeting them.

"I've been so preoccupied with work this last year that, I don't know. I guess I haven't had much of a drive, to be honest."

I don't know what overtakes me. Without warning, I grab his belt, then I cup him over his pants. "No drive? Really? Do I need to get rough? Is that how you like it?"

He doesn't respond the way I'd hoped.

He pushes my hand aside and scowls at me. "What the hell are you doing?"

"Trying to get my husband to have sex with me!"

His brows slant, and he looks at me with pity.

Great. Well, if pity sex works . . . Hey, at least I'll get something.

I want to tell my husband that I miss him. That I'd do anything to have him back. Yet, I hate him. It's extremely conflicting. So much for my day spent thinking positive thoughts about him.

At least I tried.

I grab the spatula and slam it against his chest. "If you aren't going to be intimate with me, the least you can do is make supper tonight."

CHAPTER 19

Hazel

I'm a bit stunned to find Dad standing in the kitchen when I get home. But of course, he isn't surprised to see me because I always keep both my parents in the loop about my whereabouts. If I didn't, they wouldn't let me go anywhere.

"Hey, honey," Dad says.

Holding what looks to be a sticky spatula, he wraps an arm around my shoulders and squeezes me against his chest. Then he plants a quick kiss on the top of my head. "How was school? How was your afternoon with Alex?"

I'm about to give him a very condensed version of my day, but he keeps talking. "His mom was home, right? You know the rule, Hazel."

Here we go again.

Are we seriously having this stupid talk again? It's so embarrassing. Why does my dad have to make everything so cringey?

"Dad, I've told you, like, a gazillion times. Alex is gay."

My dad smiles, and I can tell he thinks I'm naïve. "Right. That's the perfect alibi to get close to a girl."

He winks at me like he's done it himself, and I want to vomit.

Before I can say anything else, Mom comes down the stairs, eyes crinkled. She looks genuinely happy to see me, but then when she looks at Dad, you'd think she was trying to cast some wicked spell on him.

They were probably fighting again.

"Hey, sweetheart," she says. Her lips curve into a

warped smile.

It's not very nice to look at, and I feel horrible even having that thought.

"Hey," I say.

She goes to raise her good arm but then seems to rethink hugging me and pulls it back down against her side. "Good day at school?"

I nod.

"Did Alex's mom drop you off?"

"What?" I say. "No, I walked."

Her features contort so quickly that I take a step back. "You *walked*?" she repeats.

Behind me, Dad puts his spatula down and enters the conversation. I think he's about to come to my defense.

"Are you serious right now, Hazel?" he says behind me.

Okay—I was wrong.

He's usually on my side. But right now, he looks as pissed off as Mom.

"Have you not been watching the news?" Mom says. "Two girls have gone missing this year. This year! We have some sick predator piece of shit on the streets, and you're walking by yourself—"

"Calm down," I say, but I immediately regret my words.

Mom hates being told to calm down. It's basically like telling her that she's acting totally irrational. Acting *crazy*.

"Calm down?" she repeats. "Do you know grown women have been abducted in Bayton Valley? We may not be as big as Chicago or New York, but the city is big enough. There are plenty of creeps walking the streets! And the crime rate has been soaring!"

If she were a cartoon character, she'd have steam coming out of her ears.

"Your mother's right," Dad says. "You shouldn't be walking ten blocks home alone. Not right now. And especially not through the East End."

I roll my eyes.

They make the East End sound like a ghetto. I mean, sure, it isn't great. Some windows are broken, and I've heard a gun go off twice now. But all the bad stuff in the East End is drug related. And I'm not into drugs, so those types of people have no reason to come after me.

"How many times do I have to repeat myself about not walking alone?" Mom plants her fist on her hip, which tells me she isn't messing around. "I'm always willing to come get you."

Mom usually does come to pick me up. Either that or Anna drives me home. But she's been drinking more than usual lately. And if I tell that to Mom and Dad, they might not let me go to Alex's place anymore.

So really, I was being responsible. Anna offered to drive me with a slur, then stumbled while trying to fetch her keys out of her purse.

That's when I decided to walk.

"Alex could have at least walked with you," Dad says.

Mom scoffs at Dad. "Seriously? Don't get me wrong, I love Alex, but he's half of Hazel's size and twice as dainty as her. He wouldn't be much use against a predator."

I cross my arms. "I'm not dainty. And neither is Alex."

"I didn't mean that as an insult," Mom says.

She isn't totally wrong. Alex is pure feminine energy. He spends his free time drawing, not playing sports. I love that about him. It's why we're best friends. But Mom is probably right—if some creep pulled up to abduct me, I'm not sure how much damage Alex could do.

Then again, that kid's been through a lot. I like to think that if my life were on the line, a different side of him would come out.

"Why didn't you call us?" Dad says. "Your mom could have picked you up."

Because you would have smelled Anna's alcohol and cigarettes clinging to my clothes.

But I can't say that.

I wish they'd trust me. Know that I make smart decisions and not think I'm some stupid teenager.

But I know that won't happen. Dad's arms are now bulging because he's crossing them even tighter, waiting for an answer. And Mom doesn't seem any more impressed.

I'm getting really sick of them both looking at me like that. Honestly, I don't want to deal with this right now.

I take a step sideways, prepared to march my way upstairs, but Mom sticks out her good arm. "Where do you think you're going?"

"Upstairs," I say. "There's no point talking about this. I'm obviously grounded or something. You guys are making a big deal—"

Her fingers are suddenly wrapped around my wrist, and she's standing inches away from me. Her hot, minty breath assaults my nose, and her bright eyes are inhumanly wide. I want to pull away, but I'm too freaked out right now.

"Making a big deal out of this?" she says. "You're my daughter, and it's my job to protect you. Do you understand that?"

Her fingernails are now digging into my skin. Why isn't Dad doing anything? He looks as scared as I am.

All I can do is nod.

"You have no idea what kind of sick fucks are out there. No idea! You can't trust men. Do you hear me? All it takes is one bad one, and your life is ruined, Hazel. Or you're dead."

When I don't say anything, she squeezes tighter. "Are you listening?"

My throat swells.

Why is she acting like this?

"Mom, you're hurting me." My voice comes out a squeak.

She instantly lets go, and her face softens. Then, she clears her throat. "I— I didn't mean to hurt you. I'm sorry. I just need you to understand how serious this is, Hazel. You have no idea what some men are capable of."

I peek over her shoulder at Dad.

Please, help.

He stands quietly, barely making eye contact.

I can't tell if he's afraid to stand up to Mom or if he's ashamed to admit that she's right.

CHAPTER 20

Meghan - 23 Years Earlier

I don't like Mom's new boyfriend. Every time he looks at me, I feel gross. He stares a little longer than he should for a grown man. And his eyes always appear wet and shiny.

It's creepy.

Why does he watch me like that?

I'm twelve years old and only now starting to develop. Is it because of that? Are my new boobs growing in weird? I mean, a lot of guys at school look at me like that, too.

I haven't said anything to Mom about it. I'm probably making things up in my head. And even if I'm not, well, she's finally happy. I can't take that away from her.

She went almost a whole year without smiling. All she did was cry and drink. But these last few weeks, she's dancing and grinning and won't stop talking about how incredible Karl is.

Meeting him has somehow helped her get over Dad. I never thought my mom would get over him. After she found out about the affair, she was devastated.

But it wasn't only one affair.

Turns out he had countless.

The worst part is that I didn't think my father would ever do something like that. He always seemed so honest. A stand-up guy. He brought Mom flowers every other week. Made supper twice a week.

I miss my dad, a lot.

But I can't say that to Mom. I'm scared to make her more sad than she already is. She was so upset over what he did to her that she fought really hard in court, and she now has full custody of me.

No visits, either.

Something about one of his affairs being with a girl under the age of consent, which is seventeen in New York. I looked it up.

That's so gross to think about.

Mom got him in a lot of trouble for that one, and he spent a year in prison.

So how can I miss a man who does something like that? It makes *me* feel gross.

"Meghan?" Mom says.

I look up at her and then at Karl, who is hugging her from behind while pressing his rosy cheek up against hers.

Karl isn't the type of man Mom would go for. Dad has blue eyes, like me, but his hair is almost black. Karl has dirty orange-blond hair and a receding hairline and these weird brown eyes that appear black half the time. They don't match his hair at all. Sometimes I wonder if he bleaches it.

He's not in shape, either. His belly juts over his belt, and his arms are on the flabbier side. I don't understand how Mom could find him attractive. But Karl is a very smooth talker and has a very charming smile.

Mom, on the other hand, could have been a model with her dark eyes and long auburn hair. She's also slender and tall, almost surpassing Karl.

I definitely didn't get my features from her.

"Burgers or pizza tonight?" she asks.

It's Friday night, which means we get to eat something special. Something unhealthy. I spent the last year feeding myself with ramen noodles and peanut butter sandwiches since Mom was too depressed to cook.

Having Karl around also means I get to have good food again. I suppose that's a plus.

"Um, doesn't matter," I say.

"How about both?" Karl says. He pulls open one of our kitchen drawers and extracts a spatula. "I'll cook."

My mom titters, which is so embarrassing. "Oh, Karl. I didn't know you were a cook!"

"There's a lot you don't know," he says, winking horribly at her.

I make a sour face and look away, but a clanking sound draws my attention back to them.

Karl has dropped the spatula on the laminate countertop and has scooped my mother up. She's now sitting on the counter next to the sink, her long, curly hair curtaining over her back.

"Oh, Karl."

He kisses her passionately.

It's enough to make me gag with my mouth closed. I can't stand it when he does that. And sometimes, he watches me while he's doing it. It's disgusting.

"Do we have ketchup?" Karl asks.

My mom, who is still smiling like girls in my school do when they're crushing hard on one of the boys, pivots on her heels and pries the fridge door open. "I'm certain we do. I just used it the other night. Meghan, did you finish the ketchup?"

"No," I say.

Karl is watching me intently. "Are you sure?"

"I don't even like ketchup," I say.

Karl scratches his head. "We can't eat burgers without ketchup. It just isn't the same, you know? I could run to the store. But I really want to get the pizza started."

My mom doesn't hesitate. "Don't worry. I've got it."

She snatches her coat from our flimsy plastic coat rack and leans in to kiss Karl, who, once again, is watching me with those seemingly black eyes of his.

I shiver.

"I can come with you," I tell my mom.

I don't want to stay here alone with Karl in this tiny apartment. My mother has known him all of three weeks. Why is she leaving me alone with him?

"No, no, you stay here, honey. It'll give you and Karl some good bonding time. I'll be back in less than twenty minutes."

I want to protest, but she's already out the door.

Karl flashes me a brief smile. He starts shredding cheese and sprinkling it over one of those pizza crusts that come in a kit.

At least he's ignoring me.

Thank God.

I reach for my Game Boy, prepared to start playing Pac-Man, when Karl rounds the kitchen island and joins me in the living room.

I don't look up when his shadow looms over me. The guy is big—at least six feet tall, which my mom seems to love. He rakes a hand through his greasy-looking hair, then casually points at the seat next to me. "Do you mind if I—?"

Yeah, I mind.

But I don't want to be rude. So instead, I shrug.

He sits down heavily and lets out a lungful of air that smells like beer.

"Listen," he says. "I'm sure it's not easy having some random person in your apartment with you and your mom. She told me all about your dad and what happened. I just wanted to say that I'm sorry."

He rests a hand on my thigh.

I'm so uncomfortable I could scream. But I'm also too scared to react badly. What if he gets angry? What if he hurts me? Mom isn't here right now.

I flinch when he reaches for a strand of my hair and tucks it behind my ear.

"You don't have to be scared around me, Meggy."

Meggy?

He brushes his thumb against my cheek. "You're both my beautiful princesses now, and I'm going to take very good care of you both."

CHAPTER 21

Meghan

It's Tuesday, which means Hazel has soccer practice after school. It's my favorite day to do groceries since I have to go out anyway.

I tell Ziggy to behave, even though I know he'll probably jump all over the sofas and try to get into the garbage can the moment I step out. I'd bring him with me, but he'd just yap in my Jeep and annoy everyone in the parking lot.

I snatch my purse and inspect it for my key fob. It's in there. I'm good to go.

I leave through our huge two-car garage in my Jeep, extra careful while reversing this time. Almost running over Hazel's friends last week has caused my driving anxiety to go up.

When I get to the grocery store, I'm not surprised to find a parking lot full of cars. It's three o'clock in the afternoon, and it seems like most people like to do their groceries at this time. Then again, it seems like people are always everywhere.

It's annoying.

Don't people work anymore?

I park in the nearest handicap parking I see. Months ago, I was embarrassed to use my placard. But now, I don't care. I have one good arm. Pushing a cart across an entire parking lot while trying to dodge traffic isn't easy.

The double doors of Bayton Valley Grocer swoosh open the moment I approach with my rattling cart. Inside is as busy as I suspected. Why wouldn't it be? This store was built only two years ago, and it's beautiful.

Best of all—they tend to stock more local products than imported products, and their prices are competitive.

Melodic music hums overhead as one elderly couple leisurely browses the fruit aisles. They're moving so slowly, it's as if they have nothing better to do. They probably don't.

Next to them, a young mother tries to wrangle three kids, two of them small toddlers. Poor girl.

I move as quickly as humanly possible, my pace a stark contrast to the calming music coming from everywhere. But I've never been one to linger in a grocery store. Actually, I don't linger anywhere. Why do people do that? I'm here for groceries—not to get my step count in.

Hazel loves this certain type of breakfast cereal called CocoClouds. It turns the milk into chocolate milk. It's not the healthiest breakfast option, but she deserves a treat once in a while.

I walk fast down the cereal aisle, scanning the shelves. At the same time, footsteps echo behind me.

Tick. Tick. Tick.

I wouldn't normally care. We're in a grocery store. People walk—that's what humans do. But for some reason, right now, the sound really irks me. It might have something to do with the fact that I've been hearing it ever since I walked in.

Is everyone wearing heels today? Or are these same heels following me everywhere?

I turn my head sideways to spot a tall woman with long, luxurious brown hair flowing behind her back. She doesn't look at me. In fact, I don't think she even sees me.

She's crouched—something you'd think impossible in those black heels of hers and that skintight sky-blue dress—and scanning through peanut butter jars on the bottom shelf.

On the top of her head is a huge straw hat that is so large it droops all around her head.

I'm surprised the weight of it doesn't drag her down to the floor.

She's only shopping. My irritation must be due to the lights in here. Ever since my accident, fluorescent lights really affect me.

I finish my groceries and push my cart through to checkout.

Thankfully, Maya is working today. She's my favorite staff member here. A large, fierce woman with a radiant smile that could light up an entire city. Her hair is usually tied back in a ponytail, but today, she's sporting cornrows.

"Honey, let me help you with that," she says.

I thank her as she helps me load my groceries onto the conveyor belt.

When she has finished helping me, she pats me on the shoulder. Her touch is warm and earnest. There's something about this woman that makes me want to hug her and cry and talk to her about all my frustrations.

Instead, I offer her a ghost of a smile and awkwardly push my cart using my hand and my abdomen.

Tick. Tick. Tick.

There's that stupid sound again.

As I exit the sliding doors, I turn around to spot that same woman standing behind me, slowly placing her items on the conveyor belt. But rather than focus on her groceries, she's looking right at me.

At least, I think she is.

That damn hat is masking half her face, and on top of it, she's wearing oversized sunglasses, leaving visible only a pair of bright-red lips.

Who wears sunglasses in a grocery store?

Does she think she's some kind of celebrity?

I keep walking, my neck twisted from watching her while she watches me. She's stopped moving now with a can of beans hovering over the conveyor belt.

But rather than place it down, she smiles at me.

It's not warm or kind.

It's a chilling smile that has me moving a little bit faster toward my Jeep.

Chapter 22

Meghan

By the time I've finished loading my groceries—a task that only got easier once a friendly bearded man with sleeve tattoos offered to help—I hurry around my car and jump into the driver's seat.

That woman.

Who the hell was she?

I search the parking lot for a sky-blue dress and a straw hat.

Nothing.

She must have left while I was busy shoving grocery bags into my trunk.

Sighing, I rest my foot on the brake pedal and press my ignition Start button. As my Jeep's engine rumbles to life, I spot a little white piece of paper fluttering underneath my windshield wiper.

A ticket?

Seriously?

I have my handicap placard resting right on the dashboard. Angrily, I snatch my very visible placard and shimmy it over my sun visor.

This wouldn't be the first time I got ticketed. Some people take one look at me and think I'm abusing the system because I'm relatively young and don't walk around with a cane. That doesn't mean I'm not disabled.

People should really mind their own business and stop calling the authorities over things like this.

Mumbling swears under my breath, I step out of my Jeep and come around the front. The slip of paper is jammed, almost crumpled, like whoever left this was in a hurry.

I yank it out from under my wiper.

Wait a minute.

This isn't a parking ticket. It looks like a ripped piece of printer paper. There's nothing official about it. Did someone hit my car and decide to leave a note? I'd be surprised. People in Bayton Valley only care about themselves. Some days, I wish we could pack up and move to a small town. Or somewhere south, where we don't get hit by winter storms.

I uncrumple the ripped piece of paper to find poor handwriting scribbled in black marker.

What the hell is this?

I raise my eyes to the parking lot again, looking for *her*. Did *she* do this? She was looking at me funny. Or is this entirely unrelated?

It can't be a coincidence.

And judging by how beautiful that woman was, I'm willing to bet that was Valeria. The only reason a beautiful woman would be harassing me is Cole.

I would know.

I've been through it before.

And each time, I managed to get rid of Cole's mistresses. But something tells me it's going to be different this time.

That woman . . . She had to have been Valeria.

Which means I'm not dealing with some young snob who can easily be scared off.

This woman wants Cole.

All to herself.

I glance down at the note one more time.

He's *mine*. Not *yours*.

CHAPTER 23

Meghan

Hazel sits quietly in the car, sweat dripping down her dark hairline. When the sun penetrates the windshield like that, it makes her hazel eyes look yellow.

But I don't comment on how beautiful she is.

I'm too stuck in my own head over what happened at the grocery store.

Not that Hazel is going to mind the lack of conversation. She never wants to talk to me lately.

I drive us home quietly, and Hazel wastes no time disappearing into her room.

I should have said something. Tried to talk to her. I wish she'd open up to me. Maybe tonight, I'll offer to make her chicken Alfredo—her favorite. And she's been on this whole gluten-free kick lately, so I'll use gluten-free pasta.

Once I'm done with putting the groceries away, I grab my tablet and open up my SocioWeave app. It's the latest and most trending social platform out there, which means everyone is on it.

At least, I hope.

I type in *Valeria*. Usually, SocioWeave is good at pulling profiles of people in close proximity. It's a bit creepy, in my opinion, but it serves its purpose.

Unfortunately, there's a long list of *Valerias*.

And many of them are pretty.

I should have asked Cole for her last name, but I suppose that would have been suspicious.

Besides, I've dealt with his flings plenty of times and never once needed a last name.

Next to her name, I type out *Bayton Valley*, and only a few profile pictures pop up. One of an older woman who looks to be in her late sixties. Another with a flower as a profile picture. And finally, one of a young woman hugging a little boy.

I click on it.

The woman is stunning. Big brown eyes, perfect teeth, and a grin so wide and symmetrical you'd easily mistake her for a Hollywood star.

She has a petite frame, but she isn't lacking in curves. Exactly like the woman in the blue dress at Bayton Valley Grocer.

It's her.

I know it.

The question is: why the hell was she following me? Is she *that* obsessed with Cole? Does she think she'll manage to scare off his wife?

I swipe through her photos. Most of them are with that young boy, who is easily as dark-featured as she is. He looks a lot like her, too.

He must be her son.

I'm not finding any photos of a boyfriend or husband. Or wife. Who knows? It's only her and the boy.

"Single mom," I mutter, analyzing each one of her pictures.

She's at least a decade younger than me. I'm suddenly very self-conscious. I'm well aware that I've gained weight since Cole and I got married. And then there's my mouth that droops and my nonfunctioning arm.

I'm a mess.

At least, compared to this beauty.

That's no excuse. Cole is your husband and shouldn't be sleeping with anyone else.

I don't know why I've put up with his shit for so long. It's as if every time I manage to get rid of one mistress, a new one pops up weeks later.

They aren't the problem.

He is.

I'm about to swipe sideways again when Hazel appears in front of me as if having teleportation abilities.

I jump, my tablet almost falling off my bent knees.

"Hazel. Where the hell did you come from?"

"Nice to see you, too, Mom."

I get that teenage hormones cause all sorts of attitude problems, but it seems like Hazel is perpetually in a bad mood.

"Everything okay?" I turn off my tablet and sit up from my slouched position.

"Can you give me a ride to Alex's place? He invited me over for supper."

"His mom going to be there?" I ask.

"Probably."

Truth be told, I don't really care. But I'm trying to reinforce Cole's rules about not being alone with a boy without adult supervision. It's the right thing to do. I wish he'd have my back like I have his.

But Alex—I'm not worried about him. They probably spend the evenings braiding each other's hair. He's a really good kid, and he has no interest in my daughter.

"Sure," I say, not bothering to press the whole adult being around thing. I'm too angry at Cole right now to reinforce his rules. "You ready to go now?"

She nods.

I leave my tablet face down and grab my purse.

Alex's house isn't far from here. Not by car, anyway. Within five minutes, we're already there.

When I pull up to the curb, Alex's place looks as shoddy as it always does. I feel bad for the kid. His foster mom doesn't seem to put much effort into maintaining their home. Weeds are growing all over the place. And are those vines creeping up the side of the house? They weren't there a few months ago.

Green mold and mildew cling to the off-white panels, and the interlock path leading up to the front door is missing a few stones.

But my attention is quickly pulled toward a woman

with messy red hair tucked under a worn ballcap. She's kneeling in the garden of weeds, plucking out one plant after another.

Is she cleaning?

That's not Anna. And I can't imagine Anna would hire someone. She doesn't have the money for that.

And the few times that I met Anna, she was having one drink too many. I get a bad vibe from her. Like she isn't a good foster mom at all. I've been tempted to report her so that she loses custody of Alex, but Alex seems happy enough. He could end up someplace much worse.

"Anna hire a gardener?" I ask.

Hazel arches a brow at me. "What? No, that's Charlotte."

"Charlotte?" I say.

The woman, Charlotte, turns her head to look at us. She's wearing big square sunglasses with a pink frame. I can't tell if she's looking at my Jeep or at something else.

But she must spot Hazel because she immediately lights up and waves her entire arm over her head.

"Alex's aunt," Hazel says. "I told you about her."

"No, you didn't," I say.

Hazel breathes out hard, her little nostrils flaring into points. "Yeah, I did. Like a gazillion times."

When Hazel says *gazillion*, I estimate anywhere between two and four.

Which is still a lot for me to not remember. Cole might be right. I should contact Dr. Tang about my memory issues.

"She's visiting?" I ask.

"No," Hazel says. "She helps take care of Alex. She knows Anna is, well—"

I don't say anything. I'm afraid that if I open my mouth, I'll say something very mean.

"She comes over all the time," Hazel says. "And she usually makes us really good food."

"She doesn't drink?" I ask.

Hazel laughs. "No way. She's actually really cool. She

doesn't approve of Anna's drinking."

I'm happy to hear that.

It comforts me to know that a level-headed adult is around my daughter, taking care of her. I'm tempted to go meet her, but I don't want to embarrass Hazel. I'll introduce myself another time.

"'Kay, well, thanks, Mom," Hazel says.

I raise my arm, prepared to give her a hug, but she reaches for the door handle and gets out. Seconds later, she's running toward Charlotte, who gets up and stretches her arms out for a hug.

Great.

She's closer to Alex's aunt than she is to me.

CHAPTER 24

Diary Entry

I did something I probably shouldn't have done today.

But then again, it needed to be done. Cole keeps talking about his wife, and every time he does, I want to push a sewing needle and thread through his lips.

No, not really.

I'd never hurt him.

What I want is for his wife to go away and never come back. She doesn't deserve him.

She doesn't even know what she has. She's an idiot. So, yeah, I followed her. I mean, I guess I'm hoping to scare her off a bit. If Cole knew what I was up to, though, I'm not sure what he'd say. He'd likely stop talking to me.

I can't let that happen.

That man was sent to me by God himself.

He's meant to be mine.

I have to find a way to get his wife out of the picture. I mean, doesn't she know he's not in love with her? Even I know that. And he didn't have to say anything. It's all over his face.

Today, for example, I brought him a hot coffee. Two creams, one sugar, just like he likes it. He thanked me three times for that coffee. When I told him it was only coffee, he said his wife never takes care of him like that. That if he were to ever ask for coffee, she'd tell him to get up and get it himself. That she wasn't a doting housewife from the fifties.

What kind of a woman does that?

Her job is to serve her man.

No wonder he doesn't love her anymore. She doesn't know how to keep him happy.

If only Cole would get divorced, we wouldn't have his wife standing between us. He wants me. I can see it in his eyes. The way he looks at my chest, my lips, and then at my hips every time I walk toward him.

He tries to act like he isn't interested and like he would never cheat on his wife. But I know he wants me. Probably more than he's ever wanted *her*.

And once he gets a taste of me, he'll never want to let me go.

CHAPTER 25

Cole

Valeria has a lot more depth to her than I initially realized. She's not only smart, but she's hilarious. Once she's comfortable, that is.

She doesn't like Frank very much, or the rest of the managers, but that's because all they do is salivate over her. So she's given them all funny nicknames. It's an inside joke, and no one else knows it but me.

For example, Frank has now been dubbed Mr. Dro:luge, which is a portmanteau of *Drool* and *Deluge*, since he's always wiping his mouth around her.

She's the best assistant I could ask for.

Today, I get my own coffee. I don't want Valeria to think I'm taking advantage of her position. When I walk by her desk, she looks up at me with a quirky smile.

"Got your own coffee, I see," she says.

I raise my mug to chest level, showcasing the *Best Boss* part of it. "I can't very well make you do everything."

Her hypnotic smile broadens.

It's challenging to not be in a good mood when I'm around Valeria. There's something about her that brightens up my day.

"HR finalized the paperwork," I say. "We have a new office secretary starting next Monday, so you'll be officially reporting to me. Until then, you'll have to keep juggling both jobs, if that's all right."

She stops what she's doing and perks up. "Oh? That was fast."

"I'm efficient," I say, smirking. "How about lunch? To

celebrate."

She hesitates.

"It's only lunch, Valeria. Not a date. If you want to bring a friend with you, that's fine, too."

This seems to put her at ease. Although I don't know who she'd invite. She doesn't seem to want to make friends with anyone in the office.

That's not entirely true. I do sometimes see her talking to Mrs. Jones, but it seems to be more out of courtesy than anything. Mrs. Jones has a fascination with printers. I swear, she keeps old ones just to collect them. And that's all she talks about.

It may have something to do with the fact that she recently turned seventy. I imagine she's seen some pretty incredible developments throughout the years.

As if reading my mind, Valeria says, "Sure. I might invite Mrs. Jones."

I can't tell if she's joking or not. But I must have made a face because she bursts out laughing.

Thank God.

She was only kidding. Mrs. Jones is a great woman, but I could write out a list of printers, along with their serial numbers, thanks to the conversations we've had.

"Meet you in my office at eleven thirty?" I ask.

Still smiling, she nods and resumes organizing my calendar on her monitor.

Valeria is amazing.

I'm so glad I snatched her up and offered her a position before someone else came along and did the same.

As I walk into my office, I turn around to look at her. To my surprise, she's looking at me, too. But when she catches me, her gaze darts back to her screen as if nothing happened.

Chapter 26

Meghan

"Shit, shit, shit."

Water sprays wildly at me, soaking my hair, my neck, my face. I try to combat it by swatting my arm under the kitchen sink, but nothing is stopping the torrent.

How the hell did this happen?

I can stand here and panic like a helpless housewife, or I can do something about it.

Without hesitating, I run into the basement, my bare feet stomping against our carpeted steps. I round the corner and head into our furnace room, where everything that runs this house is located, including the main water supply valve. I latch onto it and spin until a clunking sound fills the house, and then, silence. The sound of water spraying upstairs has stopped.

"Thanks, Mom," I mumble.

My mother didn't know anything about property maintenance when I was growing up. She would always comment about how that was a "man's job." So I took it upon myself to learn as much as I could so I wouldn't end up in her shoes.

Helpless.

I may know how to shut off the house's main water supply, but I don't know how to fix a busted pipe. That's beyond my scope of knowledge. It's beyond Cole's, too, but he's the one who always knows which contractor to call.

So I whip out my phone and call his cell.

Nothing.

Why isn't he picking up? It's noon. He should be on his lunch break right about now. I try a few more times, but he still doesn't pick up.

"Damn it, Cole."

I head back upstairs, out of the basement's darkness, and return to the kitchen. All I wanted was a damn coffee, but the moment I rinsed out my mug, I heard the hissing sound. And then, when I opened the cabinet, water started spraying everywhere.

I've never had that happen to me before.

A leak, sure. A clog, definitely. But a burst pipe? I thought that only happened in the winter.

I try Cole's phone again.

When he still doesn't pick up, I decide to call his office. I don't make a habit of doing this, but if it's important, then his secretary will transfer me over to him.

Oh, great.

That means Valeria.

Part of me doesn't want to tap Call, but I also don't want to wait too long. Plumbers are busy. They might only be available in a few days, and I don't exactly want to go that long without water.

Chewing my lip, I press the big green button followed by the Speaker button. I hate holding phones up to my face.

It rings, and rings, and rings.

Then, a croaky voice picks up.

"AstroWyre, how may I direct your call?"

I'd recognize that voice anywhere.

"Mrs. Jones?" I ask.

"Y-yes?"

"It's Meghan," I say. "Cole's wife."

"Oh, Meghan!" she says cheerfully. "How are you doing, my dear? Sure has been a while since I heard from you."

I smile down at my phone. Mrs. Jones is probably the sweetest woman I've ever met. She was working at AstroWyre before Cole even started, which was almost fifteen years ago now. He lucked out and landed a job fresh out of college, then made his way up the ladder.

"I'm good," I say. "How have you been?"

"Oh, you know," she croaks. "Same old, same old."

"Since when do they have you answering the phones?" I ask.

"It's temporary," she says. "Waiting on the new secretary to join, and the current one is out of the office."

"New secretary?" I ask. "I thought you guys just hired Valeria."

She chuckles on the other end. "High turnover here. And your husband was a sneaky bastard."

I love Mrs. Jones.

She tells it like it is.

"He hired Valeria to be his personal assistant. So the company had to hire a new secretary. She starts next Monday."

I grit my teeth. Why the hell does my husband need a *personal* assistant?

"Is Valeria sick?" I ask.

"Oh, heavens, no. That woman looks healthier than I did at her age. I saw her leave with Cole. Something about a business meeting. He asked me to keep an eye on the phones while they're out."

A dull ache spreads in my neck, and I only then realize that I'm hunched forward, my fist clenched against our kitchen's cool countertop.

"Thank you for letting me know, Mrs. Jones."

Mrs. Jones laughs whimsically. "You've known me fifteen years, Meghan. How many times do I have to tell you to call me Jacqueline?"

"Sorry, Jacqueline," I tell her. "Thank you for talking to me."

She lets out a little hum. "Do you want me to have Cole call you back?"

"No," I say, a little too quickly. "No, don't bother him. I know he's very busy with his new position."

"New position?" Jacqueline asks, sounding confused.

Her words are like a punch to my gut.

Are you kidding me right now?

Did Cole lie about his interim promotion? I inhale a slow, calculated breath, trying not to fly off the rails. I'm starting to think I don't know my husband at all. The man is full of secrets. Like Jacqueline said—he's a sneaky bastard.

I'm about to ask her all about Cole's supposed promotion when she lets out a high-pitched chuckle. Although I can't see her, I can picture her flicking her wrinkly hand and throwing her head back, mouth agape. "Oh, you mean his promotion. To replace David."

My heart calms itself.

"Yeah, that," I say forcefully.

"Yes, yes," she says. "It's been nonstop meetings since he took over for David."

Well, I'm happy to know that some of what my husband tells me is true.

Not that it matters right now. Because he's gone out for lunch with Valeria—I know it.

Which means I'd better hurry.

CHAPTER 27

Meghan

Blue Fusion Bistro is as busy as it was the last time I saw it. I don't understand how such an expensive restaurant could still be in business. Then again, it seems to be the go-to for all businessmen and businesswomen around here.

It's almost like customers want to flaunt their success by buying their potential clients a meal worth more than their high-end clothes.

It's Cole's go-to, that much I know.

For business, and other things.

The parking lot is freshly paved. With how much money this place makes, they can afford to renovate annually.

I pull up next to a sparkling red Tesla, feeling slightly out of place with my Jeep. Every car around me is a luxury brand—Lexus, Bentley, Mercedes.

Then, I spot Cole's car. I'd recognize that thing anywhere. A slick, shiny black Lexus LC. It's such a selfish car.

Two doors.

What kind of a father buys a two-door sports car? He's thirty-six years old. Not fifty-six. His purchase can't even be blamed on a midlife crisis.

Then again, Cole has a part to play when it comes to his job. I suppose I can understand that. What would his clients think of him if he rolled up to a business meeting in a beat-up hatchback? Or in a family minivan?

Maybe I am too hard on him.

For all I know, he's meeting with important clients now. Trying to secure his position as COO.

I keep my car in Park, unbuckle my seat belt, and peer through the restaurant's windows from a distance.

Most people inside are wearing suits.

No surprise there.

Plenty of gray-haired heads, a few women with excessive amounts of jewelry hanging from their necks, and waiters who seem overly eager to please their clientele.

Then, I see him.

He's sitting a short distance away from the window at what appears to be a two-person table. I can't see who he's sitting with.

I could get out of my Jeep and cross the parking lot, but if Cole sees me, he'll drive me straight to the hospital himself and demand that I get placed under strict psychiatric care.

Been there, done that.

Not going back.

He's smiling. A lot. More than he ever smiles with me. And then he full-blown laughs with his head thrown back. This can't be a business meeting. He's not acting very professional at all.

He raises his arm and gently places it down on the table, his fingers tapping. The overhead light glints on the face of his Rolex.

Then, the server comes to pour him a glass of wine. She goes on to pour a second glass for the person across from Cole.

This is killing me.

I really want to see who's sitting across from him.

I could drive away slowly, but my Jeep isn't exactly inconspicuous. It's bright red, and Cole knows my car. He'd recognize it anywhere.

I sit for a long time, watching my husband flirt with some faceless woman across from him. I want to storm in there and catch him in the act, but he'll accuse me of being a psychopath. Afterward, he may also tell me that I made him lose hundreds of thousands of dollars in a business deal.

Yeah, right.

That's no business meeting. But my husband has a way of making me feel crazy. It doesn't help that I've literally suffered from a debilitating brain injury and can't exactly trust myself, either.

So I wait, and wait, until finally, Cole gets up from his seat and bows like a gentleman. It looks like he's excusing himself.

This is my chance.

I slowly drive across the lot alongside Blue Fusion Bistro's panoramic windows. First, I spot a hand, followed by a wrist with a gold bracelet.

And then, I see her.

Luscious brown hair, a model build, plush red lips. A true beauty. And now that I've gone through all her pictures on SocioWeave, I have no doubt in my mind that the woman in there is Valeria.

Worse, there's no one else.

No table full of business partners or clients. It's just the two of them.

I tighten my grip around my steering wheel, staring at her as I continue to slow-roll in my car. I'm so angry right now that I could drive straight into that restaurant and ram her with my bumper.

But then I remind myself that she isn't to blame for this. Cole is.

It's easy to blame the other woman, but at the end of the day, Cole is the one betraying me. Not her. Cole is really good at making women believe that our marriage has fallen apart.

I suppose that wouldn't be entirely false—our marriage is in shambles.

Not that it's a reason to ever cheat.

The truth is, if Cole were a trustworthy man, it wouldn't matter how much of a husband-stealing twat this woman is. Because he wouldn't give in.

But I know Cole.

And I know—

Bang.

I jolt forward, almost smashing my face against my steering wheel as a horrible crushing sound fills my car.

My eyes widen in terror.

Oh, no.

I was so busy looking at Valeria inside the restaurant that I drove straight into the car in front of me.

CHAPTER 28

Meghan

You have got to be kidding me.

I lean over my steering wheel to assess the damage, but I'm pressed right up against the BMW. I can't see anything.

A woman with a blond blowout rushes out of her car in a frenzy. She gapes furiously at her rear bumper, then up at me through my windshield.

"What the fuck, lady?" she snaps. "Weren't you watching where you were going?"

I roll down my window. "I'm so sorry."

Part of me wants to use my brain injury as an excuse, but if I do that, there's a good chance I'll get my license revoked. I was lucky to get cleared to keep it in the first place.

She whips a hand toward her car. The opalescent paint job looks custom. "Do you have any idea how much this thing costs?"

Probably more than three of my cars combined.

Which is surprising, because the girl looks to be in her early twenties. I can only assume she has a much older rich boyfriend or a very generous daddy.

Not that it matters.

I hit her. I'm at fault. How am I going to explain this to Cole?

I inhale a deep breath, trying to calm my nerves.

This can't be happening.

If Cole sees me out here, there's no telling what he'll do. If he doesn't see me, I could lie to him and tell him it happened while I was out doing groceries, even though I never do groceries on a Thursday.

"I'm really sorry about this," I say.

She doesn't care for my apology. She wants me to develop a time machine and undo the damage to her precious baby.

"Let's just exchange information," I say. "I'm sure it's only a scratch. It won't be hard to fix."

"Only a scratch?" she shrieks.

I'm surprised my Jeep's windows don't shatter.

"Would you keep your voice down?" I hiss.

She lets out an exaggerated laugh, and now I'm starting to wonder if she's drunk. "Oh, you want me to keep it down? Why's that? Afraid we might draw some attention to your ugly piece-of-shit car? And the fact that you shouldn't even be driving in the first place?"

She's staring at the blue-and-pink sling holding my arm in place.

That was a low blow.

I grit my teeth. "I can drive just fine with one arm."

Another big huff of a laugh. "Right. That's why you rear-ended me going two miles per hour!"

My God, this woman is annoying.

Talk about an entitled brat.

She claws at her head with her perfectly manicured nails and lets out a wordless, frustrated shriek.

"'Kay, you know what?" I get out of my car and slam the door shut behind me. "Would you take a damn chill pill, lady?"

Her face contorts so badly you'd think someone syringed lemon juice into her mouth.

"It's a car. I made a mistake. I wasn't paying attention. There are way worse problems in the world. But you're too entitled to see anything beyond the tip of your nose. You're acting like I killed your dog. Honestly, grow the fuck up." I click my fingers at her. "Get your phone out. I'll give you my insurance information, and we can part ways."

She stares at me in disbelief. I can't tell if she's going to snap, or if she can sense that if she does, I'll snap right back. Even with only one arm, I'll be the one to win this fight if it comes down to that.

She mumbles something and bends into her car. Her black skirt is so short that she's giving everyone a free show. And there are enough people now, thanks to her big mouth.

I pull out my own papers and allow her to take a picture of my insurance slips. She mutters under her breath throughout the entire thing.

While she's doing that, I inspect the front of my Jeep. Nothing.

Her BMW is almost untouched except for one little scratch that runs horizontally next to her license plate. She'll probably demand that the entire bumper be replaced and her whole car repainted over something like that.

When she has finished getting what she needs, I give her my phone number. She calls it to make sure I didn't give her a fake one, and when it rings, I raise my brows at her as if to say, *Yep, that's my real number. We good now?*

"Whatever, lady," she says.

She turns around, her hair sweeping in the air, and gets into her BMW. It's so low to the ground that she basically drops inside.

"Meg?"

My breath catches in my throat, and I stiffen at the sound of Cole's voice.

"What's going on?" he says.

I turn around and feign surprise. "Cole? What are you—"

He fluffs me off with a casual wave. "Don't even. Why are you here?"

"Fine." The jig is up. "A pipe burst at home. I tried calling your phone and your office, but Mrs. Jones said you were out. Figured you'd be here. You always are."

His forehead creases. "You showed up to one of my

business meetings over a burst pipe? Are you serious right now?"

I snort. "Business meeting, my ass, Cole. You're here with a woman."

His frown deepens, forming lumps over the bridge of his nose. "Is this about Valeria? She's my assistant. So yeah, she's here with me."

"With you?" I say. "Bullshit. You're here alone with her."

He's full-out looking at me like I've lost my mind. A creased forehead, little slits for eyes, and a big open mouth that's twisted into an upside-down smile. "What are you talking about? I scheduled a meeting with Mr. Ahdi. Do you have any idea how this looks on me right now?"

He's lying.

I saw him at the table. It was a two-person table.

"You're lying!" I snap.

"This is exactly why I don't tell you about anything at work," Cole says. "It's like you're constantly looking for ways to accuse me of—"

"Accuse you of what, Cole? Fucking your assistant?"

My voice carries across the parking lot, and Cole winces at me. He has a reputation to uphold around here.

"Can you not do this right now?" He's visibly uncomfortable. And he should be.

"You're having lunch with a beautiful woman, Cole. You may not have slept with her yet, but I know your intentions."

"Everything all right, Cole?"

I look up to see a young man with square features and light-brown skin. He's dressed even nicer than Cole and watches us carefully while holding the restaurant door open.

"That's Mr. Ahdi," Cole says through clenched teeth.

How is that possible?

I saw him, and *her*. It was only the two of them.

I did see them, right?

Or was I looking at someone else? Someone who bears

a resemblance to my husband, and to Valeria? I mean, the panoramic windows do reflect the sun rather brightly.

Cole shakes his head at me, then starts frantically fishing inside his pocket for something. What is he doing?

"I'm calling Dr. Tang," he says. "You're going to see her as soon as there's an opening."

I want to protest, but I don't think I'm in any position to do that right now.

CHAPTER 29

Meghan

The hospital room's walls are bare and stained with years of use. The vinyl flooring is at least twenty years old and full of dents. I bet if I were to run my finger along the metal baseboard, I'd have enough dust to stuff a teddy bear.

With how much money this hospital makes, you'd think they'd put more care into the aesthetics of the place.

I shift uncomfortably on my plastic chair while Dr. Tang lowers herself on a little stool with wheels, then slowly rolls toward me with my chart in hand. She looks the same as when I last saw her—purple scrubs underneath a white lab coat, glossy black hair pulled into a tight bun at her nape, and small purple-rimmed glasses perched on the tip of her nose. Atop her head is a matching purple surgeon's cap.

The woman really likes purple.

In fact, she's the only medical professional at Bayton Valley Hospital to wear that color.

But I like it.

If she weren't treating me for my brain injury, I'd like her too. But every time I come here, I'm made to feel crazy.

"Cole says you've been experiencing memory problems," she says matter-of-factly. "And delusions."

Straight to the point.

No Hi, *how are you, Meghan?*

But that's simply how Dr. Tang is.

"Memory problems, yeah," I say. "I don't think I'm

delusional."

Her small dark eyes roll up at me. "No one said you're delusional. I certainly don't think you're delusional."

I appreciate her words.

She sets aside my chart on a small pressboard desk and rests her palms on her knees. She watches me astutely for too long.

"What?" I finally say.

"Looking at your eyes." She pulls a penlight out of her chest pocket and flashes it in my face without warning.

I blink hard.

"Pupils are fine," she says.

She goes on to perform a bunch of other tests, such as testing my handgrip strength, my balance and motor function, and my blood pressure.

It takes a good thirty minutes, but by the time we're done, she sits down and lets out a little sigh. "You suffered a traumatic brain injury, Meghan. I don't expect you to be your full self."

"Ever?" I squeak.

She tilts her head pensively. "I don't like giving out statistics. That's not my job. I can tell you that many people eventually recover fully. Some don't. But you're recovering well."

I can't tell if she's delivering good or bad news. Is she suggesting that I may never get my full memory back? That I will constantly be wondering whether what I'm seeing is real or not?

I saw Cole.

And I saw Valeria.

There was no one else at that table.

"Cole seems like a dedicated husband," she says. "He's been by your side since your accident. It's normal for him to be worried."

He isn't worried.

He's pissed off that I showed up at Blue Fusion Bistro and crashed his date.

Literally.

He's probably also pissed off that now, he has to deal with the insurance. I offered to take care of it myself, but "I'm in no state," according to Cole.

She reaches for my chart again. "Your follow-up MRIs came back good. Your brain is healing. I can order another MRI to be safe."

Cole has good insurance through work. It's not like it'll cost us anything. So I suppose it wouldn't hurt. Plus, he'll be upset if I walk out of Dr. Tang's office without anything.

"Sure," I mumble.

"Did you follow up with"—she scans my chart again—"Dr. Bachmann?"

I nod.

I spent six months seeing that woman every week. Not that I minded. In fact, I looked forward to our sessions. Dr. Bachmann is a tall Swiss woman with sharp features, salt-and-pepper hair, a thick accent attached to a deep voice, and one hell of a sense of humor.

"It might be worth giving her a call again," Dr. Tang says. "She may have exercises to help you retrain your memory. Until then, I'll order that MRI. Better safe than sorry. You should be getting a call from the hospital in the coming weeks with a date and time."

I thank her for her time and leave the office.

Cole is sitting in the waiting room, his beard having grown in a bit. He scratches at it while tapping away on his phone. His dark locks drape slightly over his forehead, and when he senses my approach, he brushes it all back and tousles it over the top of his head.

"Hey," he says.

He looks rough.

Has he been worried about me? Or is it all just an act? I don't like feeling this way. Like my husband is a stranger.

He stands up. "What did she say?"

"She said I'm fine," I say. "But she's ordering an MRI as a precaution."

I leave out the part about Dr. Bachmann. If I tell Cole that my neurologist suggested I contact my psychiatrist, he'll hold that over me. It'll give him more ammunition the next time he insinuates that I'm missing a few screws.

He musters a feeble smile, and he reaches for my shoulder. I want to pull away. Right now, I hate him. He'd rather be with Valeria, and I know it.

Still, I want comfort.

What if I really am losing my mind?

What if Cole is an amazing man, and I'm pushing him away?

I allow myself to fall into his embrace. And for the first time in as long as I can remember, tears stream down my cheeks.

I'm scared.

Terrified that I'm slowly fading away.

CHAPTER 30

Cole

Who's calling Meg at nine a.m. on a Saturday morning?

She barely speaks to her mother. The only other person she ever talks to is Chelsea, but I don't even know if she still talks to her.

Sometimes, I think she's purposely trying to push everyone out of her life.

Despite this, she's been on her phone nonstop these last few weeks. She'll stand in the hallway upstairs, in the dark, and jab away at her phone while a bright-white glow illuminates the tip of her nose and underneath her eyes.

Then, when I ask her what she's doing, she says, "Noting stuff down."

She accuses *me* of cheating, but sometimes I wonder if she's having an affair with one of our neighbors. She's home all the time.

Meg rushes to her cell next to our rumbling GoldBeanz coffee machine. She swipes her finger across the screen and pulls the phone up to her ear.

Hazel pops a brow at me, watching her mother.

"Mm-hmm. Okay. Okay, thank you."

Could it be Dr. Tang? It's been weeks since her appointment, and she had her MRI earlier this week. I didn't think doctors worked on the weekends, though.

"My results are in," Meg says.

I wait quietly.

"Everything looks good." She doesn't sound excited by this. If anything, she seems despondent.

"Isn't that a good thing?" I ask.

"Not when I'm having symptoms," she says. "I was hoping they'd find a bleed or something."

Hazel stops chewing her breakfast cereal, and a little brown hunk falls back into her bowl of chocolate milk. "Seriously? You *want* there to be bleeding in your brain?"

Meg parts her lips, but Hazel aggressively drops her spoon into her bowl, and a loud clinging sound fills the entire open floor. She backs up, her chair scraping against the dining room tiles, and storms off.

Meg stands quietly, now watching our daughter with pity in her eyes.

"Shit," Meg mumbles. "I didn't mean it like that."

I want to give Meg an earful for saying something so thoughtless. Hazel watched her lie in a hospital bed with a big tube down her throat for two weeks thanks to brain bleeds.

Some days, I think Hazel is still traumatized from seeing her mother in an induced coma. Meg might blame teenage hormones for our daughter's anger, but I'm not so sure. I think she's hurting.

Deeply.

"I should go talk to her," Meg says.

"She probably needs a minute," I say.

The coffee machine beeps, so I take it upon myself to extract Meg's mug full of black coffee. "You want milk, cream, sugar? How do you like it?"

She stares at me like she wants to take the mug and smash it over the top of my head.

What the hell did I do this time?

"We've been married for fifteen years, and you don't know how I drink my coffee?" she says. "You losing track of all the women in your life? All their preferences?"

"Damn it, Meg." I slam the mug down on the counter, and a bit of hot liquid spills over my thumb. "Are we going to do this again? I have so much going on at work. My brain is all over the place. I thought we were okay."

She lets out a long breath, rolls her eyes, then grabs the mug off the counter and tears the fridge door open.

I can't believe this.

Ever since she showed up at Blue Fusion Bistro and rammed her car into some woman's BMW, well, she's backed off with her accusations.

We were fine.

So why are we back on this subject? Because of a stupid coffee? I can't remember every little thing.

Rather than try to talk things out, I grab myself a blueberry muffin off the counter and walk away.

Clearly, Meg needs to cool off.

CHAPTER 31

Meghan

I watch Cole as he leaves the kitchen with his fists clenched. He hates it when I get upset like this, but come on. Fifteen years. How am I not supposed to be upset by that? I drink coffee every day.

We used to take turns making coffee for each other. How does he not remember?

I do.

Two creams, one sugar.

I've never forgotten it, and I have a traumatic brain injury.

I bet he knows exactly how Valeria takes her coffee.

I fill mine with lots of cream—a little more than necessary—because that's how I like it. That's not difficult to remember.

Ziggy is curled up in his bed, ears flat on his head. Poor guy. He hates it when Cole and I raise our voices.

"It's okay, baby, come here."

His little tail wags, and his muzzle splits into a sharp-toothed grin. "Wanna go outside?"

He's up on all fours, bouncing around like he usually does when I offer him outdoor time.

I grab my tablet from the living room and open the patio door. Ziggy bolts outside, bounding over anything and everything in his path, including one of Hazel's pool noodles that she must have forgotten to store in the pool house.

I sit down on my woven outdoor sofa and open my AnyT-Chat app. Chels and I have been talking almost daily since I told her about Cole's new secretary. Well, his *assistant* now, apparently.

She's asked me several times if I want her to show up here. I don't want that. This is my mess, and I'm going to deal with it.

One message is from Chelsea, and the other is from my mom.

While I love my mom, we have a very strained relationship given everything she put me through as a child.

So I open Chels's message first.

So??? Any results yet?

I type in my response.

Everything came back normal.

Chels is a very busy woman with her baby, so I imagine she won't reply for another few hours.

Reluctantly, I open my mother's message.

One year.

That's all it says.

I sigh, then flinch when Ziggy barks at something in the distance. He lunges at our fence, chasing what I can only assume is a bunny on the other side.

"Ziggy!" I snap.

Then, I refocus my attention on my mother's message and scroll to the top of the thread to reread everything she's sent me over the last several months.

It's been a month, Meg. I'm your mother.

Meg! Two months! Really?

I see what I mean to you.

Maybe I should stop trying.

Three months.

Four months.

And this continues every single month up until now. Maybe I should respond. She knows I'm alive—there are read receipts, and I continue to open her messages.

Maybe Cole is right. I'm pushing everyone away. He says it all the time.

That's not true. You and Chels are closer than ever

despite you rarely ever seeing her.

Cole is the one pushing me away. And my mother pushed me away a long time ago. I offered to rebuild our relationship, but she continued to deny what happened to me.

What she *let* happen to me.

And after my accident, I started getting these horrible nightmares and sleep terrors. All about Karl and the things he did to me.

It's as if getting injured has brought all of that back to the surface. All right, it might have something to do with my sessions with Dr. Bachmann. She really delved into my childhood.

I stare at my mother's little profile icon. It's a picture of her grinning ear to ear with her cheek pressed against some man's face. I don't recognize him. But he's smiling just as wide.

Another boyfriend. After Karl left her, she started serial dating any man who would have her. I hate that about my mother. She isn't an independent woman. She's the complete opposite of what I strive to be.

Could be the reason I turned out the way I did.

I don't want to be anything like her.

It's very conflicting to love someone and hate them at the same time. My throat swells as I stare into her glossy eyes. A clump of dark-red hair rests over one shoulder. It's actually partially gray now, but only I know that. She continues to dye it red.

She looks so happy. But I know that in a few months, she'll delete the picture and replace it with something mundane like a rock or a flower until she finds herself another man to fill that void inside her heart.

I'm about to turn off my tablet when an irrepressible anger forms a knot in my stomach.

All I want from my mom is one thing—for her to admit the truth.

Admit that she didn't protect me from Karl.

But she's always made excuses. She made me out to

be a liar. Said I imagined things. No twelve-year-old imagines being sexually abused by their mother's boyfriend.

So I stopped talking about it.

Instead, I bottled everything up inside, and a part of me has continued to resent my mother for it.

I would never do something like that to Hazel.

If she approached me and told me Cole had been inappropriate with her in any way, I'd probably kill him. I wouldn't ask her if she was sure. Or try to convince her that she simply *had a bad dream.*

But I don't think Cole is capable of that. He loves Hazel more than life. He may be a cheating bastard, but he'd never hurt Hazel like that.

Even so.

I would believe Hazel's word over my own husband's side of the story. I only wish my mother had done the same.

Without thinking, I jab my finger hard against my screen's keyboard.

Admit the truth, then we can talk.

Chapter 32

Meghan

My mother read my message on Saturday, minutes after I sent it, and the only thing she could be bothered to say was, "Honey, I don't want to fight. I love you."

Every time I bring up the topic, she sneakily dodges it.

Is it that hard to admit that you did nothing while your boyfriend abused me?

Dr. Bachmann's voice echoes in my head.

"Meghan, your healing process will depend on you. Not your mother. You're longing for an apology—for an admittance of guilt. But you have to understand that you may never get it. You can either live with that and accept your mother despite her past mistakes, or you can cut ties if it's too painful."

I resented her words at the time.

Those were my only two options? Why couldn't my mom just admit the truth? Admit that she stood idly by? And then, when I finally told her, she dismissed me. Said that I missed my dad, that I was trying to take her happiness away.

That I was a *liar*.

Ziggy is sound asleep against my lap. He must be dreaming about chasing a bunny because his little hind legs keep kicking.

I'm tempted to pet him, but I don't want to wake him up. So instead, I stare at my mom's profile picture on my tablet screen and at her big, dimpled smile.

I miss her.

I *want* to forgive her, but it's so hard.

So instead, I open my chat thread with Chels and click on the most recent funny cat video she sent after telling me how sorry she was to hear that nothing came up on the MRI.

At least *she* understands.

Sometimes not having answers is worse than receiving bad news.

Immediately after, however, she admitted that she was happy to hear I was okay.

The video loads slowly. I wonder what it will be this time. She sends things like this at least once a week. It's always footage of cats doing the dumbest things, like getting their heads stuck in a fishbowl, only to then freak out and start twirling with their butts in the air.

The video keeps spinning, and right as it's about to begin, the front door slams shut.

My heart leaps in my chest, and I sit upright. Ziggy perks up, lets out a high-pitched howl, and prepares to throw himself off the sofa.

I grab him by the face and pin him down by holding his muzzle shut against the couch cushion. It might look cruel to an outsider, but I'm not hurting him. It's not like I have two arms to wrangle him with.

I consider calling out.

Hazel? Cole?

But I've seen enough horror movies to know that calling out is a sure way to end up a corpse.

A warm gust sweeps through the house, bringing along with it the earthy scent of spring.

They say break-ins happen most often during the day when everyone is out of the house.

And we aren't exactly poor. We could easily be a target for some robbers looking to sneak off with a bunch of expensive furniture.

It's 11 a.m. on a Monday morning.

Cole is at work. Hazel is at school.

My jaw tightens painfully. I should get up and hide. Something. But I can't move. What the hell is wrong with me?

My heartbeat pulsates rhythmically in my ear.

And this is exactly why I wanted a pit bull.

Not Ziggy.

No offense, Ziggy. Mommy loves you.

But I'm currently pinning him down. If I had a big dog, he'd be charging straight for the door with a bark so fierce that any intruder would think twice before robbing this place.

Heavy footsteps echo in the foyer.

They sound like boots.

Heavy boots.

Cole doesn't wear boots. He wears expensive leather dress shoes.

Awkwardly, I pull Ziggy up against my chest. He looks so contorted, and he tries to bark again, but I keep his muzzle sealed shut. He kicks and squirms, but I'm not about to let him go. If someone is here with ill intentions, I'm not letting Ziggy get hurt.

Instead, I hurry to the back patio door, my bare feet completely silent against the floor.

Wincing, I slide the patio door open a crack—which isn't an easy feat one handed while holding a squirming dog—and shove Ziggy through.

Thankfully, we had a new door installed last summer, and it's ultraquiet. Not like the one we had before that lamented like a thirty-year-old merry-go-round in a haunted park.

The moment Ziggy is loose, he starts yapping like a maniac and tries to come back in. But I quickly shut the door. He stands, clawing desperately while standing on his hind legs.

Something heavy thuds in the distance.

What the hell was that?

I don't hesitate.

I reach for our knife block and pull out the biggest chef knife there is. We rarely ever use this thing, so I know it's sharp.

I grip the metal handle tightly with my clammy palm.

The footsteps are now coming toward the kitchen.

Right toward me.

I may only have one arm, but I have an incredibly sharp knife and a dog to protect.

I'm not going down without a fight.

Chapter 33

Hazel

I jump when I see Mom standing quietly in the kitchen, holding onto what looks like a really big knife. A knife she never uses for cooking.

"Mom?" I croak.

When she sees me, her big eyes soften, and she drops the knife on the counter with a trembling hand. She breathes out shakily through tight lips.

"Y-you scared the shit out of me," she says.

A second ago, she looked terrified. Then, relieved. And now, pissed off. How do her moods change so fast?

"What the hell are you doing home?" she snaps.

Her anger only fuels mine. I called her, like, fifty times, and she didn't pick up. How is this my fault?

"And what are those?" she points at my black combat boots.

"What?" I say. "Alex gave them to me."

"He *gave* them to you? Just like that? They're brand new."

"They don't fit him," I say. "Charlotte bought them for him, but she got the wrong size and lost the receipt. They fit me perfectly."

Why is she making such a big fuss about my boots? They're just boots.

"Well, you sounded like a man coming in," she says.

Gee, thanks, Mom.

"Why are you home?" she asks.

"I don't feel good," I say.

Her features soften again.

Guilt eats away at my insides. I don't feel horrible. Definitely not horrible enough to leave school and come home. I had a headache earlier because I forgot my lunch. So I called my mom, hoping she might drive to my school to bring me some food. But she didn't pick up. So I kept calling. And she still didn't pick up.

And then, while I sat in math class, all I could picture was my mom lying motionless on the floor with Ziggy licking the froth coming out of her mouth.

But I can't tell her that.

I can't tell her that every day, I'm terrified she's going to have a seizure. She had two of them after her surgery, and I can't stop picturing them.

The way she convulsed on the floor. The way Dad shouted at me to call 911 while freaking out over her spasming body.

It was terrifying.

Some nights, I have nightmares about it. But most of the time, I see the coma version of my mom. The woman lying in a hospital bed with her eyes sealed shut and a big tube down her throat. I kept wanting to wake her up, but no matter how hard I tried, nothing worked.

"What's wrong?" Mom asks. "Stomachache? How do you feel sick?"

Is she interrogating me? I can't tell.

"Just feel sick," I say. "I can't explain it."

She doesn't continue playing cop. "You want me to make you some chicken noodle soup?"

What I really want is to wrap my arms around my mom and never let go. But she's been so angry lately that I'm afraid she'll reject my hug.

"I'm okay," I say. "I think I just need to lie down."

She nods, then hesitates, pinching lint from the bottom of her shirt. "Well, I'm here, okay? If you need anything—"

"Thanks, Mom." I turn around and go upstairs.

CHAPTER 34

Meghan

I stir the pot of steaming chicken noodle soup, clutching the ladle handle a little harder than necessary. But Cole came home late all of last week, smelling like some other woman's perfume. And now, he's late again.

He backed off for a while after I accidentally rammed my Jeep into that woman's fancy car. I think I might have scared him a bit. But he's over that and right back to being deceptive Cole.

I set the soup aside for Hazel and make myself a peanut butter sandwich. I'm sick of cooking for a man who can't be bothered to come home on time. He doesn't text or call, either.

Hazel eventually comes down, looking like she just woke from a nap.

"How you feeling?" I ask.

Her smile is strained. "Better."

"I made you some soup," I say.

She seems appreciative. "Smells good."

I finish stirring the soup. "Want me to get you a bowl?"

She shakes her head. "No, that's okay. I'll do it. Thank you, though."

And this is how I want my fourteen-year-old daughter to behave. To do things herself and not expect people to wait on her the way Cole does. I only offered because she doesn't feel good, but I appreciate her refusal of help.

I sit at the dining room table with my peanut butter sandwich, hoping Hazel might follow me. Instead, she makes herself a bowl and disappears back upstairs, into her bedroom.

I'm about to get up and grab my tablet when Ziggy goes nuts at the back patio door. Full-on psycho. He lunges and barks with drool dangling at the sides of his mouth.

Another bunny?

He doesn't usually act like that over bunnies.

I get up and gaze through the patio window. The sun has started its descent, filling our large yard with an orange glow that shimmers off the surface of the pool water.

"What is it, buddy?"

I'm afraid to let him out. When he's like this, he's in a state that I've learned to refer to as *red zone*. Nothing but his prey matters. I could yell at him, and he wouldn't hear me. Even now, he doesn't acknowledge my voice or presence.

He keeps lunging and scratching away at the door.

My eyes scan around the pool, the pool house, and our oversized shed at the back. I'm not seeing anything. No squirrel or cat.

But then, I spot something that stands out.

At the very back, up against our fence and mixed in with our cedar trees, is a dark blob. A shadow. It almost looks like someone is standing there.

No way.

I'm imagining things.

Our backyard is fully fenced with seven-foot wooden panels. No one could get in here.

But Ziggy won't shut up. And that figure isn't moving. The longer I stare, the creepier it gets. Midway up the cedars, it looks like the shape of a head with wiry, messy hair.

Then, I spot the glinting of an eye.

The sight of it causes my chest to clench painfully. This can't be real. Why would someone be standing in my backyard, watching me?

Part of me wants to call Cole.

The only person I can think of who would do something

like this is Valeria. I remember that leer she cast me at Bayton Valley Grocer. Like she wanted to kill me. Actually, no, it wasn't that. I got the feeling she wanted to torment me.

Scare me off and away from Cole.

The problem is that if I call my husband, he'll tell me I'm overreacting or, worse, *seeing things*. But it isn't only me. Ziggy is freaking out.

I could call the police, but what am I going to say? I think I see someone standing in my backyard watching me?

That's not a terrible idea.

No.

This can't be real.

I'm seeing shadows in the cedars and somehow convincing myself that a human being is standing there. Although, if it is Valeria, I certainly don't need Cole to protect me.

I can handle that bitch myself.

Without thinking about it any further, I grab my chef's knife from its block—the same one I held onto earlier when I thought Hazel was an intruder—and rip the patio door open.

Ziggy bolts out at full speed, straight toward the cedars.

Shit.

What if I didn't imagine it, and there really is someone there? Then I just put my dog in danger.

No. I've got this.

Knife held firmly in hand, I race down my back patio stairs and storm toward the cedar trees at the back. My heart is jackhammering so hard that I sense it in my palm, against the knife's warm metal.

But I'm not backing down. If this woman thinks she can come onto my property and try to intimidate me, she doesn't know me.

Ziggy stops barking and is now sniffing wildly in the cedars. His little nose points up, then down, and then he proceeds to inhale all the air around him.

"What is it, Ziggy? What do you smell?"

There's no one here.

Using the tip of my knife, I search between the branches.

It's completely clear.

In fact, I can see part of the fence through the tight row of trees. I don't see how anyone would have been standing here only to then disappear.

Eventually, Ziggy calms down and loses interest. He goes on to sniff the edge of the pool, then starts eating overgrown grass along the side of the house.

Josie must have missed that spot. I hired her through an online group in our neighborhood. She's only sixteen, but she's very eager to make extra cash. And with my one arm, I can't keep up with yard work.

I remain in my backyard for a very long time, inspecting every corner.

Someone was here. I know it.

Do you really, though? No one is here. You can't trust yourself.

Even my conscience knows better.

It was probably a cat or a raccoon. Ziggy doesn't see them very often, and when he does, he wants to eat them.

And even though I'm trying to convince myself that Valeria wasn't standing in my backyard, I can't help but feel a little safer going back inside and locking the door behind me.

CHAPTER 35

Meghan

Chels is flipping out.

Her messages keep coming through in rapid succession, each one making a high-pitched dinging sound.

You think it was her?

How would she even get in your yard?

You gonna tell Cole?

She's a psycho, Meg.

Please be careful.

I appreciate that Chels's first instinct isn't to wonder if perhaps I'm experiencing delusions. And I told her all about my delusions. They were at their peak during my first month of recovery, after my coma. I'd hear people talking in our house or see couples walking in our backyard.

Chels was the only person who suggested I'd triggered something in my brain—that now, I could see and hear spirits.

I appreciated her take on it. Chels has always been a very spiritual person. She believes in all of that stuff. And after all of the strange things that I saw after my injury, well, I'm now questioning my own beliefs.

What if she was right?

Cole's solution was to pump me full of medication. Chels, on the other hand, told me to talk to the people I saw in my backyard. By the time I worked up enough nerve to go out there and try to start up a conversation, I'd stopped seeing them.

I'm sure it was for the best.

I can't imagine how Cole would have reacted if he saw me having a full-blown conversation with an invisible person in our backyard.

I'm being careful, I respond.

I don't tell her I had a knife on me. Not through chat. In person, sure—I'll eventually tell her if the topic comes up again. But I don't want any incriminating evidence left on my tablet if something were to ever happen to Valeria.

The front door suddenly opens, and Cole steps into the house, looking more worn out than usual. He sits on the foyer bench and slowly unlaces his shoes.

I say goodbye to Chels and place my tablet face down.

I've spent the last few hours thinking about this moment. Do I tell Cole what I saw? Or will that make things worse? Every time I bring up a concern, he acts like I'm a total whack job.

So instead, I say, "Late night again?"

"What do you mean, *again*?"

His gaze is loathsome. I should have started with hello.

"You've been late every day for the last few weeks," I say. "Why don't you ever call or text to let me know? You realize I probably wouldn't get so upset if you'd just let me know what was going on, right?"

He shakes his head disparagingly at me.

Not the reaction I was hoping for.

"Late *every day*?" He removes his dark-gray overcoat and a subtle floral scent sweeps through the house. "Meg, I was home on time every day last week."

I blink at him. Is he for real right now?

"No, you weren't," I say.

With lips pressed tightly together, he breathes out hard through his nose. He's clearly trying to compose himself. "Will you be seeing Dr. Bachmann any time soon?"

Speaking of composure—I'm pretty damn good at it, too; it takes all of my willpower not to hurl my tablet at him.

He's gaslighting me.

I know for a *fact* that he's been home late every evening. Furious, I get up, phone in hand, and march toward him.

A twinge of panic spreads across his handsome features. What does he think I'm going to do? Hit him?

I open my phone's calendar and shove my screen in his face.

A blue glow spreads across his cheeks and over his five o'clock shadow. He blinks repeatedly, his pupils constricted from the light, then raises a thick brow. "Um, what am I looking at?"

I turn my phone around. I'm about to jab my finger on the screen and point out that I noted down his arrival times every day last week, but . . .

I don't understand.

I looked at the calendar last night. Most days last week, I entered an event with the title LATE.

I knew he'd use my memory against me, so I figured if I had it documented somewhere, I'd have irrefutable proof of his late nights.

But there's only one event logged last week, and it's sitting under the Wednesday column.

He stands up way more placidly than I'd expect after my baseless accusations. "Like I said. I've been home on time almost every night. I had to work overtime last Wednesday because of some last-minute meeting Vincent set up with one of our partners."

My throat swells.

I don't know what to feel anymore—embarrassment? Anger at myself?

I want to hurl my phone at the wall. But what good would that do? My phone didn't do this. The problem isn't technology or my husband.

The problem is *me*.

Something is very wrong with my memory. Chels may have made everything better for all of ten minutes by reassuring me that I'm not crazy, but she's my best friend. It's basically her job to make me feel safe and loved, and the *opposite* of crazy.

But this proves it.

Cole is right.

My brain is faulty. Something is wrong, even though my MRI results came back normal.

"I'll book an appointment with Dr. Bachmann," I croak.

Rather than get angry, Cole leans forward and kisses my forehead. "I think that's a good idea, sweetheart."

And there it is again.

That floral smell.

I may be mixing up all sorts of facts in my brain, but I'm not hallucinating the smell of another woman's perfume.

Or am I?

CHAPTER 36

Diary Entry

I'm getting really sick of that dumb bitch.

Cole has shown me pleasure the way no other man ever has. He feels so . . . He feels like heaven. The way he kisses my neck. My shoulders. The way he grabs my hips right before he lifts my skirt.

I can't get enough of him.

But his wife is getting in the way.

He keeps running home to her. One day per week with him isn't enough. I want him every night. I want him pressed up against me. I want his tongue in my mouth. I want all of him.

She's ruining that.

Why won't he leave her already?

It's not like they love each other.

He loves *me*.

He hasn't said it yet, but I can feel it. So why won't he leave his worthless marriage? He talks about it all the time. He says when the timing is right, he'll leave her, and we can be together.

There's something he isn't telling me, though.

I asked him what was keeping them together, and he couldn't seem to answer me. He keeps saying it's complicated. Then, I think he's about to tell me that, in his own way, he does love her.

But he doesn't say that.

Thank God.

I don't know what I would do if he told me he loved his wife. I think I'd shatter into a million pieces.

He loves *me*.

And only me.

If his bitch of a wife doesn't leave soon, I'm going to have to do something more extreme to get her out of the picture.

CHAPTER 37

Meghan

Hazel gets in the car with sweat dripping down her hairline. She wipes it with the back of her hand, then rolls her long soccer socks down to her ankles.

"Good practice?" I ask.

She nods, then sticks her head out of the passenger's-side window and waves goodbye to her friends.

I want to wave at them and say hi, but I'm afraid to embarrass her. She finally sits back, buckles her seatbelt, and stares straight ahead.

That's my cue.

I reverse, careful not to almost run over any of her friends this time, and leave the school parking lot.

Paper bags crinkle in my back seat as I roll over speed bumps. Thankfully, I didn't run into Valeria today. It was a normal, boring day of grocery shopping.

"Got your favorite cereal," I tell Hazel.

She doesn't hear me. She has her earbuds in and is bopping her head to her music.

Then, without warning, she rips her left earbud out. "Do you mind dropping me off at Alex's?"

Again?

She's been going there nearly every night. What's the deal? He is gay, right? Or is there something she isn't telling me?

As if capable of reading my mind, her brows knit, and her jaw goes slack. "What? What's the problem?"

"You've been going there almost every day." As the

words come out, I can't help but wonder: *has she really?* Or am I making all of this up in my head, too?

She shrugs. "So what? I like going there."

"More than you like being home," I say.

It wasn't a question, and she didn't even attempt to argue. That's what's bothering me.

But I can't blame her.

"I'm not trying to hurt your feelings, Mom. But it's just peaceful there, you know?"

We come to a red light, and I use the opportunity to look at her. "Is our home the opposite of peaceful?"

I shouldn't have asked that.

Of course, it is.

If Cole and I aren't fighting, I'm upset about something. Who am I kidding? We're always fighting.

Another shrug. "It's just different. And Charlotte used to be a chef or something. So she cooks up all sorts of stuff."

Ouch.

I used to cook a lot too before I lost function of my arm. I hope this isn't only about food. Because we can find other ways. I could ask Cole to contact a food delivery service.

Is that what I need to do? Order takeout every night for Hazel? Would that improve our relationship?

"I'll bring you." My tone comes out a little clipped. I'm not upset with her. I'm hurt.

"Mom, if it's that big of a deal—"

I force a smile. "No, honey. It isn't. If you like being there, then I want you to be wherever you're happiest."

She pulls her bottom lip between her teeth and looks away from me like she's ashamed. I know her intention isn't to hurt me. She's fourteen. And Hazel isn't like that. She's a great kid. She isn't passive-aggressive or manipulative. She simply enjoys being at Alex's place.

We reach another red light, and I rest my hand on her thigh. "Seriously, honey. It's fine. It sucks to know you prefer being someplace other than home, but I know things haven't exactly been pleasant around the house lately."

Her big eyes double in size. For a second, it looks like she's about to cry. As if she's been waiting all year for me to admit that things aren't normal anymore.

The only reason I've continued to put up with Cole's bullshit is to protect Hazel. To keep a roof over her head and a father in her life. I don't want her growing up the way I did. But if my attempt to protect her is going to cause more harm than good, then I'm not doing my job properly.

The light turns green, so I pull my hand away, and although almost imperceptible, I could have sworn I saw a little pout. A tiny flinch in her lip. Disappointment.

Do I not give my daughter enough physical affection?

Come to think of it, I've been so preoccupied with Cole and with thinking that my daughter hates me that maybe I *have* pulled away.

Cole says I've been pushing everyone away, but I think it's the opposite. I'm not pushing—I'm pulling.

I pull up against the curb, right in front of Alex's house. The garden is all cleared up of weeds, and the grass is freshly cut. Charlotte seems to be on a roll lately.

Hazel leans forward, the tip of her nose half an inch away from her phone. "Shit."

"What's wrong?" I don't bother correcting her for swearing in front of me. She's fourteen, and I have way bigger fish to fry.

"Nothing," she mumbles. "I just accidentally deleted a reminder that I put in my calendar. I have a paper due next Friday. I was trying to add a note, and I deleted it."

Before I can say anything, she starts thumbing away at her phone. "It's okay. I'll just retrieve it."

I blink. "Retrieve it?"

Without looking up at me, she takes all of thirty seconds to explain to me that you can restore deleted events to your calendar. Then she shoves her phone into her pocket and looks up at me sheepishly.

"Well, thank you for—"

I wrap my arm around my daughter and pull her close to me. She stretches awkwardly over the center console, stiff as a sheet of plywood. But then she softens and molds into me, hugging me back.

We hold onto each other for several minutes.

She smells like coconut. It must be a new moisturizer. Hazel has always loved moisturizing her skin. Her hair smells of lavender—her favorite shampoo.

God, I've missed my daughter.

"I love you, Hazel."

"I love you too, Mom."

She pulls away and quickly jumps out of the car. She shoulders her bag but doesn't look back at me. Instead, her hand quickly goes up to her cheek before coming back down.

Was she crying?

Has my daughter been in pain but unable to express it? I feel like a terrible mother.

I need to do better.

And I will.

But first, I need to find out how to retrieve deleted calendar events.

CHAPTER 38

Meghan

After spending fifteen minutes on my tablet and getting slightly distracted by Ziggy's ankle kisses, I've figured out how to retrieve deleted calendar events.

I lean forward on the sofa, phone in hand, calendar open. Now that I've restored my data, there's an event every single day of the week.

And they all say the same thing: *Cole home late.*

Is this real? Or am I imagining it?

I blink repeatedly until my eyes get watery. My phone screen isn't changing. This is very much real. But . . . how?

Did Cole go into my phone and delete the events?

Of course, he did.

Surprisingly, I'm not upset. Instead, I find myself smiling. Because I'm not crazy. This proves it. My memory has been fine.

Cole has been toying with it.

And the only reason he'd do that is if he had something to hide. The more I think about Cole and his sneaky ways, the more my smile falters.

That son of a bitch.

I know he's a cheater—but this? This is too much.

Fuming, I toss my phone over my tablet—*clunk*—and make my way upstairs. I haven't gone into my office since my accident because it only reminds me of what I've lost.

My career.

I used to love working on marketing for my new dental clinic. I even ran my own ads. A true entrepreneur, Chels had called me. But now, as I stare at my bare office, all I see is a life I'll probably never have again.

A thin layer of dust coats my slick black desk and the tops of my double monitors. Everything is powered off. Next to my monitors is a spider plant, which, miraculously, is still alive.

I wonder if Cole has been watering it. But Cole always told me that he respected my space and that he wouldn't enter my office without my permission.

Before entering, I hurry into the bathroom and fill a little paper cup with water. It isn't much, but I'm sure my plant will appreciate it.

The dirt inside the turquoise ceramic pot is so dry it looks like sand. Poor thing. I pour the water in, and the dirt absorbs it instantly.

I touch my leather chair, dust sticking to my fingertips, and roll it away from my desk. The hardwood floors have lost their sheen and taken on a matte finish. It even *smells* like dust in here.

The sun is trying to peek through the blinds, which are tightly closed. You'd think I was *trying* to kill my plant, yet somehow, it survived.

I twirl the blind rod, allowing several strips of bright yellow light to spill into my office and across my floor. Dust particles float in the air, resembling fairy magic.

Underneath my computer desk is a small cabinet with a keyhole. I pull the handle to test it—it's locked.

Good.

It should be.

I swiftly move to the blinds and reach up high, right behind the faux-wood valence. As expected, my fingers graze a little metal key that's connected to a magnet. I pry the key away and unlock my cabinet.

The interior is meticulously clean in comparison to the furniture in my office. There's no dust inside, and everything is organized by color and function—just as I like it. I push aside a heap of papers until I spot it—my little red notebook.

It's a small 4 × 7 journal with spiral coils. The first few

pages are full of random notes about finances and bills. I riffle through the pages until I reach page 142.

The number doesn't have any real significance.

I just like the way it looks. The way it sounds when spoken aloud. And it's also midway inside the journal, so even if Cole were to come sneaking around in my office, he wouldn't think to read the middle pages of some little notebook.

I sit down and roll closer to my desk, then reach inside the drawer and extract a black ink pen. I should have done this sooner, but Cole made me doubt myself.

He made me believe that my brain injury was turning me into someone else. Someone incapable of separating reality from fiction.

Admittedly, part of me feared that if I opened this journal, I'd find a blank page. And if that had happened, I'm not sure what I would have done with myself.

Because this page contains history.

Fifteen years, to be exact.

Twenty different names.

I'm not wrong about Cole. This proves it, just as my deleted calendar events did. I may have suffered a grave injury, but I'm not entirely gone. I'm still here. And I still have a job to do—to protect my daughter.

Hazel looks up to her father. If she were to find out who he really was, I think it would break her. And she's already partially lost one parent. I'm not so sure she could handle any more pain.

Then again, Hazel is like me. She's resilient. A survivor. And the truth is, I can't keep protecting Cole.

With the pen's cap still on, I draw an invisible line down the list of names. They're all written differently and with various ink colors.

Twenty women.

Fifteen years.

Alicia.

His first, before we were married. I clench my teeth at her memory. I don't hold anything against her. Cole made the decision to cheat on me. I'm not going to pin the blame on another woman. But the sight of her name brings back the memory of when I first discovered Cole was a cheater.

It was devastating. My whole world was turned upside down. I thought he was different. And then when Chels found out about it, she wanted to break his legs with that crowbar.

Okay, *that* memory makes me all warm and fuzzy.

She's such a firecracker.

She also begged me not to marry him. But I loved Cole, more than anything. And days after I found out about his betrayal, I also found out I was pregnant.

Roseline.

I never liked her, but she's the reason I discovered Cole was a serial cheater. That he'd broken his promise to remain faithful when he married me. That was a whole shitshow, but I wouldn't change how things played out.

Beth.

Lizzy.

Claire.

I despised Claire especially. She had a thick French accent and walked around as if everyone ought to drop to their knees and bow in her presence. Cole must have loved her domineering personality.

Angelika.

Ugh. Don't miss that one.

Sarah.

Okay, she was actually very likable. And probably the easiest to get rid of.

The list continues halfway down the page. I pull the pen's cap off with my teeth and lean forward, placing the ballpoint on a blank line beneath the last name.

Valeria.

It's the only one that isn't yet scratched out.

Don't worry, Valeria. Soon, you'll be ancient history, just like the rest of Cole's little playthings.

CHAPTER 39

Meghan

Sitting in a parked car for hours on end isn't fun. It's hurting my ass, and I'm getting very restless.

This wasn't such a good idea.

What if Valeria stays late with Cole again? I could be waiting until this evening.

No, I have to do this.

I reach for a snack bar in my purse—chocolate chip granola—and tear the wrapper open with my teeth. The texture is chewy yet soft, and the bar almost melts in my mouth.

I swallow it back with a chug of soda, the fizzing sensation in my mouth calming me slightly.

"Come on," I mutter.

Every few seconds, someone exits through the front doors. The glass building is exceptionally large, and so is the parking lot. It must be at least a few acres.

The sun is halfway through the sky and reflecting off the building's glass. I can still see the front doors without issue, but in the next hour or so, the reflection might be painful.

I'm parked all the way at the back, next to a brand-new Ram pickup truck and a leafy tree that looks to have been planted last year.

Every time a woman with long brown hair steps out, I perk up. But even from here, I can tell they aren't Valeria. I'll recognize her when I see her. Hopefully, she doesn't stay late; otherwise, this is going to be one hell of a long night.

Thankfully, there's no need to rush home. Not unless Cole suddenly comes out. Then I'll take off and beat him to the house. But Hazel is at Alex's, yet again, so I'm happy about that.

When I looked Valeria up, she'd posted a picture with her young son. So I'm counting on her wanting to return home to him. Then again, she could be a shit mom. Especially if she's been staying behind every evening, screwing my husband. Who knows?

By six o'clock, most of the staff has left the building. Except for Cole and Valeria.

Damn it.

What a waste of my time.

I turn my engine over and leave.

***

I tried again yesterday, and still Valeria didn't leave on time. But today is Friday. People like to leave early on Fridays, right? I considered telling Cole to be home early for whatever reason. I'm beginning to suspect that her schedule matches his.

By the time I've counted a total of five hundred and fifty-nine people having exited the building, my eyelids become heavy.

I immediately reach for my energy drink and chug back several bubbly gulps. I can't fall asleep. Not now.

Just as I'm about to reach inside my purse for my usual snack, a woman with wavy brown hair and a snug black business skirt comes walking out through the front doors. She looks over her shoulder, then descends the small flight of stairs, her hand grazing the railing almost flirtatiously.

That woman knows she's hot.

Either that, or she just had sex with Cole and is feeling on top of the world. I clench my palm around my steering wheel over and over.

She takes long strides through several rows of cars before reaching a beat-up and rusted sedan that stands out among all the other luxury brands. That is her, right? It has to be.

I shift my car out of Park and slowly roll forward, following her as she exits the massive parking lot. I keep several cars behind her. If she feels followed, even in the slightest, she may open up to Cole about it tomorrow. And if she does, it won't be hard for him to put the pieces together.

We drive into the south side of Bayton Valley and into what everyone refers to as the "poor end" of town. Most houses here are old duplexes with molded white paneling. Gardens are overgrown. Some windows are busted. Others are boarded up.

It's not exactly a safe neighborhood.

"You sure have a type, Cole," I mutter.

He likes it when women need him. When he can be their knight in shining armor. He takes advantage of that.

As I take in the neighborhood around me, I instantly feel bad for this woman's son. Then again, Valeria works at AstroWyre, which means she has ambition. If she weren't sleeping with my husband, I'd be rooting for her.

She pulls into an old driveway full of deep cracks, and her car lights turn off. The moment she steps out of her sedan, a little boy comes blasting through the front door with his arms wide open. He throws himself into her arms, and she hugs him tight, beaming.

It's very hard to dislike this woman.

While I hate home-wreckers, I'm under the presumption that Cole has somehow misled this woman into believing he's in love with her. That they belong together, and I'm nothing but an evil bitch who refuses to divorce Cole. But to follow me at a grocery store—that's a little overboard. Still, I always want to give women the benefit of the doubt. My husband, on the other hand—I know exactly how he is.

I suddenly spot an older woman with short gray hair

and olive skin standing between the house's doorframe and the partially open screen door. She smiles, watching who I can only presume are her grandson and daughter.

So she has a good relationship with her mother. Valeria must be a decent person when she isn't stalking wives and stealing their husbands.

Why does Cole always put me in this position? It isn't fair. I don't enjoy being the bad guy. But my family and daughter come first. I don't have the luxury of caring about how my interjection changes the lives of Cole's mistresses.

My focus shifts to the metal lettering attached above the sweet middle-aged woman's head. She's now lovingly reaching for Valeria and stepping on the tips of her toes to peck her daughter's cheek.

Before I can reconsider what I'm soon about to do, I take note of the address.

59 *Abbott Drive.*

As I drive away, I watch her home through my rearview mirror. It shrinks with every passing second. "I'm sorry, Valeria. But there's no other way."

CHAPTER 40

Meghan

I almost started to feel bad over the weekend.

Almost.

But I'm not backing out of this. I already told Chels that I'm going to handle my husband's indiscretions. I've handled them before. This time is no different.

On Monday, Cole went to work as he always does. When Hazel was out of the house, I drove down to the south end of town and staked out Valeria's place. I did the same thing on Tuesday.

Both days taught me something: Valeria's mother only shows up at around three o'clock, and the little boy, at three thirty. It seems that she shows up to take care of Valeria's kid. I don't stay long enough to find out what happens when Valeria comes home. I imagine they all share a meal in that tiny kitchen of hers, laughing over freshly cooked food while the little boy talks about his day at school.

By Wednesday, I'm confident in my plan.

No one is home, which means I can do what needs to be done without drawing attention to me. I get dressed in a one-piece contractor uniform Cole wore for Halloween three years ago. It's rather large on me, but with a tight sports bra and a ball cap, I mostly look like a man.

I drive to Valeria's place but park my car two blocks away. If she has a doorbell camera, it would be pretty heedless of me to park right out front of her house.

As I walk down her quiet street, I lug one of Cole's toolboxes with me and keep my head down. Only a few people are seen strolling about, but they don't appear to care about my presence.

One woman is humming a tune I've never heard while staring at the sky and walking at an angle. She's clearly high on something. It's sad despite her false sense of happiness. Across the street from her is an older woman walking a three-legged dog while smoking two cigarettes at once. The dog looks healthier than her, despite its missing limb.

Not exactly the kind of neighborhood I'd want my kid growing up in.

I readjust my sunglasses under my ballcap and walk across Valeria's front lawn and toward the back. There aren't any cameras in sight, which is surprising. If I lived in a place like this, I'd have at least a dozen cameras set up all around my house.

I move toward the backyard, between her house and her neighbor's shoddy bungalow. There's no one here. Just me.

It's perfect.

Trying to act as inconspicuous as possible, I settle among a row of trees between Valeria's house and her neighbor's, then bend down as if inspecting something on the ground.

If anyone were to see me, they'd think I was simply preparing to perform a land survey.

A crow suddenly lets out a throaty caw from one of the overhead branches, and I flinch so hard I almost drop my toolbox.

Bastard.

It's like he's onto me. Warning me to get lost; otherwise, he'll tell Valeria what I've done.

Thankfully, crows don't speak English. And from the looks of it, no one can see me—not here, squished between the two houses.

I search the ground for a nice, heavy rock.

Admittedly, I feel bad about this. But I can't linger on my feelings. I need to act, not think.

My mother was always good at reminding me of this.

"Think with your head, dummy. Stop thinking with *feelings*." She sneered as if the last word was so repulsive that speaking it aloud might induce vomiting.

Which was so ironic given how my mom cried herself to sleep after my dad left. But every time I asked if she was okay, she'd wipe her face and tell me to get out of her hair. Then, an hour or so later, she'd hug me tight and tell me she loved me.

It was never a dull moment with my mother.

This lasted for a few years, on and off. Men came and went, but she kept crying over my dad.

Think with your head, dummy.

And my head is telling me one thing—to get Valeria out of the picture. I can't stand here worrying about her life and her son.

So I bend down and pick up a large rock full of sharp points.

It's perfect.

Then, with all of my strength, I hurl it at Valeria's window.

CHAPTER 41

Meghan

I can't believe I'm about to do this.

I mean, I can—I've done it before. But every time, it makes me feel unhinged. Cole might be right about me when he says I take things too far.

No, this isn't taking things too far.

The jack is plugged in firmly. I test the Power button of my voice changer, and a little blue light comes on at the top right-hand corner.

This little gadget cost me twenty bucks over five years ago, and it's served me well.

Once I'm confident that everything is set up properly and that my phone settings have my number blocked, I dial AstroWyre and wait patiently as the line rings. A young female voice picks up. "H-hello, AstroWyre, Angela speaking. How may I direct your call?"

She must be the office's new secretary.

Even if you get rid of Valeria, Cole will probably set his sights on her next.

I push this thought away.

"Oh, hi there. I called yesterday to book a meeting with Cole Garrett." I pause, hoping to God that the voice changer is working correctly. Then again, this woman doesn't know who I am. Still. She should be hearing a man's voice on the other end.

"I was told by . . . Valeria, I believe her name was," I continue. "I was told I would receive a callback to confirm a time and date for my meeting with Cole."

"Oh," the woman says, her voice unnaturally high

pitched. "Oh, um, hold on. I'm new—"

"Is Valeria in?" I ask.

"Valeria?" The girl sounds like she's sixteen years old. I picture her twirling hair around her ear and popping bubble gum in her mouth. "Um, no, I don't think so. I haven't seen her all morning."

Perfect.

"Oh," I say. "Will she be in tomorrow?"

"Um, I don't know. I can ask Cole. I heard something about an emergency at home."

Her shattered window.

I smile against the voice changer.

"That's quite all right. I'll call back tomorrow. Thank you for your time, Angela."

"Did you want me to—"

I hang up.

***

Valeria's beat-up sedan sits in her rutted driveway. I drive slowly, leaning over my steering wheel to spot her side window. Shards of glass are sprawled in her ashen mulch, some clinging to the tips of hostas that are in dire need of water.

The busted window is covered in a red-and-blue drape. What is that? A Spiderman comforter? Did she seriously use her kid's bedsheet to cover it up?

I picture her inside her little house, frantically calling various contractors to get quotes for a new window.

Quotes she can't afford.

But she won't have to worry about that much longer.

I park my Jeep down the road and climb out. Admittedly, I put a little extra care into my appearance today. Not that Valeria is competition. But I don't exactly want to show up to my husband's mistress's house looking like a slob.

I want her to know how much of a mistake Cole is

making.

A few heads turn my way as I walk down the old sidewalk, careful not to get my heel caught in a crack. I'm so out of place here, especially with my gold chain necklace and collection of rings. It's nothing fancy, but I'm still regretting the decision.

This is the sort of neighborhood in which people get jumped. Mugged. Raped, even. I don't want to be here any longer than I have to be.

Get in, do what you have to do, and get out.

I clutch my purse snugly against my body, just in case some asshole tries to run up from behind me and take it. But Chels has taught me many self-defense moves. I once had a young man with an obvious drug problem grab my purse and try to tear it off my shoulder. He landed on the floor, cupping his balls. Although, I had *two* functioning arms then.

I don't want to find out how well I'd fare with one.

Head held high, I walk up to Valeria's front door and knock gently. From the other side, she shouts, "One minute!"

Then it sounds like she trips and catches herself on the wall. Is she one of those hoarders? Does she have heaps of clothes and boxes all over the place?

She opens the door, a sharp breath escaping her mouth. Her cheeks are flushed, and her lips, dark red. But not lipstick red. No, she's naturally stunning and seems to have everything working in her favor, including the pigment of her lips. It's hard to look away from her.

Even in sweats and a baggy T-shirt, the woman is attractive. She leans forward, inspecting the street behind me, then raises a brow.

"Um, hi," she says. "I'm sorry, do I know you?"

Right. Let's play this game.

"I'm Cole's wife."

I can't read her expression. Blank? Fear? Or maybe there's nothing at all behind that beauty.

"Oh, hi," she says. Then, she smiles ingenuously. "It's

nice to meet you."

Why the hell is she smiling at me like that?

I think back to the day she followed me at the grocery store. And then, when I sensed someone in my backyard. Part of me wonders if coming here was a bad idea.

I visualize the pocketknife in my purse. If she tries anything, I'll pull it out.

She tucks a thick strand of her brown hair behind her ear. The woman is very thin, but not in a way that lessens her curves. Her waist is cinched, and her jawline is extremely sharp.

She isn't very muscular, but I've learned from experience that size doesn't mean anything. She could take a swing at me and have twice my strength.

"Um, is everything okay?" she says.

"Peachy," I say coldly. "May I?"

I raise a brow and aim my chin at the inside of her home. The smell of muffins wafts through the air, causing my stomach to grumble.

But I'm not here for pleasantries.

She hesitates, then looks around outside, almost like she's looking to see if there are any witnesses. Is she afraid of me?

She should be.

"Come in," she says, her lips stretching into a strained smile.

I step inside, and she closes the door behind me.

Soon, this will all be over.

PART TWO

CHAPTER 42

Cole

At least two dozen women are lined up near the elevators, waiting to be interviewed. Each one of them has been carefully vetted and interviewed virtually by me before being invited to an in-person meeting.

An in-person meeting with Vincent. No, it's not standard for a CEO at a company the size of AstroWyre to hire an office secretary. But Vincent always insists he wants to be a part of it. The truth is, Vincent is worse than Frank when it comes to women. Although, he isn't a pig about it. But he isn't shy to admit that he only wants to hire the *hottest of the hottest*. He says it keeps his salesmen on their toes. Helps keep morale around the office if there's a good piece of eye candy.

Which is why he asks me to have virtual meetings with each candidate, first.

If they're over the age of thirty, he isn't interested.

As long as they have basic computer skills, he asks me to mark them down as potential candidates. If Valeria were still here, I'd ask her to send out the invitations. But she isn't. She just up and left without a word. I tried reaching out, but she never returned my calls.

What kind of a person does that?

I'd ask Angela to take care of it, but she left, too. Although with Angela, I had a feeling she didn't intend to stay long. She was always distracted and didn't quite seem to know what she was doing.

I'm hoping that the next secretary stays put. At least for six months. Is that too much to ask?

Vincent whistles at me and throws his head sideways to get me to meet him in the boardroom. If I didn't know him personally, I'd think he was working for the mafia with his thousand-dollar suit, his slick black hair gelled back, and those dark eyes beneath bushy brows that almost look taped on. Like those Velcro Halloween eyebrows. It's not like he's young; he's sixty-five years old, but the guy is in shape and very suave with any woman he meets. It amazes me how twenty-year-olds throw themselves at him.

I'm sure that has something to do with his money, and also those impressive gray sideburns of his. Women are constantly complimenting his hair.

He peers through the blinds of the boardroom by pulling down one of the sleek panels. "You can tell numbers three, four, nine, eleven, and thirteen to go home."

I don't bother asking him why.

I know exactly why. They're a bit on the heavier side (meaning they don't look like sick models), and somehow, I didn't spot this during the virtual interviews. What was I supposed to do? Ask them to stand up and measure their waist circumference for me? We'd get hit with lawsuits left and right.

If Meg knew about Vincent's hiring process, she'd probably rip him a new one. Then force me to quit this job. Then key his car.

I don't want to tell them to go home. But Vincent's the boss, and if I want to keep my job, I have to do what he says. I'm hoping that if I do everything he asks, he'll recommend me to the board of directors as the best candidate for his job when he retires.

Reluctantly, I approach the candidates and ask numbers three, four, nine, eleven, and thirteen to follow me into a different boardroom. I politely tell them that we made a mistake during the hiring process and that they cannot attend the interview.

One woman stands up and says, "Are you fucking

kidding me? Is this because we aren't sickly twigs like the other girls out there?"

I shake my head. "Absolutely not. And it isn't my decision. I'm sorry."

"Then whose decision is it?" she snaps at me.

I lean sideways, my head popping out of the doorframe, and wiggle a finger at Tommy. The guy used to be a wrestler, standing at close to seven feet tall. His head alone is nearly the size of my chest. He's massive, which makes him the perfect head of security at AstroWyre.

I walk out before that same woman can lash at me some more. Tommy handles the rest—even while she's shouting at me, he remains calm and gently guides her toward the elevators.

When I return to the small, intimate boardroom where Vincent is now sitting on the opposite side of the table, I pull up a chair next to him. Vincent pulls his cell phone out of his pocket and calls someone.

Mrs. Jones, I assume.

He always gets her to bring in candidates during interviews.

"Bring the first one," he says.

He's not sweet with Mrs. Jones. He's not mean, either, but he doesn't put any effort into being kind. Probably because he doesn't want to sleep with her.

Vincent looks at me sideways, crow's-feet spreading from his eyes. "Keep a list of your three top choices. You can have one." He sticks up a thick finger between us. I spot the indent where his wedding ring sits when he isn't in the office. "One. Got it? You can hire her directly this time. No more stealing my office secretaries."

Satisfied, I nod.

Chapter 43

Meghan

Cole has been happier than usual these past few weeks. Way happier. There's no way he's still thinking about Valeria. And if he is, he sure has a funny way of showing it.

He's even happier than when Valeria was his assistant.

If things were any different, I'd be livid. It's been two weeks since he lost Valeria, for crying out loud, and he's already chasing after his new love interest.

It gets him all riled up.

Like he's a predator, and he's hunting to catch his prey.

Hazel is never home anymore. I may have gotten rid of Valeria, but I'm losing my daughter. If I don't do something soon, I'm not sure she'll return to me.

A knock at my window suddenly jolts me out of my thoughts.

I peer sideways, wide eyed, to find Mrs. Jones beaming at me while waving a wrinkly hand. Her eyes have shrunk into little crescent moons, and if she were smiling any wider, her dentures would likely fall out.

I'm assuming she has dentures.

Those teeth are a little too perfect.

I lower my window and offer her a warm greeting. "Mrs. Jones, how lovely to see you."

She's so short that she could almost walk *underneath* my side mirror without so much as knocking one of her curls out of place. Almost.

With a wavering finger, she pushes her glasses up the bridge of her nose. "What're you doing out here? Coming to surprise Cole?"

"Yeah," I lie. "I was about to call him and ask if he wants to come to lunch."

The joy on her face slips away. Something's wrong.

"What is it?" I ask.

She clears her throat, looking rather uncomfortable. Does she know something I don't? Doubtful. I'm not here to have lunch with Cole. I'm here to get a good look at his new assistant.

"He's been in meetings all day," she says. "And I think he's taking his new assistant out to celebrate a sale they just made."

"Oh?" I say. "Well, I don't want to get in the way of that."

She's struggling. She knows as well as I do that Cole is sleeping with his new assistant, but she doesn't think it's her place to say anything.

"How is she?" I watch her reaction very carefully.

She almost jumps at my words. "Hmm?"

"His new assistant? Katya, I believe her name is."

"Oh." Her eyes double in size. "You know who she is?"

"Of course I do," I say. "My husband told me last week."

For the first time ever, Cole approached me and opened up about needing to hire a new secretary, since Valeria *just up and disappeared without a trace.* He sounded resentful when he said it. But then, his tone softened, and he observed me with scrutiny. Waiting to see if I'd flinch. If I'd frown. Something to tell him that I'm responsible for Valeria's disappearance.

But I have a solid poker face. I told him I was terribly sorry that he'd lost such a good assistant and that I hoped he'd find another one—just as good, if not better.

Judging by how happy he's been the last few weeks, I'd say the match is better. Much better.

"Well, do you want me to let him know you say hi?" Her voice quivers so much that I'm afraid she's going to suddenly collapse.

"No, that's all right." The last thing I need is for Cole to know I'm onto him again. "I'll shoot him a text."

She nods, though it looks more like a bobble. "It was very nice to see you, Meghan." She taps my car door, then turns away and starts walking toward AstroWyre's front entrance.

A woman her age shouldn't have to walk half a mile to reach the front doors. Why doesn't she have some sort of privileged parking? Every step she takes looks like it requires a great deal of energy.

I'm tempted to call out to her—offer her a ride to the front doors—but I can't drive up to AstroWyre like that. If Cole sees my car, I'm going to get an earful. The last time I tried to spy on him from my car, I crashed into that woman's BMW and was basically forced to book an appointment with my neurologist.

She's cleared me, though.

Cole thinks I'm speaking with Dr. Bachmann again, but I haven't made the appointment. Instead, I tell him I've been having weekly virtual sessions in my office.

That, combined with extra-good behavior on my part, has him totally unaware of what I'm planning.

This time around, I'm doing things differently.

When I'm finished, Cole Garrett will never cheat on me again.

CHAPTER 44

Diary Entry

I can't believe that bitch.

She thinks money is going to get me to leave Cole? I mean, it worked—I quit my job. But I'm not going anywhere. She's delusional if she thinks I'm leaving.

Besides, Cole is now bound to me.

Because there's a little secret he doesn't know. And once he finds out, it's going to change everything. It might even get him to leave his witch of a wife.

Stupid bitch.

I found a picture of her on SocioWeave today. She pretends to be happy, with her tilted head pressed up against Cole's cheek and those long blond locks of hers flowing all around her neck. I was jealous at first since I was cursed with dark hair. Always wanted to be light featured. That didn't pan out.

But Cole loves my dark hair and brown eyes. He says they're little chocolates. *His* little chocolates.

I printed out that picture of Meghan and stuck it to my wall. A little bit of red marker to the eyes, the mouth . . . She looks better like this.

Dead.

She'd probably look better dead in real life, too.

If she doesn't leave him soon . . .

Anyway.

Cole is my world, and Meghan is the Minotaur. She's selfish and arrogant and only thinks about herself. If she really cared about Cole, she'd let him go.

I'm wasting my time here.

And this is hurting my hand.
As soon as I tell Cole I'm pregnant, he'll leave her.
I know it.

CHAPTER 45

Meghan

And there she is.

Long, straight blond hair and legs for days. Although I'm too far away to hear what she's whispering in Cole's ear, his amorous smile tells me it was a sexual comment.

Something to get him all aroused.

She's practically kissing his neck.

"Katya," I mumble to myself.

I've already marked her name down in my little red notebook. Not that it matters, because Katya will be the last. After this, I won't even need that notebook anymore.

From here, I can imagine her heels ticking on the asphalt as the two of them approach Cole's Lexus. Her mouth stretches into an astonished smile when his car lights flash.

She mouths something.

"This is your car?"

At least, that's my best guess.

Cole's shoulders pull back a little unnaturally like a puppet being controlled by a puppeteer. He's so proud of himself. For what? A piece of shiny metal on four wheels?

Grow the fuck up.

My eyes narrow on Katya as she bends down to enter Cole's passenger's side. Her red dress rides up, revealing a sexy thigh.

I should be angry, knowing that my husband will—if he hasn't already—be sleeping with this woman.

But I'm not angry.

In fact, I feel more alive than I have in as long as I can

remember.

Cole drives away with his prize while I sit quietly watching him, a crooked smile on my face.

***

I don't bother following Cole. I know where he's going—either some quaint little restaurant in Bayton Valley or a motel room.

He's been avoiding Blue Fusion Bistro ever since I showed up that one day.

But it doesn't matter, honestly.

This plan is so much bigger than his little secret lunch hours. Or his overtime, which I'm sure he uses to bend Katya over his desk and have his way with her.

I just wanted to see them together.

Is that weird?

Maybe.

But it helps sustain my anger. And right now, anger is what's fueling me.

Once I'm certain Cole is far out of sight, I leave AstroWyre's parking lot and take a right turn onto Montgomery Drive.

As I turn, a white Hyundai Accent takes the same corner a little too sharply, like they're afraid of losing me.

My eyes flicker toward my rearview mirror.

It's hard to make out who the driver is. The side windows must be tinted, which always makes the interior so dark.

I squint.

Big sunglasses. Long, wavy dark hair.

This woman isn't following you. You're being paranoid.

I turn off Montgomery, then take a left.

She's still behind me. And close, too. If I didn't know any better, I'd think she was pissed off. Because now her bumper is almost touching mine. What the hell is her problem? There are two lanes. She can go around me.

I tap my foot on my brake, hoping it'll get her to back off. She backs away for a few seconds, then comes at me aggressively again.

Okay.

This bitch is *trying* to intimidate me.

Could it be Valeria? No way. I took care of her. And this isn't even Valeria's car.

But that looks like Valeria.

She rides my rear bumper, and now, I'm tempted to slam my brakes. She'll be at fault. But her aggression is throwing me off. It's causing my heart to pound uncomfortably in my chest and the steering wheel under my palms to become wet and slippery.

I take another sharp turn and hit the gas.

She follows me.

Fast.

Shit.

I swerve onto the freeway. I'll lose her there. I may not have two functioning arms, but I've always been a good driver. Especially in this Jeep.

I weave in and out of traffic, trying my best to lose her. But she's coming after me. Every time I merge lanes, she follows, her bumper almost hitting mine.

For a brief moment, I consider calling the police, but by the time they show up, she might have already rammed me off the road. I'm better off focusing on getting rid of her.

Besides, there's an exit up ahead that leads to a long stretch of back road. I doubt her little Accent will be able to keep up with my Jeep.

I just need to get away from her.

And there are never any cops there (although at this very moment, I wish there were), so it's not like I'll get a speeding ticket.

I signal left, but at the very last second, I swerve off the exit, causing several cars to honk at me.

I exhale a quivering breath and grip my steering wheel tightly, fighting to keep my Jeep straight despite my trembling arm.

I think I lost her.

My lips are about to break into a prideful grin until I spot a white bumper in my rearview mirror. It comes from above, from the top slope of the descending off-ramp.

Are you kidding me?

The second I'm on the straight back country road, I hit my gas pedal. Her car looks to be shrinking behind me.

"Eat my dust, you bitch."

I don't slow down. About two miles from here, the road forks, and several other long stretches of back roads become accessible. If I can turn on one of those without her seeing me, then I'll lose her.

My heart is now throbbing in my ears. My throat is dry, but I'm sure even if I drank an entire bottle of water, it would still be dry.

I don't understand why this is happening.

What does this woman want with me?

I glance in my mirror again, my chest aching painfully, when I spot the front of the Accent busting through a big gray cloud of dust.

My breath catches painfully.

I'm going a hundred miles per hour in a fifty-five zone. It feels unstable. I don't enjoy going this fast. All it takes is one big pothole or a deer, and I'm a goner.

Yet this crazy driver is coming in fast, easily going 110.

I could press the gas a little harder, but I don't want to go any faster. This is getting increasingly dangerous. I have a daughter to think about. I'd rather face this woman than crash my car trying to escape her.

Without warning, I slam on my brakes.

My car skids across the road, pebbles flying in every direction. She comes at me so fast I'm certain she's going to rear-end me.

But right before she does, she swerves sideways and slows down along with me.

What the hell is she doing?

I keep driving, having dropped to the legal speed limit, and the white Accent follows me on the left, dust and debris suspended in the air between us.

I want to roll my window down and shout at her, but what if she has a gun? What if she's about to shoot me through the window?

Lowering my window while keeping the wheel straight isn't an easy feat; it's not worth the risk.

Without warning, her car swerves to the left. I'm certain she's about to take the ditch. But a split second later, she swerves back toward me, full force.

The collision causes my entire body to jolt and my foot to instinctively slam on the brake pedal.

I don't even understand what's going on.

But the next thing I know, my car is flying into the ditch on my right, and the Accent disappears into a big cloud of beige dust.

CHAPTER 46

Cole

Meg's puffy blue eyes roll beneath fluttering eyelids, her gaze latching on to the space around me.

"Meg?" I say.

I get up from the hospital chair and approach her bedside. "Honey, can you hear me?"

She appears more alert with each blink.

"Nice to have you back," says Kiyana, the nurse assigned to my wife. "How you feeling?"

Meg blinks so hard that little lines crinkle across her temples. "Um."

"Airbag hit you pretty hard." Kiyana grabs Meg's chart and inspects it. "Says here you suffered a traumatic brain injury last year." She pauses, then approaches my wife. "Can you tell me your name?"

Meg stares at Kiyana a little too long for my liking. Could the airbag have worsened her injury? Caused her symptoms to return, full blown? Oh, God . . . How will Hazel handle this? Seeing her mother back in a hospital bed will break her into pieces.

She's still in school. I haven't told her anything. Not until I have more answers.

I inspect Meg's face—it's swollen, and a little red blotch darkens the corner of her eye. That airbag did a number on her.

"It was that bitch," Meg says.

I pull my face back, while Kiyana's forehead bunches.

"Valeria," Meg says through clenched teeth.

Okay—her memory isn't gone.

And her hatred is aimed at me. But I didn't do this. Why is she so pissed off with me? And Valeria wouldn't do something like this.

"You think you know who did this?" Kiyana says.

Meg nods ferociously. "Um, yeah. I saw her. Long brown hair. Big sunglasses. White Accent."

Kiyana sticks a finger up. "Hold on. Let me get the police. They've been wanting to ask you some questions."

She disappears from the small hospital room, leaving me alone with Meg.

"Honey, how do you know it was her?" I ask, trying to be as gentle as possible. "You just described over fifty percent of women in Bayton Valley. Or even in America, for that matter."

"It was her," Meg says. "Who the hell else would it be? She wanted me dead, Cole. And the only person who would want that is the woman you're sleeping with."

My brows snap together. "I'm not sleeping with Valeria."

She rolls her eyes. "Sorry, *were*."

I almost wish she *had* lost some of her memory. Maybe then she wouldn't be so vicious with me.

Even if I try to explain to her that I never slept with Valeria, she won't believe me. Not when she's like this.

"Valeria quit two weeks ago," I say. "Why would she come for you now?"

Meg lets out an overly fake laugh. "Oh, I don't know. To get rid of the *wife*? I knew she seemed way too nice. She's a good actor. Playing innocent little mother. I almost wanted to like her."

I freeze, staring wide eyed at the woman before me. Her blond hair is all matted on one side, and deep bags sit beneath her swollen eyes. That scowl on her face isn't doing her any favors, either. She looks possessed.

If I hadn't seen this side of Meg before, I'd think the accident had caused her soul to bounce out of her body before welcoming in a different one.

She's furious.

But that's not what scares me—it's the words she just used.

She *almost liked* Valeria.

Which means she's met her.

I'm well aware that she saw her through the window at Blue Fusion Bistro, but when the hell did she talk to her?

"How would you know anything about her?" I ask.

I'm afraid to know the answer.

"Are you serious right now?" Meg says. "She worked as your assistant, Cole. You don't think I've had to talk to her on the phone?"

I suppose that makes sense.

For a moment, I thought Meg had confronted Valeria. I wouldn't put it past her.

"Mrs. Garrett?" comes an authoritative male voice.

The young cop walks in with a female partner at his side. "I'm Officer Vaughn, and this is my partner, Officer Delgado."

The female cop offers a curt nod but doesn't speak. Officer Vaughn, a forty-some-year-old man with bulging biceps, veiny hands, and a meticulously trimmed afro, enters the small space. He clutches a little clipboard in one hand and a plain black pen in the other.

"Nurse Kiyana says you may have relevant information regarding the person who hit you. The woman who called 911 said she found your car in the ditch, the side of it completely totaled. Did someone ram into you?"

I'm a bit nervous for Valeria right now. I didn't know her. Not really. Would she actually be capable of something like this?

And if so, *why*?

"White Accent, four doors," Meg says. "Not new but not old, either. The car, I mean. The woman had long brown hair and huge sunglasses over her face. She looked like she wanted to hurt me. She started following me on Montgomery Drive. Then onto the freeway, and off Exit 23."

"Pasture Road," says Officer Vaughn.

Meg nods.

"Did you catch the license plate?"

The indignant look on Meg's face tells me she wants to rip this officer a new one. If she'd seen the license plate, she would have led with that.

"We're just trying to help," says Officer Vaughn.

Meg sighs. "I know. I'm sorry. I'm just really upset that this happened. I'm pretty sure it was Valeria, my husband's mistress."

Everyone's eyes are on me now, so I clear my throat. "Could I speak to you both privately?" I ask the officers.

Meg lets out a boisterous laugh. "Seriously, Cole? So you can tell them how crazy I am? Tell them all about my brain injury? Go ahead." She shifts her focus onto the police officers, a calmness washing over her. "My husband will tell you he isn't cheating on me, but he's a compulsive liar. But please. By all means. Go ahead and speak privately."

With that, I lead the police officers out of Meg's room—away from her anger and hatred.

CHAPTER 47

Meghan

Cole is on his best behavior on the drive home. Unfortunately for me, I no longer have a car. It could take weeks before the insurance pays out.

"I know this is a lot," Cole says. "But I promise you, Valeria didn't do this."

I let out a long sigh. Honestly, I'm so sick of Cole's lies. But I still welcome any information he might have. Because now that my anger is gone, I'm left totally confused.

Valeria offered me home-baked muffins while I accused her of sleeping with my husband. When I asked her about following me at the grocery store and the note, she swore up and down that it wasn't her.

What if I'm wrong about her?

Either someone else has been stalking me, or Valeria is a total psychopath.

"Go ahead, I'm listening."

I rest my head against Cole's window. I'm in a lot of pain, especially my left arm where the door rammed into me. That, and my neck. Something about whiplash. But overall, I lucked out.

No broken bones. No severe head injury. I'm alive and well.

"The police looked into Valeria," Cole makes an agonizingly slow left turn. I'm injured, but not *that* injured. "She left her rental property last week. Just took off. They managed to track her down. She's in Ohio with her mother and son. With extended family."

His jaw is tight, and his eyes keep darting between me and the road. The scary part of all of this is that I don't think he's lying.

"Okay," I say calmly. "Then why did this happen? Is there someone else you've been screwing behind my back?"

Cole smacks the steering wheel, his nostrils flaring. "I didn't sleep with Valeria, Meg. I don't know how many times I have to tell you."

But Valeria . . . she was different. Which is exactly why it would make sense if she'd been the one to ram me. She's probably a total psychopath.

I picture her beautiful face and the way she offered me chocolate chip muffins.

"My son's favorite," she'd said, watching me with a smile so bright, I almost started to view her as a friend.

I remember thinking they were poisoned but then immediately dismissed this idea, considering I showed up without warning. Those muffins were rising before I ever set foot in the house.

"Where in Ohio?" I ask.

Cole frowns at me. "That's not for us to know. I'm just telling you what the cops said. She's been there since last week. Her mother can vouch for her."

Or she's in on this, too.

"So unless she has a twin who still lives here, in Bayton Valley, it wasn't Valeria."

I'm still trying to rack my brain—trying to come up with an explanation for all of this. What if Valeria took a flight, and rented a car to attack me, and then immediately flew back to Ohio?

It's not impossible.

"Meg," Cole says sternly, likely sensing my thoughts.

"What?" I lash back. "Someone tried to kill me, Cole. And that doesn't concern you? Excuse me for wanting answers."

He takes another slow right turn, and I'm tempted to tell him to press a little harder on the pedal. I want to get home. I want to go lie in bed with Ziggy tucked at my feet and fade away into a five-hour nap.

"I know," Cole says. "Trust me, I'm freaking out about this."

Sure, you are.

Cole hasn't been happy in our marriage for years. I don't know why he stays. I suppose for the same reasons as me. To keep our family together.

But that isn't enough anymore.

"The cops are looking into it," Cole says. "They take attempted murder pretty seriously."

I'm surprised Cole didn't chalk this up to me being *paranoid.* That he isn't blaming me for the accident. It would be an easy thing to do, after all. Maybe I swerved on the road due to my lack of arm function. Maybe I'm the one who rammed into someone only to then lose control and crash into a ditch.

Why?

Why does he believe me this time, when every other time, he's found some way to question my sanity?

Is it because he knows something? Or is the damage to my car irrefutable?

I don't press him.

Instead, I watch his side profile; his jaw keeps working as his knuckles whiten around the steering wheel. He's visibly upset.

Does he actually care that I almost died?

It's hard to tell with Cole. On the surface, he does appear to be distraught over my near-death accident. But my husband is also a compulsive liar, so I can't trust what I see.

Then, I wonder: what if he's lying to me about Valeria?

What if the cops never said all those things? And instead, he called her and warned her to leave town? I mean, I'll find out soon enough. It's only a matter of time before the police find the person responsible.

Unless they aren't even looking into this.

For all I know, Cole spun his web and somehow

convinced the police that I was responsible for the accident. His lies will only take him so far, though.

If I had been the one to cause the accident, the other driver wouldn't have taken off the way that Accent did.

I have no clue what to believe, but I do know one thing—I can't trust Cole, which means I need to find out for myself if Valeria truly left town.

Chapter 48

Meghan

"Hi, Cole."

Chels's voice is like a sharp icicle. A very jagged one that might be used to stab a person. That person being Cole.

Cole steps aside so fast he stumbles on a pair of Hazel's boots, then clears his throat awkwardly. He extends an open palm toward the living room, where I'm sitting.

I tried to nap, but I couldn't fall asleep due to the pain in my neck. It's been sneaking up on me over the last few hours, growing with intensity by the minute.

"Thanks." Chels doesn't mean it. If she could, she'd shove him aside. Once she steps into view, her shiny metal baseball bat glints, and she twirls it a few times in her fist. I think she's doing that on purpose to intimidate Cole.

It works—he takes off without a word.

Not that Chels has any intention of hurting him. The bat isn't for my husband.

She stands in my foyer, legs at shoulder's width. I haven't seen Chels since she gave birth about eight months ago now. She looks great. She's clearly shed all the baby weight, not that she ever had much to begin with.

Petite as always, yet very toned. Those little legs of hers are so much mightier than they appear. When that woman wears a swimsuit, you really see the definition. Even through her tight black leggings, I see her powerful muscles.

It's not just about appearances, though—it's about

efficiency. I've seen her kick down many doors with those biological weapons.

"We doing this or what?" She drops the bat into her palm.

Today, she's sporting a blue hoodie with a big raccoon's face on the front. The total opposite of what you'd expect someone to wear on a mission like this.

I love my best friend.

I try to smile, but it hurts my face. The swelling has gotten worse.

Cole is long gone now that Chels is here, which is probably for the best. If he knew what we were planning, he'd try to stop us. Then again, maybe he wouldn't.

I legitimately think Cole is afraid of me.

And Chels.

Good.

He should be.

"Yep," I say, groaning as I lift myself off the couch.

Chels frowns scornfully at the sight of my mild bruising. "That bitch is going to pay for this."

While I admire her protective nature, we have to be careful about this. If Cole is in fact lying, and Valeria is still in town, then we can't get caught confronting her.

But now that Chels busted into my home like that, I'm afraid Cole is already calling Valeria. By the time we get there, she'll be long gone.

I guess we'd better move fast.

***

"Cole wasn't lying," I say in disbelief.

Chels leans over her steering wheel, her honey-brown eyes narrowing on Valeria's property. Well, clearly, it isn't her property anymore.

In front of her old house is a rented moving truck. But it isn't to move things *out* of the house—it's here to move things in.

Several young men sip on beers as they unload box after box, followed by a stained sofa that should probably have been tossed at the dump.

"Where the hell is she?" Chels grumbles.

"Apparently, Ohio," I say.

She turns to me. Her hair is pulled back into a tight ponytail, which stretches her subtle freckles. Sometimes, I think it's a permanent fixture on her head. She never lets her hair loose.

Okay, that's not true—I once got her drunk enough to take out her elastic, but it lasted all of thirty seconds, during which time I didn't recognize my best friend.

Chels scoffs. "Ohio. Right."

I should be angrier, but I'm not. What if Cole was being honest? What if the police are in fact investigating, and that's how they knew about Valeria's whereabouts?

Cole said something about the police looking into analyzing a few street cameras for footage. That they might be able to get a read of this mysterious car's license plate.

Sighing, Chels leans back into her leather seat, her ponytail squishing against the headrest. "You wanna go back? I can take a swing at Cole instead."

I smirk. "That's okay. I told you—I'm handling it."

She doesn't seem convinced. Chels often gets this very analytical look, like she can read people's minds. She watches me intently, trying to gauge how serious I am. I swear, that woman should have been a cop. I never in a million years imagined she'd be a stay-at-home mom, but Jack has changed her. He's an amazing guy, and I can tell Chels's priorities have changed.

It's all about family now.

As it should be.

"What did you do?" Chels asks.

"What do you mean?" I say.

"You told me you'd handle Valeria," she says. "How'd you handle it?"

"Same as all the others," I say.

Chels's head pivots against the headrest to watch the movers drag a computer desk out of the moving truck. Then, she looks at me again. "You think it didn't work?"

I ignore her question. "You know what's really weird? Valeria swore she didn't sleep with Cole. She said he kept trying and that he was very smooth and not pushy, but she had no interest."

Chels stares at me.

"She said he made her uncomfortable and that she wanted nothing to do with him."

"Sounds like a strong woman," Chels says.

"Yeah, maybe too strong," I say.

"You still think it's her? Who came at you in that car? Why would she do that if she has zero interest in Cole?"

I open my mouth but immediately close it.

"What is it?" Chels asks.

"She followed me," I say.

Her eyes bulge, and she leans against the center console. "What do you mean, followed you?"

"While grocery shopping," I say. "She tried to hide her identity with this big hat and a pair of oversized sunglasses, but I know it was her."

"Do you?" Chels says.

We lock eyes for a moment. "What are you saying? That someone else has been following me? It was her, Chels. I know it."

"What about this new girl?" Chels says.

"Katya?" I say.

"Yeah. How are you going to handle this one? Same as the others?"

I can't even stifle a smile.

This will be *nothing* like the others.

CHAPTER 49

Meghan

Hazel finishes her bowl of cereal before reaching for the red-and-brown box of CocoClouds on the dining room table and tipping it upside down.

Two little pebblelike pieces of cereal roll out, and she gives me an unimpressed heavy-lidded look.

"We're out."

I hold back an eye roll. Hazel has this habit of finishing food items and then telling me we're out after the fact.

She's lucky I love her so much and that I'm forgiving of her teenage brain. If she were a roommate, I'd have kicked her out ages ago.

"I'll get more," I say.

She gets up, rinses her bowl, then shoves it in the dishwasher. I'll have to adjust the bowl later since she always places it at an awkward angle that guarantees the dish will come out unwashed.

"Bus will be here soon," I say.

Hazel lets out a dramatic sigh and turns off her phone's screen. She slips the gadget into the front pocket of her washed-out jeans, then ignores my presence and hurries into the foyer to grab her backpack.

"Hey," I call after her.

She turns around, but it's obvious she doesn't want to look at me. Not like this, with a swollen face. Cole and I told her what happened; we omitted the part about someone trying to kill me.

She doesn't need to know that.

Still, the idea of me being injured again is clearly

bothering her.

"How about Alex comes over after school?" I ask. "You guys can hang out here."

I don't have a car to drive her. So if Alex could make his way here, it would make my life a whole lot easier.

"That's okay," Hazel says. "Charlotte is picking me up."

I sigh internally. Would it kill her to spend one evening with me at home? I've barely seen her at all these last few weeks.

"If we keep this up, you'll be moving in with Alex, his mom, and Charlotte." I try to let out a laugh, but it comes out sounding like a bark.

Hazel doesn't even smile.

"I'm only teasing," I lie.

Seriously, though. Is she going to want to move in with them? She's never home anymore.

Then, as if out of pity, she says, "We could come over tomorrow and spend the day."

"Come over tomorrow?" What is she talking about?

"Yeah, I'm sleeping over tonight. Thought I told you."

For a split second, I contemplate using Cole's argument that she's too old to be having sleepovers at a boy's place. They aren't little kids anymore.

But that would be cruel. I know nothing will happen between Hazel and Alex. And with two adults in the house—even if one of them is more like an irresponsible teenager—Hazel is perfectly safe.

"Sleepover?" Cole says, appearing from around the corner.

Today, he's clad in a crisp blue suit—no red power tie—and shiny tan leather shoes. He smells good. Too good. Like he spent the last thirty minutes spritzing different colognes until the mixture was *just right*.

"You're not sleeping over at Alex's," Cole says sternly. "We let you go weeknights, but you're both fourteen now. He's a teenage boy. It's not happening."

Hazel's brows slant almost unnaturally. "But, Dad!"

There's that whiny tone that usually gets him to give in

to anything. But not this. Not when it comes to boys.

Normally, I stay out of it.

Cole has a very strong opinion about this, and unlike him, I don't undermine him in front of our daughter. But today, after everything that's happened, I decide to open my mouth.

"Oh, would you relax, Cole? Alex has zero interest in anyone with boobs."

Hazel's jaw drops, and Cole screws up his whole face. I never stand up for Hazel when it comes to Cole's mistrust of her best friend.

But Hazel is a good kid.

At some point, we have to trust her to make good choices without confining her within invisible walls.

She's not chasing after boys in high school. She's hanging out with her best friend. And if that makes her happy, then I'm going to do everything in my power to ensure she gets to keep doing more of it.

"You're making a huge deal out of nothing." I turn away from Cole and grab Hazel's shoulder. "Honey, go ahead and sleep at Alex's place if you want."

Her black-outlined eyes dart between her father and me. This may not have been such a good idea. I can tell she doesn't want to upset her father. But at the same time, she really wants to spend the night at Alex's place.

I'm surprised smoke isn't blowing out of Cole's ears right now. He's livid. It doesn't show—not to Hazel. But I know my husband. His jaw tightens in a very subtle way when he's upset. He has this way of swallowing down intense emotions.

"M-mom's right," Hazel says sheepishly. "Alex has no interest in me."

"That means nothing," Cole says through clenched teeth. "Boys have stuck their penises in home-baked—"

"Cole!" I snap.

An uncomfortable smile tugs at Hazel's lips. "What? Pies? Yeah, I know all about that. Alex isn't like that. Actually, he thinks he's asexual."

Cole throws his head back and laughs.

I should shut my mouth—I really should. But then the words come right out. "Not everyone has sex on their mind twenty-four hours a day."

I'm glaring at him as I say it.

His cheeks darken several shades, and he picks up his briefcase. "You know what? If you both think it's perfectly safe, then I trust my girls. Okay? I hope you both have a great day."

There's the jaw twitch again.

He leans over Hazel and kisses the top of her head. He's about to do the same to me, but I narrow my eyes even more. I don't want a kiss—not from him.

He gets the message and walks out.

The second he's gone, I expect Hazel to let out a big laugh and thank me for having her back.

Instead, she frowns at me.

Why the hell is she frowning at me?

"Why'd you do that?" she says. "He looked so uncomfortable. It's like you hate him. Even I feel it. If you hate him so much, why don't you guys get divorced already?"

With that, she storms out and slams the door behind her.

I'm left standing alone in the foyer in my pajamas with a crushing sensation in my chest.

Why is it that no matter what I do, I seem to keep pushing my daughter away?

It isn't too late. You can fix this.

I hope my conscience is right.

With a little effort, I may be able to repair our bond. And the sooner, the better. Because if my daughter ever finds out the truth about me, especially with how things are between us now, I don't think she'll ever forgive me.

Chapter 50

Cole

"Remember," Vincent says, turning his head long enough to look at me. "I do the talking."

Vincent always does the talking when it comes to trying to hook a big fish. I get it. The Lodge Builders have expanded tremendously over the last three years, building small homes for thousands of people. That means hundreds of offices. Thousands of employees. Securing a deal with them would be huge.

"And all you have to do is look pretty." He winks at Katya in the back seat of his Lamborghini. She looks a little snug back there.

When she catches his dark eyes in the mirror, she forces a polite smile. Katya isn't exactly assistant material. Don't get me wrong—she gets the job done. But she's not the kind of woman who likes to be told what to do. I'm not sure why she would have applied to a job in which her primary duties are literally to follow her boss's orders.

But I understand her, which is why it works.

I flash her an apologetic wince.

Vincent parks at Blue Fusion Bistro and exits his car with a strut in his walk. So many eyes are on him. That's what happens when you drive a Lamborghini in a city like Bayton Valley.

Attention.

But he likes it. He *wants* it.

We go inside and are led to a reserved section at the back of the restaurant. Vincent does that for really important clients. And then he makes a point to tell them that he reserved half the restaurant for them.

"If I wanted my clients to have a basic meeting at some basic restaurant," Vincent said before leaving AstroWyre, "I'd let one of the sales managers meet with them. But clients like Lodge Builders? They deserve respect. They deserve to meet with the man in charge."

Vincent rarely goes out to meet with clients. It's not really his job. But I can tell he wants this deal. More than anything. It's all he's talked about for the last two years. And as if by some miracle, the Lodge Builders are now looking to open up a new branch in Bayton Valley, which is the only reason they responded to Vincent.

If they knew he called their work *stupid little houses,* they wouldn't even be considering this deal.

"Real men want big homes," Vincent once said to me. "Not some shitty little cabin made out of a storage container. They'll be out of business in a few months."

But instead, they continued to grow and grow. I personally wouldn't want to live in one of their little lodges, but I appreciate the initiative. It's offering the world something it needs more than anything right now—cheap real estate.

The waiter comes to greet us in a very professional manner and asks if we would like to start off with any drinks. Vincent orders a bottle of their *best wine* and then says he's waiting for his guests to arrive.

"If you need to use the washroom, use it now," Vincent says. "I don't want you interrupting the meeting."

Unfortunately, I drank two coffees before hopping into Vincent's Lamborghini. It wouldn't be a bad idea to take a precautionary leak.

Katya gets up at the same time as me, her chair scraping as she leans forward. Her breasts almost rest on the table, and Vincent stares at them. It's hard not to. Especially since she decided to wear a silky black dress with a plunging lace-up neckline.

I follow her toward the restrooms, and we part ways as

she enters the women's. As I'm exiting, Katya comes out at the same time. We almost walk right into each other.

"Oh, sorry about that," she says, a slight Russian accent clinging to her words. It's most noticeable when she rolls her Rs.

But her narrowing eyes aren't apologetic at all—they're seductive.

"Sorry." I'm not sorry, either.

The woman is beyond stunning with her piercing blue eyes, her sharp and defined cheekbones, and the way she easily coifs her dark hair to one side with a simple rake of her hand.

How can someone's hair be *that* sexy?

Hers is.

As she moves her hair out of her face, it drapes over her left shoulder, and my eyes are drawn to her collarbone. A thin, fragile-looking chain necklace is fastened around her neck, while the pendant piece of it rests right above her breasts, beneath one of her laces.

"Enjoy what you see?" she asks.

My mouth goes dry.

She takes a step toward me, and I don't back away. Her lips, two plush pink lines that could easily be mistaken for candy, slowly approach mine. "I could make you forget your name."

Holy shit.

I'm suddenly very much aware of the fact that I need a pillow, or a briefcase, to conceal what she's done to me. I can't go back to the meeting like this.

Just as her lips graze mine, a loud crash echoes down the corridor. My head snaps sideways to spot a waiter scrambling to pick up shards of glass on the floor.

But that's not what draws my attention.

It's the quick flash of a figure moving away from Blue Fusion Bistro's front glass doors.

Who was that?

I barely caught any of her features. The second I looked up, she stepped sideways and disappeared.

But I did see one thing—blond hair tucked underneath an oversized hat, and huge sunglasses.

Seconds ago, all I could think about was pulling Katya into the bathroom and locking the door behind me.

Now I have a sinking feeling in my stomach.

Because although I barely had any time to spot the woman, there's only one blond woman in my life.

My wife.

Which means she's following me.

CHAPTER 51

Meghan

Who the hell is ringing my doorbell on a Friday afternoon? We have a very clear no soliciting sign.

I hurry down my hallway, wrapping my robe around myself. My hair is still all wet and wavy from my hot shower.

I wasn't expecting this.

A delivery? I haven't ordered anything.

The doorbell rings again, and I curse under my breath. Now they're just being rude. This better be important.

I hurry to the front door and peer through the side glass.

Is this some sort of a joke?

My mother stands poshly, her silky red hair pulled into a neat bun behind her head. The dye job looks fresh, and I'm certain she went to the most expensive place imaginable to have it done. She's wearing a long white leather jacket that looks to have cost more than her car.

She reaches a sickly, thin hand to press the doorbell again, so I rip the door open before the sound echoes through my house.

"Mom," I say.

She sticks her nose up. "Meghan."

What in tarnation are you doing here?

"Can I help you?" Okay—I tried to use my mouth filter, but my words still came out just as harsh as my thoughts, only worded differently.

"I don't know," she says. "Can you?"

What is she on about? And why is she even here? My

mother lives a solid four hours away. I lean sideways to peer at her sparkling white Audi.

My mom has a love for all things white. She also very much enjoys money, even though she's never worked a day in her life for it. But she's a very attractive woman who has a tendency to attract affluent men.

I wonder who she's dating now.

Scratch that. I don't care.

"New car," I say coldly.

She flicks a wrist over her shoulder. "Oh, that old thing? Wayne got that for me last year."

Wayne? Who is Wayne?

She combs a thick strand of hair behind her ear again and again. She's managed to tuck it already, so why does she keep repeating the same motion?

And then, I spot it.

A big shiny ring. No, not big—gigantic. Humongous. I'm surprised it hasn't broken her finger. How is the weight of that thing not causing carpal tunnel? Who's her fiancé? *Bruce* Wayne?

"You're engaged," I say.

Her face splits into a Cheshire cat grin, and she wiggles her fingers in front of my face. "Can you believe it?"

I can. All my mother has ever wanted is to be in a relationship.

Show more excitement, damn it.

Why is this so hard? Likely because my mother outright ignored me when I asked her to be honest about my childhood. About how she never protected me from my abuser.

But what's bothering me even more is that she never showed up in person after my accident. Instead, she made it all about her and how I wasn't reaching out.

And now, here she is to boast about some happy news in her life.

Not that I'm surprised.

We've always had that sort of relationship. All the dark, terrible things are swept under the rug. Some things aren't meant to be bothered, my mother always says. *Leave it alone.*

Reluctantly, I step aside. "Um, come in?"

She shrieks and brushes past me, her heels ticking with every step.

*** *

My mother is now on her third glass of wine. She's always loved her alcohol. I glance sideways at the clock. She's been here for an hour and hasn't stopped talking about Wayne.

About what an amazing man he is.

But the fact that he bought her an Audi and a huge rock tells me all he's doing is throwing money at her. That's not love. Then again, what do I know?

Cole and I don't exactly have a healthy marriage.

I'm no expert.

Without warning, my mother stops ranting about Wayne. Her gaze narrows on me the way it used to when I was a teenager and she was drunk out of her mind. Seconds later, she'd lash out at me and ask if I'd made any moves on her boyfriend. She never remembered it in the morning and would simply fluff it off as me being melodramatic.

"I don't exactly feel like you want me here." She places her empty glass of wine on the glass coffee table between us.

What gave it away?

My bored expression?

Or can she sense what I'm thinking? That she's beyond selfish for showing up here.

I'm suddenly very much aware of my posture—slouched, one arm crossed over my abdomen, knees up. Any psychologist would tell me I'm physically trying to shield myself from her toxicity.

When I don't respond, she sticks her nose in the air and

lets out a huff. "You know, I thought you'd be happy for me, Meg. I thought—"

"You thought what?" I say, sitting upright. My feet slap hard against the floor. "That you could just show up here after over a year of not talking and that your good news would *fix* everything between us?"

She scoffs like I'm a petulant child. I hate it when she does that. It's so demeaning. "Fix? Why are you always trying to fix things, Meg? You always want to talk about every little problem and then spend hours trying to fix that problem."

"Every little problem?" I'm careful with my words. If I spoke my mind right now, I'd shatter my mother to pieces. But that's not what I want. "The problems between us aren't little, Mom. They're big. The real problem is that you're unable to even talk about any of them."

Another high-pitched scoff. "There's nothing to talk about!"

What was I thinking would happen? That she would open up? Cry? Admit to being a terrible mother? My mom will never admit to that. She'll never admit to not protecting me. Doing so would destroy her psychologically. I can't even fault her. How can anyone admit they failed as a mother? It's easier to be in denial.

Dr. Bachmann tried explaining this to me, but I didn't understand it at the time. Now, as I watch my frazzled mother with that incredulous look on her face, I realize something—I finally understand.

As much as I want my mother to validate the nightmare of a childhood she put me through, she never will. Would it bring me peace? Probably not. Satisfaction? Maybe. Then again, I don't know.

All I want is confirmation that I didn't deserve what happened to me. Deep down, I know that. But there's this innocent part of me—my inner child—that wants my mother to admit that none of it was my fault.

It was hers.

But I know now that I'll never get that.

"I don't deserve this treatment," my mother says.

She gets off the sofa, snatches her white jacket from our coat rack, and pulls her purse strap over her shoulder. "A little congratulations wouldn't have killed you, Meg."

With that, she storms out of my house.

I don't chase after her.

I'm so done with that. So done with chasing after my mother's love. She may have given birth to me, but she was never a real mother.

I inhale sharply, staring at a pair of Hazel's Converse sneakers lying haphazardly in the foyer. The sound of tires squealing echoes down the road.

What I wanted to shout at her was: *If you'd paid more attention to me rather than your cheating bastard of a husband, we'd have a better relationship.*

But I'm not like my mother. I don't want to purposely hurt her.

Slowly, I turn sideways and catch a glimpse of myself in our large foyer mirror. Most of my features come from my dad, but the upper half of my face is all my mother, minus my light eyes. Especially when I frown. Our creases are exactly alike. Several years from now, I wonder—will Hazel and I repeat history?

I've been so focused on going after Cole that I've neglected to nourish my relationship with my daughter.

I want her to remember me as being the best mom ever. Not someone who caused her pain or neglected her.

Which means I need to end things, and fast.

I pull out my phone and write out a message.

"Progress update?"

Within seconds, a response comes in.

A thumbs-up emoji, followed by a little winky face.

I delete the message.

Chapter 52

Hazel

Alex's pink dye washed out too fast, so he decided to go dark. He looks good.

"What?" he says, looking at me like I'm gross.

"Your hair," I say. "I like it."

"I hope you're not getting a crush on me," he says.

I roll my eyes and punch his shoulder. I've never thought of Alex like that. He's always been like a brother to me. And lately, even more so. We spend all our lunches and most days after school together.

Today, Mom agreed to let me sleep over. I don't like how she approached it, though—cornering Dad like that and getting him upset. Admittedly, I *am* happy that she took my side.

I should have been nicer to her this morning. I think seeing her face swelled up like that really got to me. And especially now knowing she was involved in a car accident.

But why am I being so mean lately? Mom doesn't deserve that.

No.

I know why I keep her at arm's length. Alex and I talked about it just the other night, at his place.

He's convinced that ever since her first accident, part of me thinks that the universe is planning to take her from me. And that her accident was intended to prepare me for what's really to come. If I hate my mom, it might not hurt as much when I lose her.

I swear, sometimes I think Alex is secretly an

eighty-year-old man wearing a teenager's skin suit. He's too wise for his age. I suppose going through a hard childhood makes you grow up fast.

How does a fourteen-year-old know anything about anticipatory grief? I didn't even know that was a thing. Hell, I don't know much about grief, either. The most I've lost is Hammy, my hamster. And my dad's uncle, who I met once. That didn't really affect me.

But after Alex told me about anticipatory grief, I looked it up online. I guess some people can actually show anger toward a loved one who is dying.

But my mom isn't dying.

She survived.

So why am I acting like she's going to be taken from me?

"You okay?" Alex asks.

I must have been staring at nothing again.

"Thinking about your mom again?" he says.

I nod, and he instantly sighs. "I keep telling you, Haze. Just talk to her. Sit down, have a conversation. Tell her how you've been feeling."

I suppress an exaggerated gag. I don't want to talk about my feelings. And Alex knows that. He flashes me a half-hearted smile, then says, "Oh, Charlotte's here."

Charlotte pulls up in her beat-up Dodge minivan. It's an odd gray color, and the sides are all rusted. It's weird. Sometimes, she's very careless with money—like last week, when she spent over two hundred dollars on takeout and said we all deserved a treat. But then when I see her van, I'm led to believe she's secretly very poor.

Alex slides the back door open, and Charlotte presses her cheek against her headrest and beams at us. "Hey! How was school?"

"Good," Alex says. "Thanks for picking us up, Aunt Charlotte."

She smiles sweetly at him. "Anything for you two."

I think Charlotte always wanted kids but could never have them. Because ever since she came into Alex's life, she's treated him like her own. Some days, I hope that she takes him away from Anna. That woman shouldn't be allowed to be anyone's parent. All she does every day is smoke and drink.

Alex hops into the farthest seat, and I buckle myself in next to him. Charlotte leaves the pickup area, driving way slower than my mom. I like my mom's driving, even though it scares me sometimes.

"I was thinking veggie burgers and fries tonight," Charlotte says. "Homemade."

Charlotte's vegetarian burgers are to die for. You can't even tell they're not meat. And apparently, they're very healthy.

She shoots a glance in her rearview mirror, her unique green eyes darting between Alex and me. They're both dark *and* bright. It's very odd. But also very cool.

Alex nods enthusiastically. "Sounds great."

We spend the rest of the ride to Alex's place talking about condiments on a burger. Alex argues that mayonnaise should never touch a patty, whereas I say you can't eat a burger without it. Eventually, Charlotte ends the argument by saying, "Alex, don't you know you should never argue with a girl?"

When we approach a red light, she twists her neck to wink at me.

I love Charlotte.

Honestly, sometimes I wish she were my aunt. I don't have any aunts. Mom is an only child and barely ever talks to her family. Which means I don't really talk to my grandma, either. Not that I overly mind. Grandma was never that nice to me.

But Charlotte has this way of making me feel at home. She makes me feel loved and safe. When I'm at the house with Mom and Dad, all they do is fight or bicker. My real home doesn't feel like home at all.

But I can never say that to my mom.

I can't tell her the real reason I want to spend every day with Alex is because he and Charlotte feel more like family to me than my own.

Chapter 53

Meghan

Chels is very adamant about going to Ohio to search for Valeria. She thinks this whole thing is a lie. That Cole is hiding something.

I don't blame her.

My husband hides a lot of things.

"Why don't you call the police and find out where they're at with the investigation?"

That's not a bad idea.

I mean, I was the one involved in the hit-and-run.

Attempted murder.

They should be able to keep me updated on anything they've found, right? Like who the car belongs to.

Ziggy whines at the back door for the hundredth time. Groaning, I get off the sofa to let him out, and he bolts outside with his little spring legs.

"Hazel coming home soon?" Chels asks. When I don't respond right away, she adds, "How are you two doing?"

I'm not really in the mood to talk about that.

"She's sleeping over at Alex's place tonight," I say.

Her lips make an unsticking sound, but nothing comes out. I take the opportunity to change the conversation and tell her all about my mother's visit.

Chels is a supportive friend. She uses several curse words and goes on to tell me that my mother never deserved a daughter like me. By the end of it, I feel much better about the whole thing.

I'm about to ask her about her baby boy—Arthur—when I spot Ziggy acting very peculiarly in the backyard. He's usually either running or barking, but right now, his entire head is shoved in our back cedars, and his little butt is in the air. His tail isn't wagging, either.

Instead, his rear end keeps pulling out, like he's yanking on something.

What the hell is he doing?

Cautiously, I slide open the patio door and watch Ziggy as he keeps using all of his body for momentum. Pulling over and over again on some mysterious object in my cedar trees.

"Meg?"

"Huh? Oh, sorry. Um, hey, Chels, can I call you back? Ziggy's being really weird right now."

Chels never takes anything personally—unlike my mother—and happily agrees to chat later. I hang up, slide on my shoes, and descend down our patio stairs.

"Ziggy!" I call out.

He pulls his head out of the trees, looks at me, and then yaps twice before turning to resume his conquest.

"Ziggy!"

This time, he comes out with something brown-and-red in his jaw. Something big. Well, big for *him*. What the hell is that?

A dead animal?

I wince as he canters merrily away from me and toward his favorite chewing area by the pool. A few clumps of dirt fall from his mouth, along with what looks to be a few twigs.

"Ziggy, what is that?"

I approach him, but the moment he sees me get too close, the whites of his eyes expand, and his little jaw clenches around his prize. He darts the opposite way to the other side of the pool, then lies down and continues to chew.

"Ziggy!"

I'm losing my patience.

He thinks this is a game, but I don't. Why do dogs do that? They're always running away from you unless you have food.

I spend the next five minutes chasing him around the pool and feeling like a complete idiot. Finally, I've had enough. I go inside and break off a piece of hot dog from an opened package in the fridge.

Ziggy never lets anything go.

Not unless there's a trade of equal or greater value tendered. Meat, from his perspective, is the greatest value of all.

"Ziggy!" I chime, wiggling the piece of sausage over my head.

His button nose points toward the sky, and he watches me.

"Want some hot dog?"

He knows exactly what that means. And now he's up on all fours, running around the pool without his newly found prize. I let him get close so he can get a good sniff of the meat, then throw it across my yard and toward the side fence.

Ziggy chases after the piece of meat like his life depends on it. Meanwhile, I race around the swimming pool. I'm well aware that with how fast Ziggy is, he might manage to swallow the piece of hot dog and come back to steal this mysterious object before I even lay my eyes on it.

But fortunately, the treat landed somewhere in tall grass, and Ziggy is having a hard time finding it.

I cautiously approach the object.

What on earth is that thing?

There's dirt everywhere. I don't understand why Ziggy would chew on something covered in dirt. Then, what I earlier thought was blood, now appears in plain sight.

It looks like . . . a shoe.

I lower myself to one knee and dust the dirt off its surface. Then, I pick it up and shake it some more.

It's a red heel.

Ziggy suddenly yelps behind me, and I flinch so hard that I almost fall into the pool. He must have found his treat, and now he wants the shoe back.

Rather than give it to him, I stand up, feeling lightheaded. Ziggy pulled this thing out of the cedar trees, right where I thought I saw someone standing several weeks ago.

I'm not crazy. I didn't imagine it.

Someone was standing right in my backyard, watching me.

But who in their right mind wears three-inch red heels for something like that? I rub the leather with my thumb, lost in thought.

This wasn't left here by accident.

This is a threat.

CHAPTER 54

Hazel

Alex won't stop talking about fennec foxes. About their big ears and their long snouts. Every time he talks about them, he squeezes the air with curled fingers like he's trying to harm invisible particles.

"It's my cute aggression." He munches on the cheesy omelet Charlotte made.

"I could talk to your mom," Charlotte says. She pulls up a chair and tightens her bathrobe around her body. It's a cute fuzzy robe that almost matches her poufy morning red hair. That woman has the thickest hair I've ever seen.

She never ties it up, either. She'd probably look good in a ponytail or a messy bun.

She sits next to Alex and pats him on the back. I can't tell if she's silently apologizing to him for referring to Anna as his mom, or if she knows that Anna will never agree to adopt a fennec fox, even though it's all Alex has ever wanted.

Why can't Charlotte take Alex? Why can't *she* be his mom? I want to ask, but that would be rude.

Anna suddenly makes an appearance, her matted black hair looking like some exotic animal's nest. She's wearing the same clothes she went to bed with—torn jeans and a thin T-shirt that shows all her ribs. Worse, she's not wearing a bra, and her small breasts are like little pyramids poking out of her chest.

That woman needs to eat something.

She leans over the oven and takes a sniff of Charlotte's freshly cooked breakfast. "The hell is this?"

Alex rolls his eyes, but his foster mom doesn't see him. Thank God. She'd probably freak out on him for disrespecting her. But I'm not afraid of her when Charlotte is around. Charlotte looks like she can handle herself.

And she also doesn't put up with her sister's bullshit. I respect her for that.

That's the only reason I've been here so much. Before Charlotte came into the picture, I would never have spent the night here.

"Omelet and toast," Charlotte says. "Want me to fix you a plate?"

She's being way too nice. If I were in her position, I wouldn't help Anna with anything. I wouldn't even get her a tissue if she were crying. Okay, that's not true. I just don't like her.

"Nah." Anna opens up a cupboard and pulls out a bag of pretzels. She then reaches into the fridge and scoops out a two-liter jug of dark soda.

I suppress a gag.

It's ten o'clock in the morning.

She leaves the room, her dark, sunken eyes avoiding us entirely

"Don't mind my sister." Charlotte sighs.

I can tell it bothers her. But what is she supposed to do? She's doing everything right—she's taking care of Alex. The woman is a godsend.

Once we're Anna-free, Charlotte leans forward, elbows on the old wooden table between us. It creaks under her weight, and she beams at us. "You two ever been to the Neon Arcade in Applemid?"

Alex's jaw goes slack, and his eyes are almost as round as quarters. "Neon Arcade? Everyone's been talking about that place. But it's, like, an hour away. Anna would never take me there."

Charlotte squishes her cheek against a closed fist and winks at him. "Lucky for you, I have a van."

"Are you serious?" Alex shrieks. If he gets any more

excited, he'll start fanning his face. He does that a lot. "O, em, gee. You're not kidding? Right?"

"Not kidding." Charlotte drums her fingers on the table. "We can leave in an hour."

My face splits into a grin. So many people have been talking about Neon Arcade. It's brand new, only a few months old. I can't believe she's willing to take us there.

"What about you, honey?" Charlotte says, turning her attention to me. "You interested?"

I'm about to tell her that I haven't stopped thinking about Neon Arcade since I first saw the post online, but before I can express my excitement, my phone starts ringing out of my school bag.

"Oh, sorry," I mumble.

Charlotte flicks her wrist as if to say, *Sorry? You have nothing to be sorry about.*

I reach inside my bag.

It's my mom.

Is everything okay?

I mean, I know I haven't had a sleepover in ages—not since I was seven and friends with Emily Brackins before she moved away—but that's not reason enough to check on me, is it?

"Hello?"

"Hey, sweetheart." My mom sounds a little too chipper. Not like her usual self. At least, not the version I've come to know over the last year. "How're you doing?"

I glance up at both Alex and Charlotte, feeling my cheeks warm.

She *is* checking on me. I'm almost fifteen. This is so embarrassing. "Um, I'm good. Everything okay?"

"Oh, everything is fine," she says. I can picture her pacing in the living room right about now with Ziggy following her every step. "I was wondering if you and Alex might be interested in going to see the new *Batwoman* movie that just came out?"

My mom knows I *love* Batwoman. But Charlotte just offered to bring us to Neon Arcade. And we can go see a movie anytime. But to drive to Applemid? Mom has never offered to take me. Then again, she probably doesn't even know about the arcade or the fact that I'm interested. I'm sure if I told her, she'd bring me.

"Hazel? Are you there?"

I clear my throat. "Yeah, sorry. It's just that Charlotte—"

Charlotte cuts in. "No, no, honey. If something is up, we can go to the arcade another time."

I appreciate that she cares. But the truth is, I don't want to go to the movies. I was so excited about Neon Arcade.

"Oh," my mom says. "Was that Charlotte? She said something about an arcade?"

"Neon Arcade," I correct her. "Yeah."

There's a long, uncomfortable pause. I would much rather go to the arcade, but my mom hasn't offered to take me and Alex anywhere in a long time. She's really trying.

I clear my throat again. "I mean, I guess we could go to the arcade another—"

"No, sweetheart," Mom says quickly. "That's okay. Honestly. You seem excited about the arcade. We can do a movie anytime."

She's right. But I still feel super guilty. Especially because she sounds bummed out.

"Really, Mom," I try. "Charlotte says she can take us another time."

My mom lets out a strained laugh. She's trying to be sweet. I can tell she wants me to be happy above all else.

"Nah, it's no biggie," she says.

When she says *biggie*, she's covering up her feelings.

"Maybe we can go this week?" I say. "Just the two of us."

I hear her smile—the sound of saliva popping. "Yeah? I'd love that."

I press my cheek against the phone, smiling. "Yeah, me too, Mom."

We say our goodbyes, and although I feel bad about not going to the movies with her, I'm excited at the idea of us going out—just the two of us. I can't remember the last time we did that.

Am I finally going to get my mom back?

Before I can get too lost in my thoughts, Charlotte smacks the table, and I flinch. Her smile is so broad you'd think she was as excited as we are to go to the arcade.

Maybe she is.

"You guys ready?" she says. "I'll grab some snacks for the ride, and we can leave in twenty. Sound good?"

Alex and I beam at each other.

I can't wait.

CHAPTER 55

Meghan

Poor Hazel.

I didn't mean to back her into a corner like that. I could tell she didn't want to let me down.

Of course, I'm bummed, but I want her to be happy. If going to this arcade with Alex and Charlotte is what makes her happy, then that's all that matters to me.

I smile to myself, replaying the last bit of our conversation in my mind. A mother-daughter date.

I can't wait.

But my smile slides off my face the moment I remember that I don't even have a car. What was I thinking? I was so caught up in wanting to spend time with my daughter that I forgot my car was totaled. Cole says he's hopeful I'll be receiving a rental in the next few days.

I should have it in time for our date.

Maybe we'll go on Wednesday evening. No one seems to want to go to the movies on a Wednesday, so it'll be me and Hazel without any distractions around. A perfect time to bond.

You're being reckless. Someone is after you. Are you really going to put your daughter's life in danger for a bit of bonding time?

The thought hits me like a bag of bricks dropped from a ten-story building. Then again, that would kill me, so that statement is a bit dramatic.

But my conscience isn't wrong.

Someone *is* after me.

I stare at the red heel sitting on my coffee table. I haven't even told Chels about it. She has a baby to focus on, and she's barely getting sleep as it is. I don't want to worry her.

I had planned on calling the police yesterday evening, but Cole and I got into a heated argument over Hazel's sleepover. He said I completely disrespected him and his authority in front of our daughter.

I told him to take a chill pill, which didn't exactly help. He took off for a drive, leaving me home, stranded. God knows where he went. Not that I care. As far as I'm concerned, we're done.

It's only a matter of timing things right.

Of teaching him one final lesson.

As I make myself a coffee, I call the police station and ask to speak to someone regarding my hit-and-run. I'm immediately transferred to Detective Goldberg.

"Mrs. Garrett," says the detective. His tone comes across as both friendly and assertive. "I had planned on calling you this afternoon."

"Oh?"

"We were able to obtain some street cam footage from Montgomery Drive, and we've managed to identify the license plate of the white Accent you reported."

My heart starts thumping hard in my chest.

This is it.

He's going to tell me that it's registered to some woman named Valeria, just as I suspected. Or one of her relatives. A sister? A cousin? She could easily have asked one of her family members to chase me down. Not that any sane person would do such a thing per someone else's baseless request.

"The car was actually reported stolen a few hours before your accident."

"What?" I blurt out.

The detective sighs against the phone. "We located the vehicle in the Bayton Valley River this morning. Whoever was driving it stuck a rock on the pedal and sank the thing."

Is this some sort of sick joke?

Someone stole a car, chased me down, and tried to kill me? And now there's no way of knowing who did it?

"What are you saying?" I ask.

"We're looking into Valeria Cruz at the moment. We've spoken to her mother and sister, both of which confirmed she was in Ohio on the day of your accident, but you know how family is—they can say anything to protect their own."

"You think it's still possible that Valeria did this?" I ask.

Another sigh. The detective sounds tired, but not in a lack-of-sleep sort of way. If I had to guess, he's probably pushing fifty, and he's seen a lot of weird cases. So everything he does going forward is all about jumping through hoops through which he's already been.

I imagine this job isn't very exciting for him anymore.

"Honestly, it's hard to tell. But Valeria does have previous criminal charges, so that doesn't help her case."

Previous charges?

Are you kidding me?

I was right—the woman is unhinged.

"Previous charges?" My voice jumps an octave. "For what?"

"Um," he trails off like he's distracted with something. "A few misdemeanors. Petty theft. Aggravated assault with a weapon."

The last one feels like someone clobbered me with a two-by-four. *Aggravated assault with a weapon?*

"It's all public record," he says. "Feel free to look her up online. The news articles are all there."

I most definitely will.

What has me so upset is that I didn't think to look her up myself. Instead, I resorted to searching her social media profile to see what she looked like.

I'm not usually this sloppy.

Thanks, brain injury.

"Don't worry, Mrs. Garrett—"

"Meg is fine," I correct him.

"I promise you that I'll keep looking into this."

"So you'll find out if Valeria is behind this?"

There's a long pause. Who am I kidding? I know damn well that these things don't always get solved. If my attacker was smart enough to steal a car before coming after me, then they're probably smart enough to get away with all of this.

"I'll do my very best," says Detective Goldberg.

I appreciate his honesty. At least he isn't lying to me and boasting about how he's going to *catch the bad guy*. Real life doesn't work that way. All he can do is try.

"Mrs. Gar— Meg. Do you have any reason to believe someone might be after you? Is there anyone aside from Valeria who would want revenge for something?"

I hold back a scoff.

I've scared off countless of Cole's little playthings. I think back to Mia, the assistant I got rid of before Valeria came into the picture. She was a real bitch. Rolled her eyes at every word I said, then proceeded to tell me how awful she felt for Cole since he was married to an *old wench like me.*

I had half a mind to clock her over the head with a frying pan. But I didn't. I did things my way. Could she have held onto a grudge?

There are a few others that I'd put at the top of my suspect list, but honestly, at this point, it could be any one of them.

"Meg?"

"Sorry," I say. "I— I'm not sure. To be honest, my husband has a history of sleeping with his staff. The list is long."

Another pause.

"I'm sorry to hear that."

"Don't be," I say. "I'm the one who stayed."

The detective sips on something—coffee, I assume—and says, "Some people don't understand the concept of marriage and don't deserve to be in a relationship."

Detective Goldberg deserves a medal for that quote. I want to hug him, even though I've never met him.

When I don't say anything, he says, "I appreciate your honesty, Meg. This helps. I'm going to pull up a list of previous staff at AstroWyre and do a bit of digging."

I thank him for his time and hang up.

I thought speaking with the police would put me at ease. But now, I feel worse.

If Valeria's family is telling the truth, then I have no idea who is after me. Again, it's a long list.

CHAPTER 56

Meghan

Woman arrested, man in critical condition

I blink at the headline. Underneath, Valeria's name is highlighted.

In my defense, I had to scroll through several pages to find this article. So even if I had looked her up online before all of this, I might not have had the patience to keep searching.

I click on the article.

A twenty-two-year-old woman was arrested in the parking lot of Zimton Pharmacy Friday evening after an altercation with thirty-year-old Matt Neerie. Witnesses say they saw the woman, Valeria Cruz, beating the man with a baseball bat after a heated argument between the two. Matt Neerie is currently receiving treatment at Milson Hospital for severe injuries.

I lean away from my tablet, my heart pounding.

Valeria seemed so sweet. She even offered me tea when I went over to her place. I can't picture her bashing a man's skull in with a bat.

Is she in love with Cole?

Obsessed with him?

It would explain a lot.

I want to call Chels and tell her everything, but this seems to be getting more and more serious by the minute. What if I'm in over my head this time? What if I've finally come face-to-face with a psychopath?

Chapter 57

Cole

"Holy shit," I breathe.

Katya rakes a hand through her long brown hair and smiles at me as if she's just conquered the world.

It's four o'clock on a Saturday afternoon. No one is here. Well, except for the two of us.

I buckle my pants and fasten my leather belt. I don't think I've ever had sex as good as that.

Katya adjusts her flawless red dress, then plumps up her breasts in her bra like she's trying to equalize them.

I watch her carefully. "I chose right when I picked you."

"Of course you picked me," she says, that sexy Russian accent slipping off the tongue. "You could sense the chemistry."

She isn't wrong.

The moment I laid my eyes on her, I knew I wanted her. Not only was she drop-dead gorgeous, but she was wearing this sky-blue dress that stopped right above the knees. It was rather revealing—even a little too much for a job interview—but sky blue is my favorite color.

That had to mean something, right?

She was *the one*.

I always try to find something special about my next conquest. With Valeria, it was her love of technology. To me, that was hot as hell.

And with Katya—well, she's different.

She's not like any woman I've ever slept with before. She's full of passion, and danger. Hell, she pursued *me*. I usually like it the other way around. I like it when they're shy, and I slowly get them to fall in love with me.

There's no feeling quite like it.

It makes me feel like a god.

Powerful.

There have been a few exceptions to this. Some weren't exactly shy—quite the opposite. They were wilder. Sexier. I felt less like a god and more like a commanding beast ravaging my prey.

With Katya, there's a primal desire between us. I know she feels it. Every day, I want to tear her clothes off. And the way she looks at me with those piercing blue eyes tells me she *wants* me to devour her. Which I have been doing for the last week, but it isn't enough. I want more. Always more.

Katya blows me a kiss and adjusts her panties under her dress. She reaches for my office door handle, then looks over her shoulder at me.

I should be looking at her in the face, but all I can do is stare at her ass. Those curves. My God. I'm ready to go again.

"Same time tomorrow?" she says.

"Definitely," I say.

With that, she walks out, and I'm left sitting on my desk, panting.

***

"Meg, calm down," I try.

"Are you fucking kidding me?" Meg says. "You hired a criminal?"

What is she talking about? She whips her arms in the air and starts pacing across our dark oak floors. Honestly, I thought I messed up and walked in with lipstick on my neck.

Or perhaps Katya's smell on me.

I was certain when I took off this morning, after having told Meg that I needed to work overtime this weekend, that she'd be waiting at home, fueled with rage and prepared to accuse me of *fucking my assistant.*

She wouldn't have been wrong.

But that's not what this is about.

"Valeria!" she shouts. "She beat some guy to a pulp with a baseball bat!"

I take a step back and raise a brow. "How would you know that?"

"Because I spoke with Detective Goldberg," Meg says. "Valeria has a record. She's a nutjob, Cole. You brought a nutjob into our lives!"

I reach for her shoulder, but she slaps my hand away. "Don't touch me."

All right. I get it. She's worked up right now. My best bet is to leave her alone for an hour or so and let her calm down. That always works.

"Don't you people do background checks?" she asks. "Why the hell would AstroWyre hire an ex-con?"

"She's not an ex-con," I say.

Meg stops pacing, and her whole face scrunches up. Shit.

I didn't mean to admit that I knew about Valeria's past. It's also part of the reason I pushed Vincent to hire her. Is it messed up that I find that sexy? That she has a history of being badass? It only made me want her more. There's something hot about a little danger.

"You knew," Meg says.

"It's not what you think," I say.

Meg erupts in obnoxious laughter that fills the whole house. "Of course, you knew. You've always had a fascination with a bit of danger, haven't you, Cole? That's why you fell in love with me. You just *loved* that I spent two years in juvenile prison."

She works her jaw but doesn't say anything else. Her eyes glimmer with hatred. Meg isn't proud of her past. But she's not wrong—I did find it hot when I found out that she, along with a few friends and her boyfriend at the time, kidnapped her mother's ex.

The man who abused her.

She never went into much detail about it, but I found out through a friend later on that she threatened to cut his dick off and feed it to him, piece by piece.

I don't think Meg would ever do something like that. She's always had a big bark, but not much of a bite.

After all, her abuser was left untouched. I mean, traumatized, but not physically hurt. After everything he'd done to her—something I still don't know much about—you'd think she would have cut him to pieces.

Not just his junk.

But she didn't. She let him go.

Still, when I first found out about that, it was exhilarating. And then I met Alicia, the first woman I slept with while in a relationship with Meg.

I hadn't planned to get caught. But that was all part of the rush, wasn't it? What would Meg do when she found out? *If* she found out. Tie me to a bed? Drag a knife down my naked body?

I get excited just thinking about it.

It's a rush. Or at least, it used to be. Meg has never done anything about the women I've slept with.

Meg jabs a finger in my face. "You better fix this. Call Valeria, and tell her to back the fuck off before I do something I regret."

CHAPTER 58

Hazel

Charlotte and Alex wave at me through the rusty van's windows as I walk up my driveway Sunday morning. There's a shiny blue sedan parked in front of the garage. Its hood glints under the early sun.

Is someone here? People don't usually visit us.

I pull out my key from my bag and unlock the door. When I step inside, I expect Ziggy to start barking his head off and running up to me.

But he doesn't.

"Hello?" I step into our oversized foyer and drop my bag onto the floor. It makes a soft plunk, which sounds more like an explosion in the quiet of the house.

"Mom? Dad?"

Nothing.

What's going on?

I pull my phone out of my pocket. No missed calls. No texts. Okay, this is weird. It wouldn't be a big deal if that blue car wasn't parked out front. I'd assume Mom was napping, or something.

They didn't say anything about leaving or having plans today. After going to Neon Arcade—which was just as amazing as I thought it would be—I asked if I could sleep over at Alex's again. Mom said it wasn't a problem. If she had plans for Sunday, she would have said something then.

I quickly peep inside the garage. Dad's car isn't here. Is he at work? Mom said something about him needing to work overtime. I keep my shoes on and lean forward against the staircase's railing. "Mom?"

Still, nothing.

"Ziggy?"

Would she have taken him for a walk? Mom hasn't exactly been adventurous this last year. She used to walk Ziggy all the time, but after her injury, she stopped.

The smell of cigarettes wafts through the living room, and I frown. My parents don't smoke. Who the hell is in our house?

I shouldn't be calling out the way I'm doing. Isn't that how characters get killed in horror movies? They start shouting when they think someone is looming in their house. How stupid is that? It's better to be quiet.

So I seal my lips and sneak toward the kitchen.

There's that smell again.

Cigarettes.

I lean sideways, my head sticking into the kitchen. Several pots and pans are piled up in the sink, which means my mom hasn't done any cleaning since last night.

That's also weird.

She likes to have a clean kitchen first thing in the morning.

Did something happen?

A lump forms in my throat. I want to call out to her again, but I'm too scared. Should I be calling the police?

No, you're overreacting. She probably has a friend over.

Yeah, right. The only friend Mom talks to is Chelsea, and I barely see her anymore since she had her baby.

I spot Mom's favorite mug on the kitchen counter. There's still coffee inside. She's around, somewhere.

Maybe she didn't feel well and decided to lie down. Sometimes, fatigue hits her out of nowhere. Apparently, it has something to do with her brain injury. It was really bad the first few months after her accident, but she's seemed much better lately.

The smell of cigarettes assaults my nostrils again.

Okay—where is that coming from?

A warm breeze sweeps into the house, and only then

do I notice that the patio door is open and the screen door has taken its place.

She's outside—she has to be.

I rush to the back patio door, expecting to find Mom sitting with a stranger or an old friend I don't know about. Some woman with a coffee and a cigarette between her fingers.

But instead, all I see is Mom. Ziggy is farther out back, sniffing at the cedar trees with his little tail whipping from side to side.

Mom's on the phone, shoulders hunched, a cigarette in her mouth.

I clench my fists.

Why is she *smoking*?

Mom isn't a smoker. She's talking to someone, and she seems really upset. Her hand keeps flinging in the air, and every time she ashes her cigarette, she does it angrily, like she's trying to harm her cigarette stick.

I really shouldn't be snooping, but I'm so curious—who is she talking to? I lean against the screen, listening.

"I don't know," she says. "That's the problem. How fucked up is that? Yeah, yeah, I know. I don't want to end up in prison again. But if I find that bitch, I'm going to kill her."

My eyes involuntarily bulge.

Prison?

Mom's been to prison?

And what does she mean, she'll kill her? I've never heard Mom talk like that before. I mean, I know she's had a lot of anger problems this last year, but to threaten to kill someone? It's like I don't know her at all.

Not anymore.

I quickly back away from the screen door. I don't want her to know that I overheard her.

To be honest, I'm scared of her right now.

Chapter 59

Meghan

"You can't get yourself into trouble," Chels says. "Meg, promise me."

I sigh. I don't plan to actually *kill* her. Valeria isn't worth me ending up in prison. But I'll do something. I just don't know what yet.

"You know what I mean," I say.

Chels hesitates. "No, I don't. What do you mean?"

Does my best friend seriously think I'm capable of murdering someone? I didn't want to tell her about all of this because I didn't want to upset her. But I'm starting to think she's more worried about Cole's mistress than me.

But I couldn't hold any of this in anymore.

I had to tell someone.

"Chels, would you relax?" I say. "You're acting like I'm a murderer."

Chels lets out a nervous laugh, which I don't appreciate. "You've just been angry this last year. That's all. And I know you're a strong woman, Meg. I just don't want you to let your anger get the best of you."

I want to tell her she doesn't know what she's talking about, but she does. So instead, I take a pause. Chels isn't wrong. I've definitely had a lot of anger issues since my brain injury. But on the other hand, Valeria is following me. She tried to kill me. I have every right to be furious.

"Chels, can I ask you something?"

"Anything."

"If you were in my shoes, and Jack was cheating on you . . . and one of his mistresses tried to kill you, what would you do?"

She's quiet for a moment, likely thinking her next words over carefully. Then, she lets out that raspy, childish laugh that I love so much. "Yeah, I'd want to kill the bitch, too."

***

I hate it when Hazel leaves her bag lying in the middle of the foyer like that. But it's a minor inconvenience. Honestly, I'm more happy to know she's home safe than upset about her leaving her bag on the floor.

"Hazel?" I call up the stairs.

Floorboards creak, and a cautious version of my daughter appears from around the corner. "Yeah?"

"You're home," I say with a smile. "I didn't hear you come in."

"Sorry."

Why is she apologizing? And why is she acting weird?

"You don't have to be sorry. How was the arcade?"

"Good."

I lean my weight against the bottom of the railing. "Really? Just good?"

"Really good," she corrects.

Clearly, Hazel isn't in a talkative mood. I don't know what I did this time to upset her. It seems like no matter what I do, she wants nothing to do with me.

"You want me to fix you up a snack?" I rarely offer to make her lunch. Not since she turned fourteen, and especially not since my injury. Supper—I'll take care of it. But for breakfast and lunch, both Cole and Hazel can fend for themselves.

Yet, I want her to feel taken care of, and if that means putting together a sandwich every now and then, I'll do it.

But instead of taking me up on my offer, she shakes her head. "I'm not that hungry."

I wasn't expecting that.

Every time Cole offers to make her something, she brightens up.

"Where's Dad?" she asks.

Her words are like a jab to my heart. She'd rather her father were home instead of me.

"He just left. He'll be back."

I don't tell her we got into a fight last night and this morning. Cole left about an hour ago, slamming the door behind him.

Hazel nods awkwardly. She wants this conversation to be over but doesn't know how to end it.

"I'll be in the living room if you need me," I say. "Or if you change your mind about lunch."

Her lips tighten painfully. What is that? An attempt at a smile? If so, she's failing miserably.

"Thanks." She walks away, and I'm left feeling more alone than I did when I was actually home alone.

CHAPTER 60

Meghan - 26 Years Earlier

Mom and Dad got into a fight again. Something about Dad's drinking and not coming home on time. I don't really understand what's going on between them.

I sit quietly, reading a book while Mom cooks dinner in the kitchen. She's really loud about it, too. Smashing pots around. Whenever she's upset, that's what she does. She makes a lot of noise. I don't ask her what's wrong, because she'll tell me it's nothing or to mind my own business.

But last week, I talked to my friend Stacey at school. I guess her Mom sits down with her a lot, and they actually talk about things. About their feelings. I have no idea what that's like. I wouldn't even know where to start.

Stacey asked me on the bus how I feel when my mom and dad fight, and all I could say was: bad.

"Yeah, but bad in what way, specifically?" she asked me. "My mom tells me I should identify my feelings. Bad could mean angry. Sad. Scared. Or even confused."

I've been thinking about that all week.

I wish my mom would sit down with me and talk things out. Instead, she just slams stuff.

When she catches me watching her, she says, "What are you looking at? It's rude to stare."

I wasn't staring. Not exactly. But she's being so loud that she keeps distracting me from my story about vampires. It's not my fault she's pulling my attention.

Usually, I'd shrug or not answer at all. But after what Stacey told me, I really think that's what my mom needs. To talk things out. Because she doesn't have anyone to talk to. Definitely not my dad. All they do is fight. Not talk.

"Are you okay?" I say.

First, she freezes with a pot in one hand and a dirty ladle in the other. But then she looks at me like she hates me. "What's *that* supposed to mean?"

"Like, are you okay? Mentally?"

The instant the words come out of my mouth, I realize how bad they sound. I open my mouth, prepared to correct myself, when she slams the empty pot against the kitchen counter. "Excuse me? Are you trying to say I have mental problems? Are you—"

"No!" I drop my book on my lap. "I didn't mean it like that. I just meant you seem angry a lot. You and Dad are always fighting. I'm just wanting to know if you're okay. Or if you're upset and want to talk about it. Like, to let your feelings out."

She scoffs.

I should have known this was a bad idea.

"There's nothing to talk about. Especially not with my nine-year-old daughter. And feelings are for emotionally crippled wimps, Meghan. The sooner you learn that, the better." She points the crusty ladle at me and then jabs her temple. "You should always think with your head, not your heart. Now, go read in your room or something."

CHAPTER 61

Hazel

There's a gentle knock at my door.

"Hello?"

"Can I come in?" Mom asks.

After our awkward chat in the staircase, I really didn't think she'd come up here. Could she tell I was uncomfortable? I mean, she just threatened to kill someone. How is that not supposed to make me uncomfortable?

What's worse is that I think she's capable of it. A year ago, I wouldn't have thought so. But lately, I don't know. Turns out she's been to prison. Has she killed someone before?

Apparently, there's a lot that I don't know about my mom.

"Y-yeah, come in."

My mom slowly opens the door, her fingers making an appearance before one glossy blue eye. She squeezes in through the narrow crack rather than open the door all the way.

"Hey." She rubs at her useless arm. "Can we . . . Can we talk?"

Okay, now I'm scared.

Mom never talks. Not about feelings, anyway. Dad always says that Mom doesn't *do* feelings. That she's better at discussing facts, or anything else, but to never ask her how she's feeling.

Dad always said that's why she made such a good dentist. She's great at fixing things. And when it comes to teeth, you either have rot or you don't. There's zero emotion involved.

What could Mom possibly want to talk about? With how hesitant she's being, I feel like this is going to be a serious chat.

"Yeah," I say.

She points to the end of my bed and raises both eyebrows. I nod, and she sits down. She runs a hand along my comforter, flattening a few bumps.

She's staring at my floor, at my dresser—at anything but me. I can tell she's uneasy. So am I. And the longer she sits here not talking, the worse this is getting.

"What's wrong?" I ask.

She tries to smile, but it looks fake and dishonest. "Are we okay?"

I crinkle my nose, pretending like I don't know what she's talking about. But I do know. I just didn't think she felt the distance the way I did. I guess I didn't think my mom could feel much other than anger. We have good memories together—we really do—but this last year has sort of erased all those memories.

"What do you mean?" I say.

"I mean us," she says. "I feel—" she trails off. This is so hard for her. I don't think I've ever heard my mom say the words I *feel* before.

She swallows hard, and for a second, I think she's going to start crying. "I feel like you hate me, Hazel."

Her words are like a throat punch. I could never hate my mom. I love her. So much.

To be honest, I've felt the exact same way. Like she hates *me*. Oh, God. Alex was right. He told me ages ago to talk to her. I should have listened. But I was also scared because my mom always says it's better to think with your head than with your heart.

I feel my brows slant on my forehead. "Mom, I don't hate you. Not at all. I— I—" I don't even know what I want to say or how to express myself. This is so weird. How honest should I be? Completely? Or is it better to withhold a little bit? But I've been bottling this up for so long that I can't contain it anymore.

"You're always angry," I say. "Well, you have been. And it just seems like you're either taking it out on Dad or on me. Like you're never happy with either one of us."

She takes in my words. She really does. Mom can be argumentative, especially with Dad. But right now, she's giving me space to be completely honest. And with how she's nodding, I can tell she doesn't disagree with what I'm saying, either.

"And then seeing you in that hospital bed after your accident . . . I don't know. I feel like I lost you back then."

She parts her dry lips, then licks at them, but doesn't say anything.

"Do you hate me?" I add. "Do you want to leave Dad but think it's more important to keep the family together, so you blame me?"

At this, her eyes nearly bulge out of her head. "Oh my God, Hazel. No. I mean, yes, things are strained between your father and me. But it has nothing to do with you, sweetheart. I promise."

I swallow the lump in my throat.

Why won't she admit it? Admit that she wants to divorce him?

"And you're right," she says. "I've been angry, but most of that is because of my traumatic brain injury. I'm not excusing it. But the rest, yeah, it's marital problems."

There's something she isn't telling me. I get the sense that no matter how much I pry, she won't fess up. I get it. There's a lot that stays between my parents that I'm not supposed to know about.

Sometimes, I wonder if Dad is cheating on her.

I've caught him coming home late, smelling like perfume that wasn't Mom's. But I can't picture Dad being that kind of guy. I just can't.

I'd rather not know.

For all I know, Mom is the one cheating. I mean, there's a strange car parked outside. What if there's another man hiding in her bedroom closet?

I don't know what to believe anymore.

"I don't resent you, sweetheart. Not in the least. I love you so much. You're my world. You know that, right?"

I don't, so I don't say anything.

Mom sighs, then starts patting the comforter again. "I'm so sorry for this last year. I really want us to be okay. What can I do? How can I make things right between us?"

"I have a question," I say. "Actually, a few questions. And I want the truth."

She nods eagerly. "Of course. Anything."

"There's a car parked outside. Is someone here with you? Are you cheating on Dad?"

Before she can answer, I add, "Also, I heard you outside. Why were you in prison, and who do you want to kill?"

CHAPTER 62

Meghan

Why were you in prison, and who do you want to kill?

My daughter's words take me by surprise. She wasn't supposed to hear that. She was never supposed to know about my past, either.

She asked me if I was cheating on Cole, too, but that one's easy to answer. It's her other question that has my head spinning.

She must think I'm a monster.

I can't lie to her. But I can't tell her the truth, either. She's too young. Also, she's my daughter—she doesn't need to get caught up in all of this. Cole is a cheating bastard, yes. But he's also her father. And I would never do anything to turn her against him, no matter how badly I want to make him pay for what he's done to me.

When the truth comes out—and it will—I'll be there to support Hazel through the carnage. But I'm not about to destroy her relationship with Cole simply to spite him.

I'm not that person.

I inhale a deep breath, close my eyes, and exhale. Coming in here, I did not expect to have this conversation. I knew having a serious discussion wouldn't be easy, but this is much worse than I anticipated.

"First," I say. "I'm not cheating on your father." *That shit stain is cheating on me.* "That car is my rental vehicle. Your father brought me to the car rental place this morning, before going to work."

Hazel pulls her knees against her chest and rests her

chin on them. I can tell she feels bad for having made such a bold accusation.

If only she knew the truth.

"And yes, I spent two years in juvenile prison when I was younger."

She raises her chin a bit, clearly intrigued. I don't want to be entirely honest with her, but now that she knows, she could easily look it up online. It's public record. So I tell her what's available to the public. That I, along with some friends, terrorized my mom's ex-boyfriend. I explain to Hazel that he wasn't a good person, and that even though he deserved what we did to him, I shouldn't have done it.

"It was immature, and not very well thought out," I say.

If it had been better thought out, I wouldn't have gotten caught.

Hazel nods slowly. She's not looking at me like I'm a monster, so that's a plus.

"What about the person you want to kill?"

I don't make a habit of lying to my daughter, but she can't know the truth about this. I can't tell her that Cole's psychotic mistress is after me.

A) It would break her heart to learn the truth about her father.

B) She'd be terrified for my well-being, and she just opened up about feeling like she lost me a year ago.

"It's a work problem," I say. "I was really caught up in the moment. I didn't mean it. I just found out my accountant has been embezzling money from my corporation."

Damn, I'm a good liar when I want to be.

Correction—when I *have* to be.

This is about protecting Hazel.

Besides, she has no clue who does the accounting for my dental practice. It's not like she's going to go fact check my explanation.

"Oh, shit." She stares at me in disbelief, jaw agape.

Although she hasn't yet asked, I imagine she's curious as to why I was smoking a cigarette. I'm not a smoker.

Never have been. But I have this odd habit of lighting up a cigarette during very stressful times. I keep a pack in the basement freezer, hidden underneath an old meatloaf no one dares to touch.

So while I was talking to Chels on the phone, I got this irrepressible urge to inhale some nicotine.

"That's also why I was smoking," I say. I point at my temple and stick out my tongue as if to say, *Stupid me.* "I was so stressed out that I went out and bought a pack just to have one. I haven't started a new habit, if that's what you're wondering."

She doesn't say anything, but it's clear to me that it's exactly what she was thinking. Either that or that I have a secret smoking habit no one knows about.

Finally, she releases an extended breath that sounds painfully overdue. "Okay."

"Okay?" I repeat.

She nods. "Yeah, okay. Thank you for being honest with me."

Guilt sets in. I wasn't honest with her—not entirely. If she knew everything . . . Well, there's no telling what she would do. But it would destroy her. And I won't allow my daughter to experience any more pain because of me.

I rest my palm on her calf, and she doesn't pull away. Instead, she casts me an undecided look. Then, her gaze drops to my lips, and I'm suddenly extremely self-conscious.

"Does it bother you?" I ask.

She looks away from my lips. "What?"

"My deformity," I say.

"It's not so bad, Mom."

"That's not what I asked you," I say.

She's silent for a moment, until it looks like tears are welling up in her eyes.

"No. I mean. I don't know. Sometimes."

I can now feel tears pricking at my own eyes. The downward tug of my lips isn't something I can fix.

"It's not ugly or anything," she says. "I just miss you.

Like, how you used to be, that's all."

I'd give anything to go back to how things used to be. But I can't. This is my life now.

"I miss the old me, too," I say.

Without warning, Hazel throws herself into my arms. I manage to keep myself from toppling over in her bed, and I wrap my good arm around her back.

God, I've missed her bear hugs. It's what I call them. When she uses her entire body to give me a full, tight hug. She smells like cherries and sunshine, if sunshine were to have a smell. I seal my wet eyes and press my cheek against the side of her head, not wanting this moment to ever end.

"I'm still here, sweetheart."

A little squeak comes out of her mouth.

"Everything will be fine," I say, gently stroking the back of her neck. I stare blankly at her dusty dresser mirror behind her. "Momma's here, and she isn't going anywhere."

My reflection is frightening—soulless, angry, and almost monstrous. Despite the intense love that I feel for my daughter right now, I feel something even more powerful.

Fury, and an irrepressible urge to protect her at all costs.

I stroke her head again, my pale fingers raking through her dark hair.

Hazel looks nothing like me and everything like her biological mother.

But blood means nothing.

She's mine.

And I'm going to do whatever it takes to protect her.

CHAPTER 63

Diary Entry

This isn't how things were supposed to play out. Cole was supposed to leave her. I'm carrying his baby. Why isn't he leaving his wife?

It would be so easy.

And together, we could raise our child.

But instead, Cole turned on me. Well, Meg did. I don't think Cole is behind this. He loves me. But Meg . . . All she wants is a family, even if that means stealing someone else's.

What am I supposed to do?

I mean, 100K to give up my child is a lot of money. I could always have another baby.

But I can't replace Cole.

He seemed so serious when he handed me the contract, though. Said we couldn't see each other anymore and that I could either leave and raise the child on my own, or hand her over and get paid in return.

The only reason Cole has that kind of money at twenty-two years old is that he lucked out with stocks. Okay—he's kind of a genius when it comes to investing. That's what makes him so damn hot.

Not that it matters.

Cole doesn't want to be with me.

He wants to have a family with his wife.

For now.

Soon, he'll see that I'm the one for him.

Whatever.

I'll take the money, give them their stupid baby, and

leave for a bit. But I'll be back. Cole will miss me, and then he'll be begging me to take him back.

Enjoy playing house, *sMegma*. It won't last long. You just wait. I'll return and take what's rightfully mine.

CHAPTER 64

Meghan - 15 Years Earlier

My husband sits at the edge of our small, two-seater sofa with his head bowed shamefully in his palms.

I have half a mind to throw something at him. I'm so angry. So hurt. How could he do this to me? He swore he'd be loyal after marriage.

We've been married all of three months, and he's already knocked up some bitch.

Roseline.

Or Rose, as he calls her.

What hurts so badly in all of this is that I miscarried last month. Everything seemed to be going so perfectly. We'd just gotten married. Moved into a high-end apartment on the outskirts of New York City and were preparing to have a child together.

Not only have I now lost my child, but I was also told that getting pregnant in the first place was a miracle highly unlikely to repeat itself.

Basically, I'm incapable of carrying a child.

And now, some other woman is carrying Cole's child. My life is ruined. The family I've always wanted—the happy family my mother could never give me—has slipped through my fingers.

"I'm sorry," Cole says.

I throw my head back and let out a laugh. "You're *sorry*? You're a fucking cheater, Cole! I should have known. I don't know why I married you. It was a mistake. I want a divorce. Actually, no. I want an annulment."

"Babe, please—"

I grab a picture frame off one of our side tables and hurl it at his head. He raises a protective arm, and the frame smashes into his elbow before crashing on the floor and shattering to bits.

"Shit, Meg—"

I reach for something else—a plastic water bottle—and chuck it at him. He doesn't raise his arm in time, and it hits him right on top of his head. He's lucky it didn't catch him in the nose.

"You're an asshole!" I shout.

He gets up, but that doesn't stop me. I find the TV remote next, and he raises both arms.

"Meg, stop!" He rushes toward me and grabs my wrists to halt my attacks.

Even while grabbing onto me, he doesn't hurt me. Cole's never been abusive. He's gentle and loving, which makes all of this so much worse.

How could he do this to me?

"Baby, please," he says. "I'm so sorry."

He tries to hug me, but I shove him as hard as I can. It causes him to stumble back a few steps. He doesn't try to hug me again after that.

Instead, his big blue eyes watch me pleadingly. They're a bit watery. Is he remorseful?

"You were supposed to be faithful," I squeak.

He drops to one knee and clasps two large hands together. "Baby, please. I'm so sorry. How can I make this right? I'll do anything."

I should tell him to pack his shit up and leave.

I don't want to be married to a man who cheats on me. But I'm also a total mess. I'm still grieving the loss of my child, and I'm afraid that if Cole leaves too, I'll have nothing left to live for.

The thought makes me feel beyond pathetic. I should be stronger than this. I should be more resilient and capable of living my life without the love of a man.

I'm still so young. I could find someone else and have a family with them.

Wait.

No, I can't.

What man will want me if I can't even carry a child? Cole is begging for my forgiveness. He wants us to be a family.

"Baby," he repeats. "Please." His voice breaks.

There's only one thing I want more than anything in this world.

And that's to be a mother.

I raise my chin and wipe tears from my cheeks. There *is* something he can do. Something that will ensure I get to raise a child.

"You still have those stocks that blew up?" I ask.

His brows slant, like he's reconsidering offering to do *anything* for me to stay.

"Y-yeah."

Cole may not like what I'm about to ask him, but what other option is there? If we get divorced, there's no guarantee I'll find another man to raise a family with.

And somehow, the timing of this couldn't be better.

I'll simply have to get over the fact that Roseline's child is the product of adultery. I need to look at this differently. Maybe God, or whoever is up there, led Cole to be unfaithful so that I could have a child.

It's not ideal, but it's better than the alternative.

Being alone.

Chapter 65

Meghan

I can't believe how much Hazel has grown in the last year alone. She's turning fifteen in two months, and she could probably pass for an adult.

It seems like only yesterday, I was holding my newborn daughter in my arms and singing lullaby after lullaby.

"Only two more weeks of school and two more months until your birthday," I tell her.

She smiles up at me from her phone. "Yeah, and in a few more years, I'll get my driver's license."

My jaw goes slack.

She's right.

And a few more years after that, she'll be moved out. Why does life happen so fast? I can't imagine not having my baby girl at home with me.

Then again, I want her to have the best life imaginable. I want her to meet her person, whoever that might be, and have a beautiful family with them. Or, if she doesn't want kids and a family—I'll totally support that, too. She does talk about wanting to get into medicine a lot. She might be career-driven rather than family-oriented.

Which is totally fine, too. More than fine. As long as she's happy.

Cole avoids us all morning, likely sensing how upset I am with him. If things had played out differently last week, I wouldn't even be alive right now. I'd be dead, my body lying in some casket, and Hazel's life in shambles.

All because of him.

Last night, I spent all evening playing out my options

in my head. Also out loud, with Chels. She thinks we should drive down to Ohio and confront Valeria directly to get answers. And although I appreciate her wanting to protect me, I don't want either one of us getting hurt or making this worse.

Besides, the police are looking into this. If they can find out who stole that white Accent, they'll be able to track the person down.

Part of me still thinks it's Valeria, even though Detective Goldberg said that family confirmed she was in Ohio at the time of the attack.

But like he said—family covers for each other.

So that information is useless.

It has to be her.

I mean, who else would it be? This all started happening the moment I bribed—okay, and gently threatened—her to leave town and never come back.

She may not have shown it in the moment, but I bet that pissed her off.

Before I can tell Hazel that her bus will be here any minute, she slides her phone into her bag and comes to me for a hug. I cling onto her a few seconds extra, appreciating the warmth of her body against mine.

For the first time in as long as I can remember, I feel like I have my daughter again. Like she isn't distant, beyond reach.

And all it took was a heart-to-heart.

If only my mother had been a better communicator, our relationship would be different today.

I kiss her forehead. "Are you going to Alex's tonight?"

She shrugs. "Actually, I was hoping we might go see *Batwoman*."

I smile so big it hurts my face. "Yeah? I'd love that."

We had originally planned to go on Wednesday, but Mondays are even better. The theater is always empty. It'll just be the two of us.

I follow her outside and wave lovingly as she walks down the street to her bus stop, where five or six other teens are standing. They're all ignoring each other to play on their phones.

Of course.

It's strange how much the mind changes over time.

Fifteen years ago, I thought that if Cole and I divorced, my life would be over—that I would never get to raise a child of my own due to my fertility issues.

If I knew then what I know now, I would have left Cole. There are plenty of men willing to adopt. Hell, plenty who might *want* to adopt due to their own fertility issues. Plenty of good, wholesome men. Not like Cole. But I was so convinced my life would be forever ruined. Wasted.

I was wrong.

But at twenty years old, it certainly felt that way.

Then again, even if I could go back in time, I wouldn't change a thing. I love Hazel more than anything even if she isn't biologically mine.

She can never know the truth. How do you explain to your child that they were brought into this life through adultery?

I would never do that to her. Even if Cole deserves it.

Hazel walks with a happy trot and waves at one of her friends. She's seemed a lot happier since our talk, too. I feel terrible knowing she's been bottling up all sorts of negative thoughts and feelings when all we had to do was talk things out.

Today, she's pulled her hair back into a high ponytail and is wearing black leather combat boots. She's really into this emo style lately. It suits her, though.

I could never pull off something like that. Not that I'd even try. In the distance, Hazel whips out her phone and starts thumbing it.

She's probably texting Alex, who gets on the bus a few stops before her.

If I were a stranger and spotted her standing next to me, I wouldn't think we were related. She looks nothing like me. Not really. She's an equal mix of Cole and Rosaline.

Chels is the only other person in this world who knows the truth. Frankly, I'm surprised no one else has figured it out. I mean, Hazel is dark featured. She has dark hazel eyes, which is why we named her Hazel.

Almost everything I've read online says it's nearly impossible for two blue-eyed parents to have a brown-eyed child. I suppose miracles happen, but still.

I retreat from the door, not wanting to push my luck with her. Things may have improved between us, but if I stand there in my pajamas waving at her, I'm only going to embarrass her in front of her friends.

The moment I close the door, something loud chimes in my pocket.

A text?

At eight in the morning?

I reach into my pocket and extract my phone.

Wednesday @ 6 p.m.

Immediately after, a second text comes in.

83 Prairie Drive.

CHAPTER 66

Diary entry

I can't believe it's already been fourteen years since sMegma tried to push me out of my daughter's life. And Cole's.

Today, I watched Hazel get on the bus. She looked happier than usual. Which is weird. Lately, she's been looking depressed, and I blame Meg for that. It's always the mother's fault. Not that Meg is her mother to begin with.

I hate watching my own blood from the sidelines like this. Like I'm some criminal.

She looks so much like me. And Cole. She's like the perfect combination of us both.

If Cole knew I was in Bayton Valley, I don't know what he'd do. The contract was clear—I was to leave and never come back. Never have contact with my child again.

Then again, I've already broken the contract countless times, and Cole hasn't done anything about it. I think the whole thing was Meg's idea. Not his. Because every time I've reached out to him, he's been very kind.

Okay, more than kind.

We have a tradition now. Twice per year, we meet up at the Dauntmilton Hotel and spend the night together. He tells Meg he has to go on a business trip.

It's the best sex of my life, and it makes it so hard to walk away when it's all over. But Cole insists that his daughter comes first. *Our* daughter, he says. But then he reminds me that Hazel can never know the truth; otherwise, it would destroy her.

I've been watching Hazel for a while now. Not every day, but most days.

She's like a mini version of me. Dark hair, hazel eyes, plush lips. Meg always had average lips, bordering on thin. Not like mine. How does no one else see it?

Hazel looks everything like me and nothing like Meg.

But the problem with Hazel is that, although she looks like me, she exudes Megness. She's exactly like her fake mother.

Some days, I wonder what life would be like if Hazel knew who I was. Not that it matters. I don't have a bond with her. Meg got in the way of that.

All these years, Cole has said that when Hazel gets a bit older, he'll leave Meg. Now, he's saying he'll leave once Hazel turns sixteen. But if he hasn't done it by now, he never will.

Every time I bring it up, hoping he might leave Meg a little sooner, he says, "You don't know Meg."

He's wrong.

I know what she's capable of.

He's clearly not happy with her. Plus, she siphons all the good out of him. When we first met, he was so ambitious. He'd made a few hundred thousand dollars off the stock market and could talk to me for hours about how he planned on expanding his riches. I mean, sure, he's finally making his way up in AstroWyre, but that's all thanks to me. He just doesn't know it.

For so many years, I kept trying to convince myself that Cole was always going to be a twice-per-year fling. My one true love that would always be unattainable.

But lately, as I've watched Cole from the sidelines, I've come to realize that I love that man with all of me. With my heart, mind, and soul.

We're meant to be together.

We created a child.

I could get into a lot of trouble for being here, but I don't care. Cole belongs to me. And maybe with time, Hazel will feel like my daughter again. I'm not going

anywhere until I get him back.
Until I get them both back.

CHAPTER 67

Hazel

"Nice ride," I say, grazing my fingertips across the dashboard.

This car *smells* new.

Brand new.

"Are you gonna get to keep it?"

Mom glances sideways at me, the paralyzed side of her mouth twitching as she tries to pull it up into a smile. "Unfortunately not. This is a rental. Nice though, huh?"

I nod. It's more than nice. It's super luxurious. I play with the air vents, then touch all the buttons at the center console. Mom doesn't smack my hand away like she used to when I was a kid. Not that she'd do it hard. It was a soft, playful tap, and she'd tell me to keep my hands to myself and not touch other people's belongings.

I'm glad she did that; otherwise, I might have ended up like Brendon, the most annoying kid in my class. He's always touching everything, taking people's things, and getting inside of other people's *bubbles*, as Mom calls them.

"Are you getting your old car back?" I ask.

Mom hesitates. She bites her lip, her eyes flicking sideways briefly. "It's totaled. I can't." She sounds really down about it. But before I can ask what car she's going to get next, she straightens up a bit, and her next words come out sounding much more chipper. "But that's okay. My Jeep was seven years old. I'm excited to get the new model. As soon as the insurance money comes in, I'll upgrade." She pauses at a red light and looks at me.

"Would you want to come?"

"Car shopping?" I ask.

She beams. "Yeah."

Even though I can't drive, I love cars. I still remember when Mom bought her Jeep for the first time. She was so excited. She took me off-roading with it, and I remember screaming as she drove over big lumps on the forest path.

"Yeah, I'd like that," I say.

She squints at the road ahead, looking happier than I've seen her in a long time. But every few seconds, her smile vanishes, and she looks into her rearview mirror, then her side mirrors. She does this the entire ride to the theater.

Is someone following us or something?

When I talk to her, she's all smiles again, like nothing is wrong. But something is very wrong. I just don't know what it is.

Normally, I wouldn't say anything. I'd keep my mouth shut and pretend it never happened. But after the chat we had, well, it's really opened up my eyes to how helpful it can be to talk things out.

To not hold everything in.

"Is everything okay?" I ask.

There's that forced smile again. "Yeah, why wouldn't it be?"

She's being dishonest with me about something. Clearly, she doesn't want to talk about it. But if I don't get a straight answer, I'm going to spiral in my head again and think my mom is lying to me.

"You seem nervous," I say. "Like someone might be following us."

The tension in her shoulders reduces visibly. I don't think she even realized how stressed out she looked.

"Oh," she says. "Yeah, I guess I am nervous. You know, driving again."

My lips unstick. "Oh. Because of the accident?"

Mom and Dad told me that some white car accidentally merged into her, and then sped off. Something about a possible drunk driver. And that the police are now looking into it.

It's hard to imagine someone drunk so early in the day. But I'm sure it happens. It infuriates me that someone would get behind the wheel when they can't even walk straight. I hope they find the piece of garbage that did this. I hope they lose their license for life and go to prison for a very long time.

"Yeah," Mom says. "I'm okay, honey. I'll get over it. Just scared me, that's all."

I feel bad now.

I should have waited at least a few weeks before asking to go to the movies. I didn't really think about how Mom might feel driving after the accident. The airbag bruised her face up a bit and caused some swelling, but other than that, she was okay.

Thank God.

Mom pulls into the theater's parking lot, parks, and grabs her purse. "You ready?"

I'm more than ready. I've been waiting months to see the new *Batwoman* movie. Apparently, this one has not one, but *two* Jokers. Something about a clone. It's been getting really good reviews. I'm stoked.

Mom leads me up the concrete stairs to the huge theater, and the mouth-watering scent of popcorn sweeps into my nose. Up above, the sky is blue and cloudless, which I find are the worst days for movies. It's always better when it's rainy so you don't feel like you're wasting the day.

But today, despite how beautiful it is outside, it's the perfect day, because I get to spend it with Mom.

She smiles over her shoulder at me, and I'm about to go through the doors when I sense someone watching me in my periphery.

I turn my head to spot a woman standing near a metal garbage can, far away from the row of glass doors leading inside the theater. She leans against the building with a can of soda in one fist and her free arm crossed over her chest. She takes a sip, her dark eyes boring into me.

I freeze, watching her.

She looks so familiar, too.

Who is this woman?

Her hair, long and dark brown, is nearly the same cut as mine. Atop her head is a large, floppy straw hat that *almost* masks the upper half of her face. If she were to tilt her head just a little bit, I wouldn't be able to see her eyes anymore.

She winks at me, then slips on a pair of oversized sunglasses, rolls away from the wall, and disappears around the building.

Chapter 68

Meghan

Trying to make lasagna with one hand isn't easy.

But it's one of Hazel's favorites, so I have to try. Cole hates lasagna, but I don't care. This isn't for him.

I slather my sauce over my dry pasta at the bottom of my pan, and Ziggy lies next to my feet, panting while staring up at me. He thinks I'm going to drop him something.

Well, when he's that cute, I can't resist.

I flick a piece of cheese off the counter, and his jaw snaps. He licks his chops with gratitude.

I'm about to reach for the ricotta when my phone starts chiming at the edge of the counter.

"Damn it," I mutter.

My hands are full. Or . . . hand.

Maybe it isn't important. I lean sideways and peer at the text scrolling across the screen.

Bayton Valley Police Department.

Okay—it's important.

I quickly lick tomato sauce off my pinky and answer the call by swiping sideways. It takes a few slimy jabs, but I manage to put the call on Speaker.

"H-hello?"

"Mrs. Garrett?" comes Detective Goldberg's voice.

"Yes," I say.

"Am I catching you at a bad time?"

I glance at my hand covered in tomato sauce, at the pile of shredded cheese on the counter, and at the partially opened ricotta container. "Not at all."

"Good," he says. "I wanted to let you know that we were able to confirm Valeria's whereabouts on the day of the accident. She was, in fact, in Ohio. Turns out she had a doctor's appointment approximately one hour before the hit-and-run, and she was present for that appointment."

A doctor's appointment? *Please don't let her be pregnant. That's all I need right now.*

I don't know how to respond to him. How is this possible? I was certain Valeria was after me. But in retrospect, maybe I *wanted* to believe it was her. It's easier to pin the blame on someone with a face than to have some mysterious, nameless figure threatening me.

I mean, she offered me tea and a muffin, for crying out loud. And she swore she didn't even sleep with Cole. Her exact words were: "Honestly, I'm kind of relieved. He wouldn't stop trying to flirt with me, and it was getting to be a bit much. He even kept me working late most nights when all I wanted to do was come home to my son."

She'd made it sound like the ten grand I offered her was going to change her life. Well, she's gone, so apparently, it did.

Not that it bothers me any. It's not my money—it's Cole's. Every year, I go on a *health retreat* for a week, which comes with a twenty-thousand-dollar price tag.

I've managed to convince Cole that after everything he's put me through, it's the least he can do. I spend the week at a five-star hotel instead and cash the rest of the money. Since he's been averaging about two playthings per year, it's worked out well. Ten thousand each.

"Mrs. Garrett?"

"Meg," I correct him.

The detective clears his throat. "Right. Sorry." There's a long pause. "I've been going over the staff list since Mr. Garrett started his employment with AstroWyre. It's going to take some time. They've hired a total of thirty-nine assistants over the last fifteen years."

Thirty-nine?

I have about twenty women on my list. How many more

were there that I didn't know about? I grit my teeth, locking eyes with Ziggy who can't stop staring at the counter full of food.

He has no clue what's going on. All he cares about is getting another piece of cheese.

Despite the serious conversation I'm having with Detective Goldberg, I flick another chunk of cheese off the counter, and Ziggy catches it midair.

"Is there anyone in particular that you remember?" he asks. "Anyone I should start with?"

That's a tough question.

I mean, a few of them gave me a hard time. Some told me to get out of their house, and things almost got physical. But for the most part, they were civil. Several of them admitted that they never wanted to sleep with Cole, and that they felt like they'd be fired if they didn't.

And then, of course, there's *her*.

Roseline Hayes.

Hazel's biological mother.

I'd be lying if part of me didn't think she was responsible for this. But I haven't seen or heard from her in thirteen years. Not since she broke our contract and confronted me in front of H Mart that one day.

Could it be her?

But why now?

Sure, there are several names I could give him, but Roseline is the only one who has high stakes in this.

A daughter.

In her sick brain, if she gets rid of me, she'll get to have Cole and Hazel in her life.

Who knows?

That woman has some serious issues.

I'm so thankful every day that Hazel doesn't take after her psychologically.

I don't want to tell the detective that Hazel isn't mine, but this might be extremely valuable information.

What if it is her?

And here I am, withholding valuable information

simply because I don't like the world knowing that Hazel isn't related to me by blood. Deep down, I'm terrified that the information will somehow slip from someone's mouth and fall into Hazel's ears.

But if Roseline is back, then she's a threat. And my daughter's safety is more important than my secret.

"Roseline Hayes," I say. "Hazel's biological mother."

Detective Goldberg doesn't respond for so long that I start to wonder if the line cut out. Did he not hear me?

"Detective?"

"Sorry, I'm noting this down. You're saying that Roseline Hayes is Hazel's biological mother?"

Hearing the words aloud is like a sharp knife to my heart. "Yes. We have a contract in place. She isn't to make any contact with us or Hazel. It was a closed adoption. We lived on the outskirts of New York City at the time, in Leerville. Before AstroWyre expanded and moved to Bayton Valley."

A chafing sound follows, and I picture Detective Goldberg nodding against the phone's receiver while scribbling down notes.

"Hayes. Got it. This is very helpful. Thank you, Meghan. I appreciate your cooperation."

By cooperation, he means my honesty. But let's be real. It's not like I could have kept my closed adoption a secret from a detective. He would have figured it out. And it's not like he's going to go blabbing to Hazel. This is his job. It's crucial information, and now that he has it, it's going to help him dig into Roseline.

I hope it isn't her.

That woman is *crazy*.

But if it is, I need to be prepared.

CHAPTER 69

Meghan - 13 Years Earlier

Hazel is crying so hard her face resembles a tomato. I wipe her tears away and offer her a soother. She won't latch on. She keeps crying and crying.

"It's okay, sweetheart," I say.

I buckle her into her car seat and reach for Dolphy, her favorite plushy. It's a pink dolphin, and she loves it to bits.

"Look who it is," I say.

Behind me is a cart with at least a dozen grocery bags, some of which contain frozen items. We're in the middle of August, and the sun is beaming rather hard on them right now. In a few minutes, my popsicles will be nothing but sticky juice dripping out of the box.

But I don't care.

Hazel is more important than keeping popsicles from melting.

I wiggle the little dolphin close to her face, then tap her nose with the dolphin's snout and make a loud kissing sound. She gasps, her little pink lips forming an O, then stares wide eyed at Dolphy.

"Oh, that's right," I say. "Dolphy wants love." I give her another kiss, and another, until she starts giggling.

She grabs onto Dolphy, and I seize the opportunity to pull out of my minivan and gently close the door. I start loading the trunk with the bags when the sound of footsteps against asphalt approaches me from behind.

They're fast and frantic and cause a jolt of tingly anxiety to spread through me. I look back, my long ponytail swinging over my shoulder.

No.

No way.

What the hell is *she* doing here?

"M-Meg?" Roseline says.

She tries to play friendly as if she just *happened to be in the neighborhood*. But anyone with half a brain could see right through it. She isn't here by accident. And this isn't a coincidence, either.

She followed me here.

I drop one of the bags into my trunk and stiffen before glaring furiously at her. "Roseline."

She isn't supposed to be anywhere near us. It was part of the contract. After she gave birth, she moved away to Montana to go live with her grandparents.

Did she move back to Leerville?

My heart is pounding so hard that her footsteps sound muffled. I'm not afraid of Roseline. But I'm afraid of losing my daughter.

I used to wake up drenched, having dreamed that Roseline used the money we gave her to hire a world-renowned lawyer. That she'd come back to take Hazel away from me.

Is that what's happening here?

"How are you?" she asks sheepishly.

"What are you doing here?" I say.

She tucks her dark-brown hair behind one ear, then proceeds to grab the rest of her long, wavy hair and pull it over one shoulder. It's the exact same shade as Hazel's. When the sun hits it, there's a hint of red.

She's clad in a beautiful sky-blue dress—Cole's favorite color—and heels that belong in a nightclub.

Roseline has always been a beautiful woman. I imagine Hazel will grow up to be quite stunning herself. And looking at her now, you can't even tell she gave birth a year ago. She's got a tight waist and hips for days.

Why is she so done up, though?

Was she hoping to run into Cole?

Her dark eyes dart from side to side like she's looking

for him.

Of course, she was.

"Cole isn't here," I say.

She plays with her hair again. "Oh. That's okay. I'm not here for Cole."

Right. Well, she sure as hell isn't here for *me*.

I stand protectively between her and the van, then cross my arms. "What do you want, Roseline?"

"Can I just see her, hold her?" she asks. "Please."

For a split second, I consider allowing her to see Hazel. I mean, I understand—she gave birth to her. But the whole point of a closed adoption is to give up the child as if they were never yours to begin with. It was all very clear in the contract.

I'm terrified that if she holds her, she'll fall in love with her and fight to the death to have her back.

No, she can't do that. The contract is tight.

It's still a fear I have.

"Roseline," I say, trying to sound as compassionate as possible. "I understand where you're coming from, but you can't be doing this. You can't just show up and ask to hold Hazel. She's *my* daughter now."

A glimmer of hatred flashes across her sharp features. "She was mine *first*."

I draw my shoulders back and clench my fists. Am I going to have to call the police?

"Please don't make this any harder than it has to be," I say. "Move on with your life, and let us do the same."

"All I want is to hold her," she says.

She isn't sweet anymore. She's livid, as if I'm denying her some innate right. She doesn't have rights to Hazel. She lost those when she signed that contract. And to be honest, she should have thought about all of this *before* sleeping with a married man. It's not like she didn't know.

"Please leave," I say.

Her features contort into something frightening, and without warning, she throws herself at the opposite side of my minivan. My heart lurches into my throat as I hear the door slide open.

I bolt to the opposite side, where Roseline is now halfway into my van, leaning over Hazel and attempting to undo the car seat harness. Hazel, meanwhile, is crying at the top of her lungs.

Although a low move, I grab Roseline by the hair and rip her out of my van. She comes flying out, arms flailing, and falls backward before landing on the pavement. Her head smashes into the car parked next to me, and she lets out an involuntary yelp.

I'm shaking so badly that my legs might give out. I slam my van door closed and fumble with my key's remote until I find the lock button.

My van beeps, and the headlights flash.

Locked.

Roseline slowly gets up, her frighteningly dark eyes glued to me. I don't care how angry she thinks she is. I'm a thousand times more upset. This is my daughter we're talking about.

"I only wanted to fucking see her!" she snaps at me.

Bullshit. She was undoing the car seat harness. She wanted to steal her.

A few heads turn our way, and several shopping carts stop rattling across the parking lot as a small audience starts to gather.

Without thinking, I grab Roseline by the throat and slam her into my van. Her head bounces off my passenger's window, and she looks more stunned than angry now. Like she didn't think I had it in me.

I press my forearm up against her chest so she can't get away. She could hit me. Let her. She has no idea how far I'm willing to go right now.

"If you ever come near me or my daughter again, Roseline, I swear to God, I will kill you. Do you understand me?"

Little droplets of saliva sprinkle out of my mouth and onto her cheek. She turns her head sideways, wincing, but not answering.

I apply a bit more pressure. "Do you hear me?"

"Y-yes," she finally says.

When I let her go, she stumbles away from me and then readjusts the strap of her dress, which is hanging low on her shoulder. She fixes her hair, too, and almost trips on her heels while walking away.

When she's finally at a safe distance, she turns around and gives me a death glare. One that tells me—*this isn't over*.

CHAPTER 70

Meghan

I pull into the parking lot next to the Bayton Valley High School soccer field.

I can't stop thinking about Roseline and the fight we had all those years ago. That look in her eyes—the rage—put me on edge for almost a year after our altercation.

Almost every night, I woke up and raced to Hazel's crib to ensure she was still there.

It didn't help that Cole kept calling me *paranoid*. Telling me that I was being *a little dramatic*, and that Roseline had no intention of taking Hazel from us.

When she turned two, my paranoia diluted. She hadn't done or said anything in almost a year, so she was over it, right?

Then, the years went on.

Still, we heard nothing. And now, Hazel is fourteen years old. Almost an adult.

I watch her in the distance with her knee-high socks as she waves goodbye to her friends. Her cheeks are all rosy, and she's panting to catch her breath.

Above, the sky is dark gray and swollen. Right when Hazel reaches the passenger's door, a few heavy globs splash on my windshield.

She pries the door open and hurries inside.

"Whoa," she says, dropping into her seat. "Talk about good timing."

A half-hearted giggle escapes her mouth.

"Good practice?" I ask.

She nods. "Yeah. Clark got hit in the face with the ball. It was hilarious."

My eyes bulge at her.

Clark is one of the goalies, and they've never gotten along. He used to jab her in class with a pencil. So while I understand that part of her would be happy that her frenemy got hit, I don't see how someone getting hurt warrants a laugh. People can kick pretty hard in soccer. That's a recipe for a concussion.

She probably doesn't mean any harm, but given who her mother is, I'm a little more on edge about her comment right now.

"What?" She reaches for her seatbelt and buckles herself in. "He didn't get hurt."

"A soccer ball to the face, and he didn't get hurt?" I don't believe it.

She rolls her eyes at me. "We aren't playing professional soccer here, Mom. The ball bounced off Anisa's knee last second. He was stunned more than anything, but totally fine." Her brows almost hug above the bridge of her nose. "And it was funny because of the face he made. Like he ate a bag of lemons or something."

She makes every effort to hold back a smile that's threatening to take up half her face.

All right—I can understand how that would be funny.

I pat her knee, and we leave the parking lot without running anyone over.

"We have a game this Saturday, by the way."

This Saturday?

Damn it. Did I not check the schedule? I should have known this already.

Hazel's eyelids get heavy. "You forgot."

"Yeah," I say honestly. "I'm sorry, sweetheart. What time?"

She uses her soccer jersey to wipe sweat off her forehead like she always does. "At three."

Before I can say anything, my phone lights up in its vent holder.

1 *New Message*

The number looks random, but I recognize it, and it sends my heart into overdrive. Why now, of all times? When Hazel is right beside me.

Hoping that Hazel didn't see the notification, I snatch my phone from its holder and tuck it between my thighs on the seat.

I stare straight ahead, driving as if nothing happened. But in my periphery, I can sense Hazel staring at me.

Don't look over. Pretend nothing happened.

"What was that?" Hazel asks.

I glance cautiously her way. "What was what?"

She grimaces. "You got a message from someone and freaked out."

I have exactly two seconds to come up with the best lie possible.

"Some conversations aren't for your eyes, Hazel."

She scoffs and crosses her arms over her seatbelt.

Damn it—that didn't work.

"You think I'm an idiot," she says.

"What? Sweetheart, I don't think that—"

"Are you and Dad having sex talk or something?"

I don't say anything.

"Was it even Dad?"

"What?"

Shit. This isn't going well. But at least she didn't see who the message was from.

"Are you cheating on Dad? You can tell me."

I'm so distracted by her words that I almost rear-end the car in front of me.

Hazel's head rocks back and forth. "Mom!"

"Sorry," I mumble.

I pull into a fast food restaurant's parking lot and park the car. This isn't a conversation to be had while driving.

"I am not cheating on your father." I don't mean to sound so hostile, but given the current situation, that accusation is a slap in the face. And that's the second time she's asked me.

Cole is cheating on *me*.

And because of it, someone wants me dead.

Unless this person after you has nothing to do with Cole and everything to do with you.

I blink at my own thoughts. I'd never even considered this. I mean, I did piss off a lot of people in my youth thanks to my big mouth.

"Then, who texted you?" Hazel asks.

I sigh.

"Because you're acting all secretive, and I don't like it."

I'm thankful that Hazel is lashing out at me rather than bottling it up as she has done with everything else this past year. But I'm her mother—not her best friend. I don't owe her an explanation for everything.

I want to tell her that I'm entitled to my privacy, but that would only cause more strain between us. Things are finally looking up.

I put my lying cap back on, even though it makes me feel like garbage.

Pouting, I rest against the center console and tilt my head. "I can't tell you because it's a *surprise*, honey."

Her anger slowly dissolves, only to be replaced by confusion. One brow goes up while the other remains firm.

I draw invisible circles on the console between us. "Isn't it someone's birthday soon?"

Her mouth goes agape, and she winces guiltily. "Oh, shit. Mom—"

I fluff her off. "It's okay. I get it. I was acting a little sketchy. But you have to realize that I'm going to be a bit sketchy in the months leading up to your birthday."

You're a terrible mother, lying to her face like this.

No, you aren't—you're protecting her.

"I'm sorry," she says.

Almost a little too suddenly, I squeeze her thigh. "Don't be sorry, honey. You didn't know."

She's quiet as we leave the parking lot. It isn't until we turn into our neighborhood that she says, "You're not hosting a big surprise party with a pony and stuff though, right? I'm turning fifteen, Mom. Not five."

I let out a genuine laugh that fills up the entire rental car. I can't remember the last time I laughed like this. "No, honey, I promise."

The truth is I've been so distracted with Cole and this mysterious woman that I haven't even thought about Hazel's birthday.

But she doesn't need to know that.

"Okay, good." She grabs her backpack and soccer duffle bag and heads inside the house.

Meanwhile, I'm left feeling totally conflicted.

Hazel has no idea what I'm about to do to her father. But there's no other way. I can't stay with Cole. But I can't just up and leave him, either. Cole is friends with some hotshot lawyers in New York City.

One time, during a heated fight, he told me that if I ever *broke our family apart*, he'd fight tooth and nail to receive full custody of Hazel.

I'm not about to let that happen.

CHAPTER 71

Meghan

Tomorrow, 6 p.m. - 83 Prairie Drive.

It's a brand-new message; I deleted the previous one. I haven't written the address down anywhere in case someone finds it.

Instead, it's stored in my memory.

I've repeated the address countless times in my mind since receiving the first message.

83 Prairie Drive.

That's where all of this will end.

Am I going too far? Possibly. But there's no other way. Cole's pushed me into a corner. I suppose I could shut my mouth and continue living this way until Hazel is old enough to move out, but I'm miserable with Cole.

I don't deserve this.

We haven't had sex in over a year—not since my accident. Some days, I think he's repulsed by me. Sure, I've put on a bit of weight, but not that much. And even if I had—so what? He's my husband. I wouldn't care if he gained weight.

I do still love him—I truly do. But Cole isn't husband material.

I swipe sideways on my phone to delete the text message. I still can't believe I'm going through with this. How will it play out? Will he scream? Beg for mercy?

It doesn't matter.

There's no turning back now.

Hazel comes gliding into the kitchen, humming a tune I don't recognize. I immediately pull away from my phone and lean my back against the kitchen counter.

"Smells good." She cranes her neck to peer inside the oven. "Is that lasagna?"

"Sure is." I slip on my oven mitt. "And it's ready."

The front door suddenly opens and slams shut. A warm breeze rushes through the house, and Hazel leans her entire body back to peep into the foyer.

"Dad?"

Cole? What is he doing here? He's never home this early. Hazel leaves the kitchen to greet him, and a moment of silence follows. He's probably giving her a big hug.

As much as Cole irritates me, I do appreciate how much love he gives Hazel.

Cole takes long strides into the kitchen, his jaw tight and his shoulders drawn back despite fake crinkles in his eyes. He had no intention of being home this early.

"You're home early," I point out.

He clears his throat. "Yeah. Wanted to have supper with my girls."

Sure.

Katya probably had to leave early, or she outright rejected him.

"What are we having?" he asks.

I didn't think he'd be here. To be honest, I thought he'd get home late, open the fridge, and find cold lasagna in a Tupperware container. I'm not usually passive-aggressive, but I would have loved to have been a fly on the wall at that moment.

The two things he hates most of all are cold leftovers and lasagna.

"Lasagna," I say.

His lips curl, but only briefly. As soon as Hazel steps back into the kitchen, he cups his palms together and forces a smile that looks like it belongs on a villain's face. "Great."

Right. He'd probably rather eat expired canned peas.

They both help me set the table, and we all sit in silence

to start the meal. Hazel keeps rolling her eyes, and I'm surprised drool isn't spilling back out onto her plate.

Cole, however, winces with every bite and reaches for his glass of red wine to wash it down.

Who doesn't like lasagna? Store-bought—understandable, sure. But homemade? I make a damn good lasagna even with only one arm. All of that gooey cheesiness, the tender pasta, the thick succulent meat sauce, and best of all, the crispy cheese on top. I always broil mine and make it extra crispy.

"Good soccer practice?" Cole asks, breaking through the silence.

Hazel chugs down her glass of chocolate milk—which is a very odd choice with lasagna, but whatever—and nods eagerly. "Very good. Clark got hit in the face with the soccer ball."

Cole snorts. "That's awesome."

I don't even bother shooting him a nasty look. Instead, I'd rather enjoy this meal with our semblance of a close-knit family.

Hazel's eyes are now squinted, and she's laughing hard while trying to recreate the story for her father. He laughs along with her and even tries to make the sour face she's talking about. The one Clark made while getting smashed in the face with a ball.

If I didn't know everything I know about Cole, and about what's to come, I'd probably smile along with them.

I don't remember the last time we all sat down and enjoyed a meal like this. Hazel has been gone most evenings lately, and Cole is always home very late.

So this is nice.

I sip on my red wine, watching Cole. His bright eyes flicker my way, but only momentarily. It's like he's afraid to look at me. Like he can sense what I have planned for him.

No, there's no way.

If he knew what I had planned, he wouldn't be here, enjoying his meal like this.

Enjoy your family meal, because this will be your last.

CHAPTER 72

Meghan

Birds chirp outside my window at the crack of dawn. I stare at my ceiling, where a spider is clinging to the remnants of a web for dear life.

Or maybe it's about to have a bunch of babies. I've never liked killing bugs. I let them out whenever I can. A few times, however, Ziggy came running from behind me and crushed the ladybugs I placed out on the back deck.

I don't do that anymore—I place them on leaves, high up so Ziggy can't hurt them.

Ignoring the spider, I get out of bed. I have way more important things to worry about today.

Like teaching Cole one final lesson.

83 Prairie Drive.

Or was it Plain Drive?

Just kidding.

It's Prairie Drive. I haven't forgotten it.

6 p.m.

Is it wrong that I'm excited? Does that make me a bad person?

No. Cole brought this on himself.

I spend the morning with Hazel as she recites a list of birthday wishes. A Batwoman phone case. That one's easy—I know exactly where to get it. A new school bag for next year. I'm not wasting a birthday gift on that. I'll buy her one this summer for school. But it's sweet that she's willing to receive it as a birthday gift.

She mentions a specific brand name hoodie that I know costs about eighty dollars. I appreciate that she's never asked for this out of nowhere. Yes—Cole and I both make good money—but Hazel doesn't act entitled. She knows that if she wants something brand name, she can either save up her allowance, work for it, or ask to receive it as a gift.

She learned that at eight years old, thanks to me. Not Cole. He'd buy her whatever she wanted, but I nipped that in the bud real quick. If it weren't for me and my cracking down on entitled behavior, I'm afraid to know what kind of a teenager Hazel would be right now.

"Made you a coffee," Hazel says.

I freeze in the kitchen, stunned by the kind gesture. Hazel used to do thoughtful things sporadically before my accident, but this last year has been horrendous. My anger, combined with her distance, really put a wedge between us.

So to see her standing next to the coffee machine with a proud grin on her face makes my heart swell.

"Aw, thank you, honey. That was very thoughtful of you."

"I try," she quips. "Sometimes."

I grab her face and plant a firm kiss on her cheek. I haven't done that since . . . Well, I can't remember. She always acts like she's disgusted and wipes it off, but she likes it. It's all over her face seconds later.

God, I missed her.

Soon, it'll just be you and me.

I've thought long and hard about this. I don't want to hurt my baby girl, but it's the only way. Cole's indiscretions have literally become a threat to this family. The pain will be temporary. Besides, Hazel is almost fifteen. She'll understand.

She gets ready for school, and just as she's leaving, Cole descends our wooden staircase. He rubs his eyes. If he hadn't had the extra two glasses of wine after supper last night, he'd have woken up at a decent time.

"Hey," he groans. "Have a good day at school."

They hug, and Hazel is out the door.

Cole's eyes meet mine, and he freezes, his hand cupped over the sphere-shaped staircase finial.

"Hey," he says.

"Hi."

I turn around to go enjoy my coffee in the backyard with Ziggy. I stay out there until Cole is gone. He always leaves before eight. To be safe, I wait until eight thirty.

Sure enough, he's gone by the time I get back inside. I'm thankful.

Because if he decides he wants to talk or make amends, I might get soft. My brain will start firing at a mile per minute, trying to come up with a different solution than the one I have planned for this evening.

But I can't go back on my plan.

It has to happen tonight.

***

Tonight - 83 Prairie Drive.

I've received these texts every day since Monday. It's like a countdown. Every time I see the message, my heart flutters. I panic a little bit. This is all about to become very real.

You're going too far. You can still back out.

No way. Someone—possibly Roseline—tried to kill me. Cole is the reason this has gone too far.

I spent my day pacing around the house and tidying up. It's the only thing I can do to keep my brain from wandering. From considering backing out of all of this.

I glance at my phone's clock: 1:32 p.m.

Only a few more hours.

I step outside with Ziggy, who takes off as if he wasn't out only an hour ago, and sit on my patio sofa. A little ladybug lands on my lap, and I gently flick it off.

This is torture.

Every minute is like an hour.

If only I could fast-forward life and get this over with.

No, who am I kidding? I don't want to *get it over* with. I want to enjoy it. Revel in it.

I'm about to get up to make myself a coffee when my phone starts ringing on the shiny glass patio table. I spent half an hour cleaning that thing yesterday—it better still be sparkly.

Bayton Valley Police Department.

I hastily accept the call. "Hello?"

"Hi, Mrs. Gar— Meg?" It's Detective Goldberg. "How are you doing?"

Let's skip the small talk, and you tell me if Roseline is behind this.

"Good. How are you, Detective?"

"Good, thank you." There's a three-second pause that feels interminable. "Sorry for the delay. You know how it is—I can't do my job without a warrant. Anyway, I was able to confirm that Roseline Hayes was in the area on the day of the hit-and-run."

I was expecting this. In fact, I played this out so many times in my mind. But all of that mental practice wasn't enough to soften the blow.

My heart is pounding in my ears, and Ziggy's barking suddenly sounds very distant, like he somehow managed to get into the neighbor's yard.

"She's used her credit card throughout the city for the last two years, on and off. There's no direct proof linking her to the hit-and-run, but if you're telling me the two of you have history, and a contract stating that she isn't to have any contact with—"

He keeps talking, but his words become jumbled.

She's been around for the last two years?

I sit down, afraid I might tumble over, smash my head, and drown in my own pool.

This can't be happening.

Two freaking years?

"Meghan?"

"Y-yes—" But I don't even know what to say.

"I imagine this news is a bit of a shock," he says. "What

I'm about to tell you next might be even more of a shock."

There's *more*?

"Do you have someplace to sit down?"

Oh, God. How bad is it? Did she secretly give birth to twins? Does Hazel have a long-lost sister we don't know about?

That's all I need right now.

CHAPTER 73

Meghan

"I found a few credit card transactions at the Dauntmilton Hotel," says Detective Goldberg. "Actually, several. There appears to be a pattern. Twice per year. The interesting part is that she books the presidential suite every time."

The Dauntmilton Hotel. I know that place. It's about an hour's drive out of the city. There's a brand-new casino next to it, but I've never cared much for gambling.

Why is he telling me all of this?

"Has your husband been in contact with Roseline?"

Detective Goldberg may as well have thrown a chair at my face. Twice. What the hell would Cole be doing talking to Roseline?

I lean forward, elbows digging painfully into my thighs. "Wait. What does Cole have to do with this?"

"March third and November eighteenth, last year," he says. "Do you happen to remember where your husband was on those days? Do you have a shared calendar?"

Why do those dates sound so familiar?

"Hold on," I tell him,

I open up my calendar app and navigate to March.

There are little gray dots spread out for that week, from the second of March to the fifth of March.

Cole: Business Trip

I don't have any other details. I think he'd mentioned it was in Colorado. But I also remember not caring very much. We'd gotten into a huge fight a week before the news. I was glad he was leaving. And besides—part of me figured he'd spend the whole trip screwing his assistant.

I scroll back to November.

Another business trip.

No way.

Could Cole really still be sleeping with Roseline? He knows the risk involved. He wouldn't do that. Or maybe he would. The man loves living on the edge.

What if the two of them are conspiring to take Hazel away from me?

I grit my teeth.

"Meghan?" says the detective.

"I have two entries in my calendar," I say coldly. "He went on apparent business trips."

"Are you able to confirm those?" he asks.

"What do you mean?" I say.

"Any plane ticket transactions? Hotel receipts?"

I hold back a scoff. Detective Goldberg doesn't know my husband very well. Cole doesn't share his finances with me. He sends me a chunk of change every month as a contribution, and I take care of paying the bills.

He doesn't tell me what he spends his money on. It's *his* money. He certainly isn't going to share receipts with me.

"No," I say. "There's no way to confirm."

It's getting hard to swallow my anger. But the more I think about it, the more it makes sense. What are the odds of Cole going on business trips twice in one year at the very same time as Roseline's hotel stay? And she booked a presidential suite. How many more signs do I need?

The math adds up.

"Can't you search his credit card transactions?" I ask.

"I'm afraid not," he says. "I'd need a warrant for that."

Slowly, I lean back and gaze at the billowy sky. "That's okay, Detective. I'll find out."

"Call me back when you do?" he says.

My voice comes out way calmer than it should in a situation like this. "Absolutely."

CHAPTER 74

Diary Entry

I can't believe him. First, that Valeria bitch, and now, Katya. I mean, I always knew Cole had a streak with the ladies.

But he told me I was different.

That I was special. And I'm also the only one who gave him a child. Doesn't that count for something?

So why does he keep having affairs with all of these women rather than return to me?

If he were with me, I'd keep him happy. I wouldn't push him away, like Meg. He'd have no reason to cheat.

I thought leaving him a dead rose on the hood of his car would remind him of the love we lost. Okay, I also wanted to scare off Valeria. I think it worked because Valeria never slept with him. Or maybe she had no interest. I'm not sure.

I bet Cole tried convincing Meg that he never slept with Valeria, but given his track record, there's no way she believed him.

But she didn't see what I saw. He left work frustrated almost every evening. He'd slam his car door and take off, wheels squealing throughout the entire parking lot before driving off to some shoddy motel.

I bet he went home smelling like perfume anyway.

But he wanted Valeria.

So he kept making her work late while he tried to sway her. Clearly, it didn't work.

I still remember when he brought Valeria to that fancy restaurant and Meg showed up. That was hilarious. She's so stupid. She crashed her car into some chick's BMW.

I was too far away to hear what was happening, but it looked like Cole won the argument. He came out with some guy who acted like he knew him. Maybe he did. I have no clue.

But Cole kept throwing his hands in the air and pointing at the guy as if Meg had interrupted some important business meeting.

If I didn't hate Meg so much, I'd actually feel bad for her. Because Cole was definitely alone with Valeria. He kept reaching across the table, and she kept pulling away.

If Meg had been patient a little while longer, Cole would have gotten Vincent to fire Valeria. Instead, Meg got involved. Stuck her big nose where it didn't belong.

I still smile when I think of the crushed rose I left Cole. Because I'm sure he thinks Meg was behind it. He's made many comments about how "I don't know Meg like he does," which tells me he's scared of her.

It's kind of funny, actually.

I've been terrorizing Meg, hoping that if I scare her a bit, she'll get fed up with Cole and leave him. I mean, she should really reinforce her fence panels. That's on her.

The funniest part in all of this is that she thinks Valeria is behind it because we look so much alike. Some might say she's a dead ringer for me. What can I say? Cole has a type. Slim, curvaceous, and dark featured.

And to make things even funnier—Cole thinks his wife is terrorizing him. Honestly, I laugh out loud when I think about it. I'm pitting them against each other.

I was the one at the restaurant window spying on him and Katya, but I wore a blond wig under that ugly hat. He must have thought I was Meg. Maybe if I keep doing this, he'll get scared enough and decide to leave.

Or it'll have the opposite effect.

I hope not.

But I'm desperate. I can't keep standing on the sidelines anymore.

Chapter 75

Cole

"Two creams, one sugar," Katya says.

She winks at me and leans forward, allowing her cleavage to land right in front of my face. Her perfume—a soft floral scent with a hint of pepper—pervades the air around me, calming me instantly.

It's hard to stay mad at her.

But what did she expect would happen after yesterday? She told me to meet her in my office after hours and that she'd give me the time of my life. I waited for over an hour, and she never showed.

Then, when I tried calling her, she picked up and casually said there'd been a family emergency. Her tone didn't exactly scream *urgent* to me.

Katya uses her manicured fingernail to push my coffee mug toward me. She pouts her plush candy-red lips. "To apologize . . . Are you upset with me?"

Her Russian accent is beyond sexy.

"I don't like being made to wait around like that," I say honestly. "It's very disrespectful. You could have sent me a text."

"Family emergency." Her sharp blue eyes are on me, and it's impossible to look away.

I'm convinced Russian women show emotion differently. Katya never seems bothered by anything. She doesn't even appear remorseful for the situation she put me in.

"I'll make it up to you." She traces a sharp nail up my throat and across my jawline.

I shiver. "When?"

"Tonight," she says. "My place."

Her place? I don't typically leave the office to spend time with my assistants. I'd prefer to do it here, behind closed doors.

"What's wrong with here?" I say.

She pulls away and rests her hand on her perfectly curved hips. "I don't see handcuffs here, do you?"

Holy shit.

I always knew Katya had a dark side; I just didn't imagine she'd be into this sort of stuff. I tried to get Meg to be a little more wild in the bedroom, but it never got as far as I wanted it to.

"Or a whip," she adds.

If she doesn't stop talking, we'll have to leave work and go to her place *now*.

"Okay." I can't even keep the excitement out of my voice. "Your place. After work."

She winks at me and leaves my office.

This day couldn't go by fast enough.

***

The sun has started its descent. We chose to wait until after five o'clock so that everyone was out of the office. Especially Frank. Vincent, I'm not so worried about. We're the same, he and I.

But Frank?

He'd be the first to open his big mouth at a Christmas party. He'd probably nudge Meg and make some idiotic comment about how my assistant is competition. Then he'd wink horribly, mouth agape.

It could also be someone else entirely. A woman from a different section that I've never paid attention to. Someone willing to give Meg a call and tell her all about what I do after hours.

Not that it's anyone else's damn business.

And not that it matters today, anyway, because Katya told me she'd prefer to drive her own car and to keep up. Katya's very independent like that.

I lower my sun visor as the orange rays beam down through my windshield, almost blinding me. Up ahead, Katya drives her silver Mustang. It's a hot look. There's nothing quite like a woman driving a sports car.

Her engine revs as she waits at a red light.

She's impatient.

Which means she wants this as badly as I do.

What will she do? Tie me up? Or does she want to be tied up? They say dominant personalities like to be dominated in bed. Speaking from experience, I'd say that's true. And Katya is *definitely* a dominant personality. She always looks like she's in control of everything, even when everyone around her is panicking.

Last week, Vincent yelled at our new office secretary for messing up a mass email. He did it in front of everyone. But Katya just sat there watching poor Harper, arms crossed with zero expression. She's unreadable. I think that's what makes her so damn sexy.

She turns left at the light, her Mustang's engine rumbling throughout the city streets. It's a powerful purr that has me revving my own engine with torturous anticipation.

I follow her to a quiet neighborhood, and she pulls up in front of a yellow house with cute white-paneled windows. Very suburban. Does Katya seriously live here?

The grass is meticulously groomed. With the way Katya carries herself and with how much she prides herself on hygiene, I can't imagine her cutting her own grass.

She probably has some tanned, shirtless gardener that does it every week while she sits drinking a cocktail on that little white patio, secretly watching the hunk through a pair of big sunglasses.

Her Mustang's engine cuts out.

She steps out, playfully tossing and catching her key fob while I get out of my car.

"This is your place?" I ask.

"For now," she says.

I raise a brow.

"Come on," she says. "Let me give you the grand tour."

I don't want a tour. I want her to bring me straight to the bedroom so I can have my way with her. But I suppose that might come across as rude, and I get the feeling Katya is the type of woman who would tell me to piss off if she felt insulted. So I obediently follow her inside.

The place smells musty—old, even. It smells like my grandparents' place. And I haven't been there in ages, but I remember that smell.

I take off my shoes and follow her inside.

Fabric sofas. Carpet. Easter-colored walls. Yellow linoleum flooring.

This is *not* the type of place I ever imagined Katya living in. It goes against everything she exudes.

She mentioned handcuffs and a whip. Does she have some secret sex dungeon in the basement? Is this eighties decor all for show?

Slipping out of her heels, she turns around and watches me carefully. Her legs are sculpted and smooth, which tells me she just shaved. She must have planned for today.

"What's wrong?" she asks. "You seem confused by my decor."

"Um, I am," I say.

She shakes her head and laughs. The sound comes out raspy and hot as hell. She leads me into a kitchen full of yellow oak cupboards and cheap vinyl countertops.

Not exactly mood setting.

"Inheritance property," Katya says. "My grandmother died a few months ago."

"Oh," I say. "I'm sorry."

"I'm not," she says. "It brought me here, to Bayton Valley. And then I met you."

She reaches under the kitchen sink and pulls out a dusty bottle of rum. She then proceeds to search the kitchen cupboards as if for the first time. "*Blyat.*"

The word comes out sounding Russian, and I can only imagine it's some sort of curse.

Her laid-back composure returns after the fifth cupboard, from which she pulls out two whiskey glasses.

Then, rolling her R, she says, "Drink?"

CHAPTER 76

Cole

We stand quietly as I inspect her grandmother's former kitchen. There are countless framed pictures of people I don't recognize. They seem happy.

Aren't people always happy in pictures?

It would be rather odd to display pictures with everyone glowering.

"Family?" I ask, even though this is killing the mood. I had expected to be jumped the moment we set foot inside. Not placed in direct view of a bunch of family photos.

Katya turns to look at the pictures on the wall but doesn't focus on them for long. "Oh, yeah."

Clearly, she isn't close with her family.

I sip on the rum while she watches me. Why isn't she drinking?

"Good?" she asks.

I nod.

"Drink more," she says.

My lips curve upward. "Are you trying to get me drunk?"

"I am." She doesn't mirror my expression. Is this her idea of a joke? I can't tell with her.

I take another swig of my drink and place the glass down, its base making a soft clink against the cheap counter.

Her eyes twinkle malevolently. "Come."

She leads me upstairs, and we can't move fast enough. I'm tempted to scoop her up and race up there myself, but she'd probably physically assault me if I manhandled her like that.

When we reach the bedroom—a medium-sized room with black bedding and drab gray dressers—she grabs me by the collar of my shirt and pulls me in for the hardest kiss I've ever experienced. And it's enough to distract me from the ugly furnishings.

It's so passionate.

So raw.

When she's done with me, she shoves me toward the bed. "Take off your pants."

I do as told and rip everything off until I'm buck naked.

She reaches into a drawer and pulls out two sets of handcuffs. "You sure you're ready for me?"

I nod so fast I almost pull something in my neck.

I've never wanted anything more in my life.

She fastens one cuff around my left wrist and locks me to the bedpost. She goes on to do the same with my right wrist.

"You sure you want this?" she asks.

I nod again.

"Say it," she says.

"I— I want this. I want you. So bad."

She winks at me. "Then you're about to have me."

***

My head rolls, occasionally hitting the wooden headrest behind me.

Katya is incredible.

More than incredible. I wish I'd met her sooner. And although I expected a wild ride from her, I didn't expect it to drain me this much.

"Tired?" Katya asks.

I blink hard. "Yeah, actually. Can you uncuff me?"

She purses her lips, chin raised.

Why is she looking at me like that?

"Come on." I wriggle my wrists, but they're fastened tightly on both sides. "Uncuff me."

But she's still looking at me in a way that's making me increasingly uneasy.

What's going on?

I blink hard.

There are now two Katyas.

"What—" I try.

She moves toward the bed, climbs atop, and straddles me. "There, there." Her warm finger presses over my lips. "I'll take good care of you. Cross my heart." She gestures across her chest, then plants a kiss on my forehead.

Then, everything around me starts to fade. Sound leaves the room entirely; Katya's figure darkens, and the bit of light creeping through the curtain grows dimmer until there's nothing left but blackness.

CHAPTER 77

Hazel

My mom is acting really weird.

She keeps pacing and mumbling stuff to herself. I only came downstairs to grab a snack, but now I kind of feel bad leaving her alone like this.

"You okay?" I ask.

"Hm?" She looks up at me from her phone. "Yeah, honey. Of course."

She's lying.

She's hiding something. Or maybe she'd rather not talk about it.

"Okay," I say, even though I don't believe her. "Well, I'm here, if you, like, wanna talk."

Her lips pull into a firm smile. "Thanks, sweetheart. But I'm okay. Just dealing with a work issue right now."

Mom talks about work like she's still working. But she hasn't worked since her accident, so it's really confusing when she makes comments like this.

Or is she going back to work? I don't see how. Her arm still doesn't work.

"I thought you didn't have work anymore," I say.

She hesitates, eyes darting between me and her phone. "Well, I don't, but I still own the business. So I do have to deal with issues as they come."

I suppose that makes sense.

When Mom first started her practice several years ago, she barely took a break to sit down. She was constantly on her phone or in her office. It only slowed down once she hired more staff. But I guess it makes sense that she still has to make the big decisions.

Ziggy suddenly appears at the patio door with a red heel in his jaw. Mom doesn't wear heels. At least she hasn't in years.

"Um, what's that?" I ask, pointing at the door.

Mom lets out a little chirp when she sees Ziggy's jaws wrapped around the shoe. She slides the door open so fast it slams against the frame.

She then rips the shoe out of Ziggy's mouth.

"I don't know how he got that," she says. She leans forward, inspects our yard, then pulls her head back in with a scowl. "Ziggy! Bad boy!" She huffs and looks back at me. "Went into the garbage again."

"Where'd the heel come from?" I ask.

I swear, it looks like she's frozen. Like I shot some sort of ice laser beam at her. She's just standing there, back round, dirty red heel grasped firmly in her fist. What's she doing?

"Mom?"

She snaps out of whatever daydream she was in. "Yeah? Oh. This? Found it in the backyard a few weeks ago. I think some kid threw it over as a prank. Probably because Ziggy has such a big mouth."

It wouldn't be the first time people threw stuff over our fence. It doesn't happen often. We live in a safe neighborhood. But there are these two eleven-year-old twin brothers that go around wreaking havoc everywhere.

If anyone did it—it was them.

Mom suddenly shrieks, and I flinch. "What? What is it?"

"Sorry." She reaches into her pocket to grab her phone. "I left it on vibrate."

Wow.

She really is on edge.

Talking to her might not be a good idea right now. Maybe what she really needs is to be alone.

"I'm gonna go upstairs," I say.

She nods absentmindedly, eyes glued to her phone.

The pale skin of her face lightens as she stares at her screen. She looks so stressed out.

Poor Mom.

"I— I'll be upstairs," I repeat.

She ignores me.

I should have gone to Alex's. I thought spending time at home after school would be nice, but Mom clearly has something going on, and Dad isn't home. Again.

Sighing, I go upstairs to my room.

CHAPTER 78

Meghan

Now.

Now? That's all the text message says. It isn't six o'clock yet. Have the plans changed? Did something happen?

It's now five thirty, and 83 Prairie is a ten-minute drive away. Which means there's no time to waste.

When I peer up from my phone, Hazel is gone.

How long ago did she leave?

I hurry to the staircase and call up to her. "Hazel, honey—I have to run out."

Muffled footsteps echo from the second floor, and her head juts out from around the corner. "Okay."

"Just have to deal with the accountant situation." I feel terrible lying to her, but there's no way she can know what I'm about to do. "I'll be back in a bit."

She nods, although I can tell she looks disappointed. Of all days, she chose today to stay home with me. And now I'm about to leave to do something terrible to her father.

It isn't too late to back out.

No way. He's put me through hell our entire marriage. Made me feel worthless. Unwanted. I'm done with him.

"I might go to Alex's place for supper," she says.

If it were any other day, I'd be bummed to hear this. But today, it might be for the best.

"Sounds good, honey," I say, walking toward the front door. "Will Charlotte be picking you up?"

I can't believe I haven't even met this woman yet. Does that make me a bad mother? Then again, I trust Hazel. And she's spoken very highly of her. Still, I make a mental note—when this is all over, I'll introduce myself. Heck, I might even make a new friend.

"Yeah, probably," she says.

Good.

I say my goodbyes and hurry to my rental car. My hand is shaking so badly that I'm thankful this car's starter utilizes a fob and not an actual key.

I leave the driveway and make my way over to Prairie Drive as fast as legally permitted. The last thing I need right now is to get pulled over. The neighborhood is quaint and very clean. People seem to pride themselves on their lawns and gardens.

Not exactly what I was expecting.

After slow-rolling down the street, I manage to spot number 83. It's a small yellow house with white-paneled windows and a meticulously groomed exterior. Again, not what I was expecting.

But there's Cole's car.

This must be the right place.

I park quite a ways down from him. If there are any street cameras or doorbell cameras, I don't want my rental next to his Lexus.

Once parked, I sit in my car, fighting with myself.

You can still back out.

No, you can't. Everything is already in motion.

This mental back-and-forth is agonizing. My gaze shifts to my dashboard clock: 5:42.

I swing my door open and step out with wobbly knees. Every step toward that cute yellow house aggravates my nausea.

I can't believe I'm doing this.

But I made a promise to Cole when we married, and I've let him get away with too much for far too long.

He needs to learn.

When I reach the yellow house, I grasp the door handle. It turns, as it should.

I step inside.

The house looks like it belongs to someone's

grandmother.

Reluctantly, I step backward and peer sideways at the house number one last time—83.

And this is Prairie Drive.

I checked it at least six times on my phone's GPS. Besides, Cole's car is out front. That confirms everything.

This has to be the right house.

The whole place smells *old*. Dusty, with a hint of laundry detergent. Something they used to sell decades ago. I can't quite put my finger on it.

A little foyer table is pressed up against the pastel green wall, and on it is an envelope with my name scribbled in black marker.

I reach for it and open it up.

Inside is a small USB key. This is it. I can't believe I finally have it.

"Hi, Meg," comes Katya's voice.

Chapter 79

Meghan - One Month Earlier

Coming here was a mistake.

But Cole isn't around, and Hazel is at Alex's place. Is it so wrong that I want to get out of the house, too?

Maybe talk to someone?

Anyone who isn't Ziggy?

I thought I'd be relieved after I got Valeria to leave town. But of course, AstroWyre hired some other girl within twenty-four hours.

It's a never-ending cycle. Honestly, I'm exhausted.

I take a sip of my cold beer and lean against the slick wooden bar top.

"This seat taken?" comes a woman's voice.

She has a Russian accent and a flirtatious smile on her lips. Is she hitting on me? I mean, not that I would mind. I'd welcome the attention since I'm not getting it anywhere else.

"No," I say.

She sits down and asks the bartender for a shot of vodka, which comes out sounding like *vudka*.

"You look depressed," she says.

Wow. Is it that obvious?

"Marital problems?" she asks.

I raise a brow. Seriously—is it *that* obvious?

She throws her chin out at my wedding finger. "You have a ring, but you keep playing with it. Like it bothers you."

"It does," I admit.

I've only had half a beer. I'm not sure why I'm opening

up to this total stranger. This very beautiful stranger. She could be a model. Actually, she probably is. Sitting next to her makes me feel super ugly.

She leans in toward me, then glances over her shoulder to ensure no one is listening. "Is he cheating on you?"

What kind of a person outright asks something like that? My marital life isn't any of her business.

Yet, I find myself opening up to her.

Telling her everything about Cole.

Because by the end of the night, I'll probably never see her again. And it feels good to get it all off my chest.

"I can make it all go away," she says. "Five grand, and I'll catch your husband on camera sleeping with me. It helps to have the proof. Trust me. This is what I do."

I blink at the fuzzy version of her.

I'm on my fourth beer now. And it may be my booze brain, but somehow, I feel like coming here tonight was fate. Like I was meant to meet his woman—Katya.

A smile splits my face. "What do you mean, it's what you do?"

"For a living," she says. "I help women leave their cheating husbands. You're all the same, you know. You come here to sulk. I find at least two of you per week."

I'm not sure whether to feel insulted or seen.

"Let me get this straight." I'm outright laughing now. "You help women like me by sleeping with their husbands?"

This is insanity.

She purses her lips and elevates her chin. "Would it not help you to have proof of his cheating? It will help you in court. Look it up."

She's not wrong.

I have looked it up—many times.

"So you'll sleep with him and record it?" My mouth is dry now despite all the beer I keep pulling into it.

"Yes, and I can also scare him. Teach him a lesson." A glimmer of excitement flashes in her eyes. This woman isn't all there. There's something off about her.

"What kind of a lesson?" I ask.

She knocks back her fifth shot of vodka and slams it down on the bar top between us. Then she lowers her head, a gorgeous yet malevolent smile warping the lower half of her face. "A lesson he'll never forget."

CHAPTER 80

Meghan

Katya steps out from the darkness, her hair disheveled and her forehead grimy. She's clearly been doing a lot of physical work. She's as stunning as the day I met her. It's no wonder Cole hired her, especially if she wore a snug sky-blue dress at her interview like I told her to do.

"As promised." Her accent is as thick as I remember it from a few weeks back. She wiggles her finger at the USB key in my fingers.

I glare at the little thing, fuming inside. I'm both enraged and satisfied. It's a very odd feeling. But this is exactly what I wanted—it's what I asked for.

"You can tell it's him?" I ask.

She nods. "Absolutely. The angle is perfect."

I slip the USB key back into the envelope, then fold it over twice before tucking it into my purse. "Thank you."

She nods without any hint of emotion on her face. I knew Katya was badass when I met her—a little crazy, even. I mean, that's why I hired her. But it's admittedly unnerving to see her *this* calm right now. It makes me think she's incapable of feeling any real emotion altogether.

"Cash?" she says.

As promised, I pull another envelope out of my purse and hand it to her. She elevates her chin, grabs it, and rips it open. Then, she starts counting the cash.

"It's all there," I say. "The second third. And I'll give you the final envelope after this is over."

She nods and jerks her head sideways. "Ready?"

No, I'm not ready.

But I'm here now, and there's no backing out.

This has to happen.

I swallow what feels like a clump of vomit and nod.

"Good." Katya reaches for the basement door's handle. "He's down here."

CHAPTER 81

Cole

"Wakey, wakey."

I crack my eyes open and blink several times to rid them of crust. And what the hell is in my mouth?

A gag?

I blink down at my wrists.

They're fastened to an old wooden chair's armrests. A chair that was easily built in the sixties, when furniture wasn't cheap and flimsy. That means standing up and trying to Hulk my way out of these restraints isn't an option.

The room around me is damp and smells of mildew. Worse, it's dusty. And I'm allergic to dust. So now, I can barely breathe since my nose is clogging up.

Where am I?

An attic?

A dungeon?

Wooden beams are angled overhead, and the only light in the room is coming from a battery-powered emergency lantern.

What's going on?

I try to push the gag out of my mouth with my tongue.

"Ah, ah, ah," comes a deep, almost robotic voice.

A voice changer?

I snap my head sideways, and a high-pitched squeal slips through the cracks of my gag.

What in the *hell*?

I can't see my captor's face thanks to a disturbing mask—a dead pig's head. But the person underneath is clearly a woman—small build, tight yoga pants, average-sized breasts underneath a loosely fitted black top.

She's in shape. And probably perfectly capable of digging my grave with her bare hands.

I blink hard.

How did I get here? Or am I dreaming?

Wait—no. I was with Katya earlier. What happened? Why can't I remember? Is she okay?

The woman in the mask is sprawled on a lounge chair wrapped in plastic, legs dangling over the armrest. She tilts her head sideways, and the pig mask shifts almost imperceptibly.

Little bits of flesh hang around the neck area, and the animal's jaw is sealed shut, a smile seemingly pulling at the corners of its snout. Its skin, a bright pink, is splattered in blood.

Then, the smell hits me. It's very distinct, and it reeks.

That head is *fresh*.

I snap my eyes shut, willing the sight away as my heart hammers inside my chest. This can't be real. I must be dreaming.

"You just couldn't stop, could you?"

I seal my eyes shut tighter.

This isn't real. It isn't real.

The sound of sharp heels clicking against cement flooring follows, and I can't resist opening my eyes again. She stands tall, now holding onto the battery-powered lantern in one hand.

In the other is a Japanese-steel chef's knife.

I try to suck in a breath, but there's barely any oxygen coming in through my single functioning nostril. The other is completely clogged now.

A crushing sensation fills my chest.

Lack of oxygen? Or panic? Both?

She moves closer to me.

Click. Click. Click.

I jerk sideways violently, trying to free my hands. I can't

die like this.

The ropes around my arms dig into my skin, and I wince in pain. This woman, whoever she is, knows how to fasten restraints. Even my ankles are tied.

Katya?

No, it can't be.

She would never do something like this.

The woman leans in so close to me that the foul smell of the pig's head slips into my partially clogged nostril. I gag, then gag again when I feel how deep the cloth is shoved inside my mouth.

Without warning, the woman in the mask rips out the rag. I cough several times, then suck in so hard it hurts my chest.

The knife in her hand glints. I'm about to protest, but she brings its point to my neck. The tip is sharp and pressed right up against my jugular.

"Any last words?"

CHAPTER 82

Meghan

"Any last words?" Katya says.

I knew the woman was unhinged—at least a bit, to accept a job like this—but I didn't expect things to play out this way.

The pig mask and all.

It's very disturbing.

But it's doing exactly what I'd hoped—scaring the hell out of Cole. Part of me feels bad for him, especially with how he's wriggling around, trying desperately to free himself from that old wooden chair.

The other part of me . . . Well, I'm reveling in this.

"P-please!" Cole begs. "Don't kill me."

I step out from behind stacked boxes in the dark, and Cole's eyes seem to triple in size.

"M-Meg?" His voice cracks. First, it sounds like he's confused. But then, it's almost as if he thinks I'm here to rescue him. "Meg!"

When I don't say anything, the confusion returns. He's putting the pieces together—realizing that I'm the one behind this, and I'm not here to save him.

"Cole," I say.

Despite the anxiety I've felt all day, I'd say I'm handling this pretty well. In fact, I don't even have anxiety anymore. Katya's calmness may have rubbed off on me. This all feels *right*.

"What are you doing? Please, Meg. Please—"

"Oh, shut up," I say.

His lips flatten into a line.

"You did this to yourself, Cole." I reach into my purse and extract the envelope Katya gave me from earlier. "And now, I finally have proof that you're a cheating bastard."

He doesn't even try to argue.

How can he? Katya took a video of the two of them having sex. It's all I wanted—all I needed—to move forward with the divorce.

Isn't it strange?

I knew my husband was cheating on me. I've always *known*. But I've never caught him in the act. And somehow, that lack of proof always led a minuscule part of my brain to think—*What if I'm wrong?*

That tiny bit of doubt held me back.

That, and Hazel. But she's fourteen, almost fifteen. I can't wait any longer.

Plus, court is never in favor of an adulterer. Cole is screwed, and not in a good way, for once.

"What's that?" Cole wriggles again, but it's clear that Katya knows how to tie knots. The moment he speaks, Katya digs her knife up against his throat again.

I admire her work.

She knows how to keep scaring him.

Cole swallows hard. "W-what? You're going to kill me, Meg? Take Hazel's father away from her?"

Katya presses the knife a little harder, and I can't repress a smile. I'm about to tell him that if he cooperates, I won't kill him. Even though the plan was never to kill him. All I want to do is traumatize him. Teach him a lesson for all the times he cheated on me.

But before I can say any of this, he opens his big mouth. "You're making a mistake, you know that? You won't get away with this, Meg. You won't—"

Without warning, Katya pulls a small paring knife out from her belt and brings it down hard, right through his thigh—all the while still pressing the chef's knife to his throat.

I flinch hard, and Cole's head snaps back as he bellows.

His mouth opens wide, revealing his upper back molars.

"F-f-f-f-fuck!" he shouts.

His eyes are now quadruple their usual size. He pants through gritted teeth while staring at the knife. His pupils are so dilated there's barely any blue left.

"Respect your wife." Katya's voice comes out sounding like a man's thanks to the voice changer I gave her.

I'm too stunned to say anything. This wasn't part of the plan. I never wanted Cole to get hurt. I hate him, but I still love him in a messed-up sort of way.

Katya was supposed to rough him up a bit—scare the living daylights out of him—not stab him with a kitchen knife.

Katya leaves the knife in place, and Cole is now hyperventilating. Tucked into her belt is another paring knife, and I'm afraid that if Cole opens his mouth again, she'll jab that one into his other thigh.

I want to say something—tell Katya that she's crossed a line—but I don't.

"Roseline," I move toward him, ignoring Katya's frightening pig head.

Cole sucks in several rapid breaths, chest heaving. "W-what? W-what about her?"

"Have you been seeing her?" I ask.

Cole is a mess. Sweat drips down his temples, and he's lost so much color that his face has taken on a deathlike pallor. Is he losing blood? Should I be worried?

But I imagine that's why Katya left the knife in place—so that he doesn't bleed out. I've heard that you should never pull out an offending object and that it should instead be stabilized until a medical professional can extract the weapon in a controlled environment.

Blood spills out all over his thigh, but it's not dripping. It's . . . collecting. Pooling. I imagine if he had pants on, and not just briefs, the material would have soaked it all up.

I'm sure if Katya were to rip out the handle, the situation might quickly escalate.

Cole squints at me. It's his famous look he gives me when he's about to tell me that I'm imagining things. Having *delusions* again.

"Don't bullshit me, Cole. I know all about you deleting my calendar notes. Trying to make me think I'm losing my mind. My memory. You crossed a line, you know that? You had me thinking my brain was completely fried. We're done, Cole. Do you hear me?"

I'm the one breathing hard now. I'm so angry I could slap him across the face. I want to, but I hold back.

"So tell me," I continue. "Have you been seeing Roseline? Twice per year?"

A look of sadness washes over him. "Yes."

Bastard.

I knew he was, but to hear him admit it causes a blinding rage to burn inside of me. Instead of punching him in the nose, all I can do is laugh. The sound fills the entire basement. Now he's really looking at me like I'm crazy.

"You're unbelievable, you know that? Do you have any idea the danger you've put Hazel in? Bringing that psychopath back into our lives?"

He stares at me. He has no idea what I know about Roseline. That she's been lingering around Bayton Valley for the last two years.

"She's been following me, Cole. Probably following Hazel."

His brows bunch, and he shakes his head. "What? No, that's impossible. Roseline wouldn't—"

"Wouldn't what?" I snap. With fists clenched, I take a step toward him. "She's the one who came after me. Did you know that? She was also in our backyard, Cole. Watching me."

His lips part, but nothing comes out. He appears to be genuinely taken aback. This is all news to him. He must not have thought Roseline was capable of something like this.

"I— I'm sorry, Meg. I'm so sorry."

He can apologize all he wants.
But it isn't enough.
Not yet.

CHAPTER 83

Roseline

This place reeks.

Honestly, I hate spending most of my days in this dump. But I do what I have to. It's not like I have much money to live on. Not while on welfare. I pay my bills, and that's about it.

Loud footsteps echo upstairs, followed by the sound of a couple bickering. Damn triplexes. Sometimes, I think this place is going to crumble if someone sneezes too hard. It's a total ramshackle property with a shit landlord who doesn't care to maintain the place.

Whatever.

This isn't my life for much longer.

I'm so close. I can feel it in my bones. It's like my cells are vibrating at a higher frequency.

A soft buzz in my entire body.

I pull out the little black stool tucked away under the vanity desk and sit down. I lean forward, gazing at my dark-brown eyes.

"There you are," I say to myself. "Beautiful as always."

I kiss my fingers and touch the mirror. Then, I prepare my makeup kit and lay everything out in front of me. I've done this countless times over the last year. I could probably put my face on with my eyes closed.

I grab my contact lens case from the corner of the desk, twist the caps off, and gently pull out the wet, floppy lenses.

One drop in each to moisturize them, and I place them over my eyes. I blink the solution away and smile at my reflection.

My makeup process takes about half an hour, which isn't all that bad. But by the time I'm done, my cheeks are less defined, my lips less full, and my brows much more filled in. Unfortunately, I went through that stupid brow-plucking fad as a teenager and now have what I like to call spider legs. Few brow hairs remain. As soon as I can afford it, I'll get microblading done.

I slide on a pair of oversized jeans and a plain flannel top. Not what I would typically wear. In fact, I don't know how anyone wears clothes so . . . ugly. It's beyond me.

You're doing this for Cole.

I elevate my chin, twirling in front of my mirror at my now shapeless body.

If I can't get Meg to leave Cole, then I'll get Cole to leave Meg. And I know exactly how to do that.

The last touch, which is probably my favorite part in all of this, is my wig. I pull my long brown hair into a tight bun at the base of my skull and adjust the wig over my head.

There.

Perfect.

I snatch my car keys from my coat pocket and leave my disgusting apartment. Overhead, Tyler is smoking off the highest balcony. He's sporting a crusty wifebeater like he always does and doesn't even bother to nod at me when I wave up at him.

Honestly, I'm not sure why I still make the effort.

I guess I'm hoping I don't get kicked out of this place. Not before I get what I want.

I drive deeper into Bayton Valley, past kids playing basketball and an elderly couple walking a dog the size of a cat.

This place is cute. People seem happy here. The city as a whole is well maintained and always very clean. Well, aside from the east side, which is where I currently live.

But as soon as Cole is mine, we're moving far away from here. I enter the richer end of town and make a left.

I've been here several times before, but today is special. Very special.

I pull up to the curb and park, then flip my visor mirror down to ensure everything looks just right.

My contacts are still in place—bright and green. My hair, red and poufy, really adds that final touch to my overall look.

Once I'm confident with my appearance, I pull out my phone.

I'm here.

Seconds later, Hazel comes running out of the house with a smile so wide, you'd think Santa Claus was picking her up.

She pries my rusty van door open, lighting up the moment she sees me.

"Hey, Charlotte!"

"Hey, honey!"

I'm not usually this chipper. But for Hazel, I make the effort. I have to.

"Thanks for picking me up," Hazel says.

I wink at her. She thinks I'm taking her back to Alex's place. But the truth is, Meg has made this whole setup a breeze.

She didn't even bother trying to meet me. What will Cole think when his daughter disappears? When he finds out she's been kidnapped by the very woman Meg knew about, but never spoke to?

He'll blame her. He'll never forgive her.

CHAPTER 84

Meghan

Cole is looking extremely pale. I'm wondering if I've gone too far. He clearly needs a hospital.

"P-please." His head rolls.

I glance worriedly at Katya, who shrugs me off as if Cole is complaining of a paper cut. "Meds are still making him drowsy. He isn't dying."

How can she be so unemotional about this? She stabbed him so easily. But I can't let my love for Cole get in the way of my plan.

"Cole," I say.

His eyelids flutter.

I step toward him and grab him by his prickly chin. "Look at me."

His cheeks squish between my fingers, and he lets out a foul-smelling moan.

"I have a list of seven women willing to testify in court against you."

This wakes him up. The tiredness that made him look so pathetic only seconds ago washes away instantly, which leads me to wonder if it was all an act.

"That's right," I say. "They didn't *want* to have sex with you, Cole. Not my list of seven, anyway. But you apparently made several suggestions that they'd lose their jobs if they weren't up to the task of getting closer to you as your assistant."

His Adam's apple bobs.

"Which means your career is over, and you'll likely end up behind bars for sexual assault."

"Meg, you can't do this. What about Hazel? She needs her father."

"Wrong," I snap at him. "She *needed* her father, and you weren't there to do your job. Instead, all you wanted was to shove your dick in any young woman with a nice body. Should have thought about your family before breaking it apart."

"No, Meg, please!" His voice breaks, and he starts full-blown crying.

He looks beyond pathetic sitting in that chair, head bowed forward, tears streaming down his face. Cole has an ugly cry. His mouth is inverted, and he looks like he just siphoned ten lemons through a straw.

Do I feel sorry for him?

No.

I thought I would, but I feel worse for Hazel. Because the truth will come out. And although I don't want to hurt her like this, I can't help but think of the women Cole slept with. The ones I reached out to over the last week. Many of them sobbed as they recounted what happened to them. And five out of the seven admitted that they only slept with Cole because they had little mouths to feed and were in desperate need of the money.

What if Hazel ever ends up in that position? At the mercy of some powerful man? I'd want that man's wife to get involved. I wouldn't want her sitting on the sidelines to *protect her children from the truth.*

This is the right thing to do.

"Where's your phone?" I ask.

Before he can answer, Katya nudges her chin at a set of keys and a cell phone resting on an old wooden shelf. I walk toward the shelf, pick up his phone, then bring it to his face to unlock it with Face ID. It takes a few tries thanks to that ugly grimace he's making.

But finally, it unlocks.

I search through his contacts.

Surprisingly, there aren't that many women's names. I imagine he deletes them after he's done with them. I scroll to the R section for Roseline, but she isn't in there.

But I'm not stupid. He probably gave her some other name to mask her identity in case I ever decided to search his phone.

"Which one is Roseline?" I say.

He sniffles.

"Which one?" My tone comes out far more menacing this time.

"J-Jimmy," he says. "Jimmy Stason."

Of course he'd give her some random guy's name. If I were to ever question him on it, he'd tell me it's a client of his. Potentially a coworker. It's not like I know everyone he works with.

I press on Jimmy's name and pull the phone up to my ear. I'm not sure why, but a faint smile is tugging at my lips.

Because soon, this will all be over.

CHAPTER 85

Hazel

We've been driving on the freeway for a good twenty minutes. Where is Charlotte taking me? She's being very quiet, too, which isn't like her. Usually, she's super chatty and full of energy.

But there's something weird about her right now.

She looks either angry, or determined, and very distracted. I can't put my finger on it.

Her phone suddenly starts playing some rock song, and she struggles to reach into her pocket.

It's not my business, and I shouldn't be watching her, but I could have sworn the caller ID said *Cole*.

No way.

It can't be.

It's not like my dad is the only person named Cole.

"H-hey," she answers awkwardly. Her eyes flicker toward me.

Okay, she's being totally weird.

But then, out of nowhere, her eyes almost pop out of their sockets. She slams the brakes and swerves the steering wheel so hard that my shoulder slams into the door.

"What the hell?" I shout.

She pulls off the freeway, her tires squealing the entire time as she cuts off three cars behind us. The moment she's off, she pulls up alongside the curb, parks, and jumps out.

My heart is still pounding a mile per minute.

She almost made us crash! What the hell was that

about? I inhale deeply, trying to steady my heart.

What could be so important that she would drive like a total maniac? She could have killed me. Maybe I don't know Charlotte as well as I thought. Because Mom would never have done something like that.

It was like Charlotte forgot about me in that moment. Like she didn't even care that I was in her car.

Through the windshield, she paces up and down the road, constantly scratching at her red hair. For a second, it almost looks like she's readjusting it the way you would a hat. Hair isn't supposed to move like that.

Despite how frantically she's walking about, she returns to the car with a tight smile on her lips.

My jaw is so tense it's hurting my neck. "What was *that* about?"

She rolls her eyes theatrically. "Would you relax? It was a bit of a sharp turn. Besides, you should be happy. Today's your lucky day."

I'm too stunned to say anything. She's never spoken to me like that before. Like I'm nothing but some annoying little brat. And what's that supposed to mean? *My lucky day?*

Without another word, she blasts the music on the radio, does another unpleasant sharp turn, and speeds toward the freeway's onramp.

Rather than go north, however, we're going south—back toward Bayton Valley.

I'm even more confused now.

She said she was taking me out someplace, as a surprise. But if we aren't going there anymore, then how is it my lucky day? That would mean *not going* has made my day a lucky one.

Where was she really planning on taking me?

I swallow hard and discreetly pull out my phone.

Mom, can you please pick me up ASAP? Charlotte is being weird. I should be at Alex's place in 25.

Chapter 86

Meghan

I'm shaking so badly I'm afraid I might fall over.

But I heard her—Hazel. She was with Roseline. How is that even possible? She was supposed to get picked up by Charlotte.

When I asked Roseline about it, she told me I was imagining things and that she was driving with her niece.

But that was Hazel—I know it.

Oh, my God . . . Did Roseline kidnap her? Hazel is a tough girl. She takes after me. Those muscular calves alone from all that soccer would be enough to render someone disabled for a few days. Maybe even permanently. I can't picture thin little Roseline getting a good grip on my daughter.

Doesn't mean she didn't have any help.

I can't think straight.

"Why the fuck was Hazel with Roseline?" I snap at Cole. His face blanches.

He's as clueless as I am and visibly frightened by this revelation. That's the good father in him. The only side I'm going to miss.

"Wh-what?" He sits up a bit, despite the knife in his thigh. "How do you know? Are you sure?"

"Why do you look so scared, *Cole*? Is Roseline going to do something?"

"I— I don't think so. But I don't know. Oh, God. I don't know."

He's panicking as badly as I am.

But Roseline seemed genuinely happy with our phone

call. I told her I was leaving Cole and that she could have him so long as she left me and Hazel alone. She agreed without a second thought. In fact, she cut me off midsentence to agree to my terms.

I don't think she cares about Hazel. All she wants is Cole.

"I have to go," I blurt out, even though I have no idea where I'm going.

The police station? Alex's? Maybe I'm wrong, and Hazel is perfectly safe with Alex and Charlotte.

Katya stands there, pig mask still flawlessly in place. It reeks, but my nose has somewhat gotten used to the smell.

"Will you get him the help he needs?" I say, pointing at his leg.

Katya nods.

Before we came down here, she reassured me that Cole would stay alive, *no matter what happened.* I should have realized she had something harsh and gruesome planned for him at that moment. She also made it a point to tell me that this house belongs to some woman she doesn't know—someone who passed away two days ago.

Katya is smart. She knows what she's doing. So I have to trust that she'll keep Cole alive, as promised. Besides, I'm sure she wants the rest of her money.

But that's what makes this moment so ironic.

I made her promise me she wouldn't kill Cole. Apparently, she's *gotten rid of* husbands in the past. The offer was there. However, Cole isn't abusive. He's never laid a hand on me. Death didn't feel like the right punishment for him.

But now, part of me wishes I hadn't refused her offer.

After learning that Roseline has my child with her . . . I want to kill Cole.

I open my palm at Katya, silently requesting her second paring knife. She hands it to me, and I lean into Cole, pressing the tip against his throat.

"I swear to God, if you or Roseline ever come near me

or Hazel again, I'll kill you both. Do you fucking hear me?"

He nods so fast that a droplet of sweat leaps from his face and lands on my chin.

But it isn't enough. Not with this amount of rage inside of me.

My daughter is in danger. All because of him.

Without warning, I clench the paring knife's handle and bring it down hard into his other thigh. He lets out an ear-splitting cry, head tilted back, mouth entirely agape.

He starts hyperventilating again. "Once that heals over, you'll have a scar to remember me by."

He's breathing so hard I'm not sure he even heard me.

Then, a text chime pulls my attention away from my distressed husband.

Mom, can you please pick me up ASAP? Charlotte is being weird. I should be at Alex's place in 25.

Chapter 87

Meghan

Alex's place is about ten minutes from here; it takes me all of five minutes to get there. My tires squeal throughout the entire neighborhood as I accidentally climb the curb before parking.

No one bothers to look my way. I bet they're used to reckless driving around here. This isn't exactly a quiet, family-oriented neighborhood. The more I look around, the more I regret allowing Hazel to come here.

But it's Alex we're talking about.

Her best friend.

How can I deny her that?

I open my phone, staring at the screen.

"Come on, Hazel. Where are you?" I mumble to myself.

I know she said twenty-five minutes, but that in itself worries me. If she is with Roseline as I suspect, why would they have driven out that far? Was Roseline planning on taking her away from me? Did I call just at the right time? None of this makes any sense.

She said *Charlotte* was being weird. Is Charlotte actually Roseline? She looks nothing like her. Roseline is petite, and Charlotte, a little on the plump side.

Then again, I haven't met her up close.

Maybe Roseline and Charlotte are working together.

Or maybe Roseline was telling the truth and wasn't with Hazel at all.

Impatient, I use my good thumb to write out a message. ETA?

It takes her a few minutes to even read the message,

and when she responds, it isn't clear.

15 mn bout.

The errors in her message are causing me to spiral. Why is she writing like that? Has she been drugged? Something's wrong. Hazel has always taken after me—she excels in grammar and punctuation and isn't one of those lazy teenagers that write everything out in code or half sentences.

How the hell am I going to survive fifteen minutes waiting for my daughter to be returned to me safely? I'm kicking myself for not setting up the LifeEv app on all our phones. Cole didn't want it. He said it was intrusive and a breach of privacy to know someone's whereabouts at all times.

But that's not how I see it.

I think it's perfectly healthy to be able to track your immediate family members. Besides, family members shouldn't be doing sneaky shit. There's no reason not to have the app. But he somehow managed to talk me out of it like he does everything.

Did.

That ship has sailed.

After several minutes pass, I want to check in again, but I'm afraid to cause more trouble for her. Maybe she wrote the message out that way because she's hiding her phone. Who knows?

Instead, I reverse and park almost a block away so that I'm not spotted.

Now, all I can do is wait.

CHAPTER 88

Hazel

Charlotte climbs the curb with her rusted minivan the second we pull up to Alex's place. If I hadn't texted my mom, I'd be freaking out right now.

But I saw her car parked down the road. She's either still in her car, or she's inside Alex's house. I'm not sure yet.

"Go on, get out," Charlotte says.

There's zero hint of kindness in her voice. With the way she's talking to me, I'm convinced she hates me. What did I do to her? What's changed? She was so sweet with me. She was like a second mom.

I get out of the van, but Charlotte is ahead of me, beelining it to the front door.

Right as she reaches for the handle, my mom's face appears through the glass storm door. She kicks it open, almost cracking the plastic in half.

Charlotte takes a big step back.

"You must be Charlotte," my mom says through clenched teeth. She's forcing a smile, but I know that scary smile—she's pissed.

Livid.

Behind her, Alex is standing awkwardly with his fingers clasped together, his neck stretching as he tries to peer over my mom's shoulder.

"Yeah, I am," Charlotte says weirdly. Why is she talking like that? Like she's trying to change her voice? "You must be Hazel's mom."

Mom doesn't even blink. I don't know what she's

thinking, but it's pretty terrifying.

"Where did you take my daughter, *Charlotte*?"

Charlotte forces a strained laugh. "Oh, well, I was about to take her to—"

"Don't bullshit me right now," Mom says.

I step away from Charlotte and hurry to my mom. She wraps a protective arm around me, making me feel safer than I have in my entire life.

She kisses the top of my head, then pulls her arm away and steps out of the house, dropping down a few inches to meet Charlotte face-to-face. Mom isn't much taller than her, and she only has one functioning arm. Despite this, I'm more afraid for Charlotte's well-being than my mom's.

"You had no right to take her anywhere," Mom says. "Alex here says he wasn't even aware you were bringing her anywhere. He took the bus home, yet you decided to pick Hazel up. Why is that?"

She takes another step, and Charlotte steps back.

"Know what else is funny, *Charlotte*?"

Why does she keep saying her name like that? Like she's making fun of it?

"I had a nice chat with Anna while you were driving Hazel back here. What kind of lunatic pays to pretend to be someone's sister?"

"What?" I blurt out.

Alex lets out a strangled chirp next to me. Though he looks more hurt than anything.

"It's not what you think," Charlotte says.

"Oh no?" Mom takes another step, and before Charlotte can do the same, Mom reaches for Charlotte's red hair and tugs sideways.

I slap a hand over my mouth.

Charlotte screams painfully and reaches for her hair. When she stands up, she looks really weird. Her red hair has shifted to the side, and under it are locks of brown hair.

Is that . . . a wig?

"Took me a few minutes to piece it together," Mom says.

Charlotte looks over at me and parts her lips. "You don't understand, Hazel, you're my—"

Crack.

Mom lowers her fist while blood gushes out of Charlotte's nose. Charlotte reaches for it, but the blood is so intense that it's spilling through the cracks of her fingers.

Mom doesn't seem to care.

She's beyond enraged. I can see it in the way she breathes—her shoulders go up and down rapidly; her back is tense, and her good fist is so tightly closed that her knuckles have transformed into micro weapons.

She suddenly grabs Charlotte by the collar and pulls her right up to her face. She whispers something, but I can't hear what she's saying. I think she's threatening her.

At her sides, Charlotte clenches her fists. She's getting ready for something. To hit my mom? To grab her?

"Mom!" I call out.

Charlotte lets out an angry roar and raises her right fist. But she doesn't stand a chance. My mom's head rocks back and then forward with full force.

A sickening crack follows.

My heart leaps into my chest, and I suck in a sharp breath.

Charlotte's eyes roll into the back of her head, and her body goes limp. Slowly, Mom lowers her to the ground.

I've never seen anyone get headbutted before.

And I never thought I'd see my mom headbutt someone.

"Mom!" I cry out.

I throw myself against her, and she wraps a solid arm around me. Alex slowly steps out of his house. Even Anna, who is usually passed out around this time, comes out looking groggy. She pulls a cigarette out of a front pocket of her shirt, along with a lighter, and lights up a smoke.

"Never really liked that lady," she groans.

"You said she was your sister!" Alex shrieks.

Anna shrugs, her bony shoulders rising a few inches. Then she sucks on her cigarette and lets out a big white cloud into Alex's face. He coughs and swats at the smoke.

"She was payin' me five hundred bucks a month to play along."

"And you didn't think that was suspicious?" Mom says. She's glaring hatefully at Anna now.

But all Anna does is shrug again. "Why would I care? It was free money."

Mom's nostrils flare. She's scary to look at right now, with speckles of blood on her chin and across her fist. She breathes hard, her eyes filled with fury as she watches Anna. Part of me thinks she's ready for a second headbutt.

But before Mom can do anything, the lament of sirens fills the entire neighborhood, and from around the corner comes a cop cruiser with flashing red and blue lights.

"How—" I start

Mom glances over at Alex. "I called the cops after I spoke to Alex and Anna. I knew Charlotte wasn't who she was pretending to be."

I stare at the woman on the ground. She's knocked out cold with blood all over her face, and her mouth is partially open.

Now that I'm looking at her carefully, she does look a bit off. For example, her clothes are about three sizes too large. It doesn't show when she's standing or moving around, but when she's lying flat on the ground like that, I can see all of the excess material.

Why would she do something like this?

"Who is she?" I ask.

Mom wraps another arm around me. "It's a long story, sweetheart, and now isn't the time."

I watch in terror as two police officers step out with bulletproof vests and palms resting on their duty belts.

"This her?" asks the female officer.

Mom nods.

Charlotte groans as the officers proceed to pull her hands behind her back and fasten them with cuffs. I don't understand what's happening. Why is Charlotte being arrested?

What exactly happened today?

Mom hugs me tightly, and I melt against her chest.

"You're safe now, sweetheart."

I don't know what Charlotte had planned, but somehow, I get the feeling that if Mom hadn't gotten involved, I might not be here right now.

Chapter 89

Meghan - Three Months Later

Jack grins proudly over my barbecue grill, shoulders drawn back. He looks cute in my pink apron, with big muscular arms bulging out on either side. What's even cuter is that he happily wore it and didn't make some stink about pink not being manly enough.

That's what makes a man attractive, in my opinion.

A guy who isn't insecure about who he is—who doesn't think that what's sociologically thought to be a female color will somehow strip away at his masculinity.

I couldn't be happier for Chels.

Jack really is the perfect guy for her. I watch from the comfort of my outdoor sofa as Chels comes out through the patio doors, a tray of drinks in hand. She places some fruity cocktail on the glass table in front of me and winks at me, then proceeds to give her husband a glass. He slurps half of it in one gulp, then wipes his beard with his thick forearm.

He thanks her with a kiss, which he can only do by bending down a whole foot. Chels is tiny.

"Burgers are almost ready," Jack says.

Hazel perks up in the distance. She's playing soccer with little Arthur on our lush green grass while Alex is busy running on all fours with those scrawny limbs of his. It looks really odd, especially with Alex's stringy hair flapping all over the place. But it's working—Arthur is full-blown belly laughing.

The kid looks more like Jack than Chels with his red locks and freckled face. He's cute—really cute. I can't believe how fast he's growing.

And now that he's past the one-year-old mark, Chels seems a lot more comfortable going out and doing things with him. Before that, she said he was fussy and it made it almost impossible to go anywhere, hence why we barely saw each other.

"This way," Hazel says, kicking the soccer ball.

Alex stops being silly and stands up before slapping tufts of grass off his knees.

Arthur giggles and chases him with a waddle, his chubby little legs barely keeping him upright. It warms my heart.

As Jack removes the burgers from the grill, Chels comes to sit next to me. She looks much more rested than the last time I saw her. There's even a glow to her.

"So," she says, resting a warm palm on my knee. "What are we celebrating? How're you holding up?"

She looks both weary and hopeful.

How mean would it be to say, "Better than ever now that Cole is gone?"

I bite my tongue. Especially since Hazel is within earshot. She misses her father.

"I'm doing okay," I say. "The trial went better than I thought it would."

And by *better*, I mean fantastic. I attended earlier today, which is the reason we're celebrating right now.

"Roseline is officially out of the picture."

Chels's jaw drops.

"You should have seen her, Chels. It was like she was trying to conjure up some new superpower: death by eye laser beams."

Chels doesn't smile. I don't blame her. I came pretty close to losing my daughter, and before that, my life. I still get a chill at the thought of it.

I feel sick to my stomach just thinking about Detective Goldberg's testimony today.

But none of that matters anymore. I'm out here, enjoying a barbecue with good friends, and Roseline is rotting away in prison.

"How long of a sentence did she get?" Chels asks.

I glance sideways at Hazel, who appears to be distracted by Arthur's cuteness. Then, I smile. "Fifteen years."

I don't even remember all the charges specifically, but I do remember a mention of impersonation. Turns out, Anna really does have a sister named Charlotte, but they stopped talking over a decade ago. Then, there was something about criminal harassment—the fact that she hung around and stalked my family for two years—vehicular assault, and kidnapping.

Chels's mouth is still agape.

To be fair, I can hardly believe it myself. Cole and Roseline really do make the perfect couple—both convicted criminals.

"So she is the one who hit you with that car?"

I nod. "Detective Goldberg managed to get footage from a small Italian restaurant's parking lot where the car was stolen. And then of course, I called him the day, well, you know—" I flick a finger in the air, not wanting to rehash the day I headbutted Roseline square in the face. Although, Chels would probably like it if I did share the story again. She loved it the first time around.

But that's not the part that haunts me.

"Anyway, they also found the car, and given Roseline's connection to Cole and the fact that she had motive to want to get rid of me . . . It all added up. But the final nail in her coffin was the matching DNA they found in the stolen car."

I leave out the part about how they searched Roseline's minivan and found a trunk full of rope, a tarp, and a shovel. Roseline's intentions for my daughter that day were far more gruesome than anyone knows. There's no point sharing something so dark with my best friend who is already constantly terrified of something happening to her child. It'll haunt her the way it still haunts me every night.

Chels gasps silently, her fingers over her parted lips. "My God. She could have killed you, Meg."

Her eyes are watering now.

"Well, she didn't," I say smugly after swallowing the lump in my throat. "That bitch is rotting away now."

Chels throws her arms around my neck. I can't tell if she's crying or not. She's never been one to be emotional, but ever since having Arthur, she's really changed. When she pulls away, her eyes are wet and pink.

Childbirth is something I'll never get to experience, but honestly, I don't mind. I love Hazel more than anything. It doesn't matter where she comes from.

I catch her watching me in the distance, a gentle smile on her lips. Thankfully, she's nothing like her biological mother. That's not something I ever have to worry about.

"What about Cole?" Chels says. "You said six years?"

I nod solemnly. Him being in prison isn't what bothers me. It's that Hazel had to find out the truth about her father. She struggled with the whole Roseline part of it. She still doesn't know that Roseline is her mother, but I explained that Roseline is obsessed with Cole and that she thought using Hazel might help her get closer to him.

It was a very lengthy discussion the day of Cole's trial. She asked to come with me, but I refused.

I didn't want her to hear all the accusations against him from former assistants. I'm thankful that Cole wasn't outright vulgar with his assistants. He didn't make any verbal threats or physically force anyone to do anything sexual with him. But given his pattern and the fact that he found a way to have women fired if they didn't sleep with him within a certain time frame—well, that gave the jury plenty of ammunition to put him behind bars for sexual assault through coercion.

I take a sip of Chels's drink, salivating instantly. It tastes like berries, lemon, and a hint of heaven. She has a way of masking the vodka perfectly.

"I'm so happy for you, Meg," Chels sips her own drink.

I smile wider than I have in so long. I'm surrounded by

love and happiness. I was so terrified that Hazel would break down after losing her father, but here she is, living and thriving despite the pain.

She's a survivor, like me.

And now that Alex is living with us, he's filled a void caused by Cole's absence. Taking him away from Anna to foster him was one of the best things I've ever done.

"Mom!" Hazel suddenly cries out.

I flinch so hard that part of my red cocktail splashes out of my glass and lands right between Ziggy's eyes. He sneezes and lurches off my lap.

"Your arm!" My daughter's eyes are huge, and she's pointing right at me.

My arm? What is she on about?

"It moved!"

I twist up my face. "What?"

"Your left arm. I just saw your fingers move."

I look down at my limp arm. It's usually wrapped up in a cloth sling, but sometimes that sling gets so damn uncomfortable with all of the sweating and chafing that I'd rather lug my arm's dead weight around.

With my good arm, I grab my left wrist and prop my arm up onto my lap. I have zero sensation. Did Hazel imagine it? The doctors said I had less than a one percent chance of ever recovering function again.

I don't want to squash her excitement, but there's no way my arm, or fingers, moved. They haven't since my injury. There's no reason they'd start now. "Hazel, I think—"

My index finger suddenly twitches, and I jump in response. An unexpected laugh slips out of my mouth.

"Mom!" Hazel shrieks again.

Alex is beaming next to her, watching the whole thing with his mouth split open in a grin. He looks as excited as she does.

Chels inches closer to me. "Meg, try it again. Try to move your finger."

The strength it takes makes me feel like a young

witch having gained powers on her sixteenth birthday. I shout in my head, willing my finger to move, but nothing happens.

"Try to stick your finger upward," Chels says.

My index finger shoots straight up. My eyes bulge so hard in my head that the strain nearly triggers a headache. "Holy—"

Hazel cheers, and Chels gives me a big hug around my neck.

"You think you'll get function of your entire arm again?" Hazel asks.

I manage to curl my finger down, then stick it straight back up. It's the strangest feeling. As if my arm isn't even my own. I don't have the answer to Hazel's question, but I have one thing I haven't had in a long time—hope.

I smile up at Hazel's baffled, expectant eyes. "I'm gonna give it all I've got."

The love around me is palpable. I want to reach out and hug everyone all at once.

But a group hug would be, as Hazel says, *cringey*.

As I stare at all the gleaming, crinkled eyes around me, I realize that I don't need a husband to have a family, and I don't need my children to be made up of my biology, either.

This is my family, and family isn't always blood, my mother being a prime example. I haven't cut her out of my life, but I've made a conscious decision to no longer chase after her love, her acceptance, or her admittance of her inadequacy as a mother.

All that did was hurt *me*.

Ziggy suddenly barks and jumps back up onto the sofa. He just wants a piece of burger, but I ignore his intentions and instead appreciate his warmth against my lap.

Chels raises her cocktail glass at me, her tanned skin glowing beneath the blazing summer sun. "To a new life."

I raise my glass and clink it against hers. "To a *better* life."

CHAPTER 90

Roseline

This place is worse than I imagined prison would be like. Everything is cold and hard, and everyone always looks so depressed or pissed off unless they're beating someone up.

Then they're smiling.

My bunkmate, Jazine, snores like an overweight pig and doesn't let me have the top bunk. Instead, she rolls around up there, causing the springs to constantly creak.

I tried to take her spot once, but she ripped me out of the bed and punched me square in the nose.

Like I needed that.

My nose is already permanently crooked thanks to Meg's big head. I can't believe she headbutted me like that. Who does that?

I'm pissed off at her, yeah.

But I'm more angry at myself, and at Cole.

If he'd left her sooner, none of this would have happened. And if I'd pushed her a little harder that night at the Afterglow Tavern, she'd be dead.

That was the real plan.

Instead, she got a bad concussion, some disfiguration, and loss of one of her arms.

Boo-fucking-hoo.

She was supposed to die. Who the hell survives a metal staircase that steep? There's a reason they put signs everywhere and a gate to close off access. I pushed her right over the gate.

Worked out well, too, because the place was so

damn crowded, no one saw what happened. Not even Cole. They figured she was too drunk and someone accidentally bumped into her.

A bit of Rohypnol helped destabilize her.

I'm honestly kicking myself for not having done the job right. All of this could have been avoided, and I'd be with Cole right now. After all, he's the reason I tried to kill her. It would have solved all our problems.

But I saw on the news that he's going to prison, too.

Something about sexual assault.

It's all bullshit, though.

Women just want his money. It's all a big conspiracy—I know it. They want a payout. Sure, Cole has slept around, but he loves *me*. I would never do something like that to him. I'd never betray him.

All I have to do is wait until he gets out of prison, because he'll have good connections to get me out sooner. He's always had connections.

I'm patient.

I'll wait my entire life for him if I have to.

Fifteen years isn't that long. I don't even care about Meg anymore. She wants nothing to do with Cole—all the better for me. Apparently, she finally left him.

I don't know the full story, but someone told me she took him to the cleaners.

That's okay. I was never with Cole for his money. Plus, Cole is resilient. Especially with me by his side. I mean, if it weren't for me, David—the original COO of AstroWyre—would still be alive and Cole would never have moved up to take his place.

Cole doesn't know what a good teammate I am. But that's okay. He doesn't have to know. All he has to do is bounce back from this and get me out of prison so that he can finally prove his love for me.

And he will.

I know it.

I'm confident he'll make the right decision and finally commit himself to me.

But if he doesn't . . . he'll end up like David, and like how Meghan should have ended up.

Dead.

Because never again am I letting anyone else have him. The only thing that will ever keep Cole and me apart is death.

And once he's lying there, cold and pulseless, I'll tuck him into bed and crawl in under the sheet next to him.

I once saw this picture online of two skeletal corpses holding onto each other in a casket.

That's so romantic.

Pure, true love.

After I'm done swallowing a bottle of pills, I'll press my head against his cold chest and hold him tight.

Nothing else will matter after that.

Because once I die next to him, we'll be together forever.

The choice is his.